Reading Up a Storm

A LIGHTHOUSE LIBRARY MYSTERY

Eva Gates

D0021105

AN OBSIDIAN BOOK

OBSIDIAN
Published by New American Library,
an imprint of Penguin Random House LLC
375 Hudson Street, New York, New York 10014

This book is an original publication of New American Library.

First Printing, April 2016

For more information about Penguin Random House, visit penguin.com.

ISBN 978-0-451-47095-9

Printed in the United States of America
10 9 8 7 6 5 4 3 2 1

Penguin
Random
House

NATIONAL BESTSELLING
LIGHTHOUSE LIBRARY MYSTERIES

"A smart whodunit. . . . Lucy is a likable heroine among an engaging cast of supporting characters, including Charles, a Himalayan with attitude who can't seem to help sinking his claws into a murder."
—Sofie Kelly, *New York Times* bestselling author of the Magical Cats Mysteries

"Charming . . . a book lover's dream."
—Krista Davis, *New York Times* bestselling author of the Domestic Diva Mysteries

"A library in a lighthouse? *And* a cat? Sign me up! A fun read for all cozy fans."
—Laurie Cass, national bestselling author of the Bookmobile Cat Mysteries

"A first-rate cozy mystery . . . plenty of twists and turns to keep you reading until dawn."
—Daryl Wood Gerber, national bestselling author of the Cookbook Nook Mysteries

"A must for Austen fans, cat lovers, and library devotees!"
—Laura DiSilverio, author of the Book Club Mysteries

"Lucy Richardson is a funny, smart, and resourceful sleuth. . . . A well-written and entertaining new series."
—Mary Jane Maffini, author of the Charlotte Adams Mysteries

"[A] charming, entertaining, and smart series . . . [featuring] an unusual (and real) setting and [a] colorful cast of characters that set it apart from other bookish cozies."
—*Library Journal* (starred review)

Previously in the Lighthouse Library Series by Eva Gates

By Book or by Crook
Booked for Trouble

AUTHOR'S NOTE

The Bodie Island Lighthouse is a real historic lighthouse, located in Cape Hatteras National Seashore on the Outer Banks of North Carolina. It is still a working lighthouse, protecting ships from the Graveyard of the Atlantic, and the public is invited to tour it and climb the two hundred fourteen steps to the top. The view from up there is well worth the trip. But the lighthouse does not contain a library, nor is it large enough to house a collection of books, offices, staff rooms, two staircases, and even an apartment.

Within these books, the interior of the lighthouse is the product of my imagination. I like to think of it as my version of the Tardis, from the TV show *Doctor Who*. It is large enough for your imagination also.

Chapter 1

It was a dark and stormy night.

I've always wanted to say that.

Tonight was the perfect opportunity to do so: a ferocious storm was fast heading our way. It wasn't going to be a hurricane, I was glad to hear, but since I live this close to the ocean, even a smaller storm can be a terrifying thing.

Fortunately, the full strength of the tempest wasn't due to arrive for a couple of hours yet, so we were able to continue with our carefully laid nefarious plan.

The big clock over the circulation desk struck six, announcing closing time at the Bodie Island Lighthouse Library on a Monday. Charlene, our academic librarian, wasn't working today, but she'd come in a few minutes ago on a made-up pretext to keep our boss, Bertie James, in her office. I peered out the window. Night had arrived early as thick clouds heralded the approach of bad weather. A steady line of headlights flashed between the rows of tall red pines on either side of the driveway, and cars were pulling into our parking lot. Fortunately, Bertie's office was in the back of the building, where she didn't have a view of the road.

"Coast clear, Lucy?" said a voice above me.

I turned and glanced up. Ronald Burkowski, the children's librarian, was peering over the railing of the iron stairs, spiraling like the inside of a nautilus shell ever higher to the upper levels.

"All clear," I said.

He came down quickly, balancing two large boxes and several bulging shopping bags. A huge bunch of colorful balloons streamed behind him. I went to the door and greeted guests with a finger to my lips while Ronald, with the help of Connor McNeil, arranged the balloons, set out paper cups and plates, and hung a silver banner that read HAPPY ANNIVERSARY across the door.

I observed the preparations with sheer delight. It was ridiculously funny watching everyone greet everyone else, decorate the room, and lay out snacks and drinks, all while trying not to say a word or make a sound. Butch Greenblatt held the door open for my cousin, Josie O'Malley, who was staggering under the weight of a huge white box. She laid the box on a side table and opened it. I peered in with great expectation, and I was not disappointed. "It's marvelous!" I gasped.

"Shush," Ronald whispered.

Josie's cake was decorated to represent five books, stacked on top of one another. The icing resembled old leather, full of intricate scrolls of red or gold; the top and bottom edges of each "book" were white for the pages, and the titles were written in ornate black script. A small souvenir figurine of the Bodie Island Lighthouse stood on the topmost book, and the number 10 was written in ornate cursive beside it. "You've outdone yourself," I whispered. "It's much too beautiful to eat."

"That's what they always say," my aunt Ellen said with a soft laugh as she helped Josie carefully peel away the walls of the box. "Until the first cut."

We were gathering to celebrate the tenth anniversary of Bertie James's coming to work at the Lighthouse Library. Bertie was not one to stand on ceremony, and she hadn't even mentioned the occasion. It was only when a longtime friend of hers, Pat Stanton, had called to ask what we were doing to mark the event that we, the library employees—Ronald, Charlene, and I—heard about it. Two weeks of frantic, and secret, organization had begun.

By six fifteen we were ready. The main room of the library was packed. Everyone shivered in anticipation. We eyed one another, waiting. I switched off the lights, plunging the room into near darkness.

"When's Bertie coming?" Eunice Fitzgerald, the chair of the library board, sat in a wingback chair near the magazine racks, her back straight, cane held in front of her in knarred hands.

"Shush," people chorused.

"Thanks a lot, Bertie," bellowed the normally soft-spoken Charlene.

The assembled partygoers tittered. Charles, another library employee, crouched on the shelf closest to the door to the hallway. He looked as though he was getting ready to pounce the moment Bertie came into the room. I had an image of flying books, falling bodies, a screaming Bertie, and headed to cut him off.

Charlene appeared, saw us all waiting and, trying to

suppress her giggles, called, "Wow! Look at this! Bertie, get out here."

The sound of footsteps in the hallway, and then Bertie's head popped around the corner. She stopped dead, her mouth hanging open.

"Surprise!" we all yelled.

Charles made his move, but I was ready for him. I leaped into the air and the full weight of the Himalayan feline hit me in the chest. I staggered backward as sharp claws dug into my sweater. I crashed into Charlene, who fell into Bertie, who would have hit the floor had not the six foot five, two hundred pound Butch Greenblatt been approaching our library director at that moment to offer his congratulations.

Butch grabbed Bertie and kept her upright. "This is a surprise, all right," she said, smiling happily in Butch's embrace.

He blushed and mumbled apologies before letting her go.

I put a squirming Charles on the floor. *If looks could kill.* He stalked off, brown-and-tan tail held high.

The crowd surged forward, everyone wanting to give the guest of honor a hug and a peck on the cheek and wish her the best.

"Nice one," Ronald said to me. "You almost flattened our boss."

"Blasted cat," I replied.

"You can help me with the refreshments," he said as the thirsty crowd turned and headed our way.

In the fifteen minutes between library closing and Bertie's entrance we'd cleared off the circulation desk and set up a makeshift bar. Ronald had poured drinks while Charlene and I had passed around canapés. We'd laid bowls of mixed nuts and platters of cheese and crackers on the tables for partygoers to help themselves.

As I served the food I chatted to our guests. Everyone congratulated me on managing to surprise the unflappable Bertie. The room was full of longtime library patrons, members of the board, and Bertie's close friends, but the one person I'd been hoping to see hadn't arrived yet. I kept checking the door, but no one was arriving late. I put an empty platter of one-bite crab cakes onto a side table and pulled out my phone. No bars, meaning no signal. That was normal: it was difficult to get cell reception inside these thick old stone walls. I made my way slowly across the room, exchanging greetings with partyers. I opened the front door, and someone threw a bucket of cold water into my face. The storm had arrived.

I wiped rainwater away with one hand, and checked my phone with the other. I had a text. Sorry. Storm coming. Don't want to leave Mom in case electricity goes out. S.

Phooey. I was disappointed, but I understood. I hadn't known Stephanie Stanton for long, but we'd quickly become friends. She'd come home to Nags Head late in the summer to look after her mother. Pat Stanton had been involved in a serious car accident when a drunk driver hadn't noticed a red light on the Croatan Highway. The drunk got off without a scratch, but Pat had suffered two broken legs and numerous cracked and broken ribs. Her recovery was going to be long and difficult. She was out of the hospital now, but clearly couldn't manage on her own, and Stephanie was Pat's only child. Pat had been a longtime patron of the library and she and Bertie were very close. She'd told Bertie she intended to consider the accident to be a blessing. At last she could spend her days doing what she'd always dreamed of having time to do—just reading.

Despite Pat's determination to look on the bright side, caring for an invalid was always difficult. I knew Stephanie needed the break, and had hoped she could make the party.

Take care, I texted back.

"It was on a night like this one," Louise Jane McKaughnan was saying to Mrs. Peterson when I'd put my phone away and picked up another round of treats, "that the great ship went down. They say . . ."

Louise Jane was a font of knowledge about the history of the Outer Banks. What she didn't know (or didn't consider dramatic enough) she made up. Usually under the guise of "they say."

"Delightful party, Lucy. Any more of those crab cakes?" Theodore Kowalski, six foot tall and rail thin, peered at me through the plain glass of his spectacles as he chewed on the end of his unlit pipe. He was a passionate lover of literature and a keen and knowledgeable book collector. For reasons known only to himself, he wanted people to think he was English, and dressed like a country squire heading off to the Highlands for a spot of grouse shooting. Theodore was also dead broke, and could be counted on to appear at any library function at which food was served. He was in his mid-thirties, only a couple of years older than me, but dressed and acted as though he was in his fifties. I guess he thought that made him seem more serious.

"I'll check," I said. "You know not to light that pipe in here, right?"

He beamed at me, clearly pleased. Theodore didn't smoke; the pipe was all for show. Although somehow he managed to ensure that he had tobacco stains on his teeth and the scent of it clung to his Harris Tweed jackets and paisley cravats like barnacles to a barge. "I'm afraid I won't be able to make book club on Wednesday, Lucy. So sorry to have to miss it."

"And we'll miss you," I said dutifully.

"An important business matter. Can't be helped."

Aunt Ellen joined us and nabbed a meatball. "Great party, Lucy. Bertie looks so happy."

"I have exciting news," Theodore said.

"What's that, Teddy?" Ellen asked.

"I've found a buyer for those Agatha Christies I've been trying to unload . . . I mean sell. I've my eye on a set of Dashiell Hammetts in mint condition that I'd like to add to my collection." As I said, Theodore was broke. He earned what money he could from buying and selling books. Unfortunately for his bank account, he was far more interested in buying than in selling. When I first began working here, Bertie had warned me to check his bags and coat when he left the library. He was known to sometimes decide that a rare or valuable volume would be happier in his home library than in this public one.

"How nice," Aunt Ellen said. "Good luck with it. Do you think Bertie was genuinely surprised, Lucy?" She took a second meatball. Ellen and Bertie were longstanding friends. It was through my mother's sister that I landed the job of assistant librarian a few months ago.

"I hope so," I said. "You can imagine how difficult it was to organize all this without her knowing. At five she said she was leaving early today. I just about fainted. Fortunately, quick-witted Ronald told her that Charlene had just called to say she wanted to come in at six to talk something over with Bertie, so Bertie agreed to stay."

"I suppose a chap has to go in search of crab cakes himself," Theodore huffed and strolled away.

Ellen chuckled. "You just can't get good help in the colonies these days. I see Eunice here, and some of the other members of the library board, but not Diane or Curtis. Did they send their regrets?"

"Gee. It seems that we forgot to invite them. What a shocking oversight."

Ellen laughed. It was no secret that Diane Uppiton and Curtis Gardner were not exactly Bertie's allies on the library board.

Butch approached us, holding a bottle of beer in one hand and a plate piled high with canapés in the other. "You up to a walk on Thursday morning?" he asked me.

"Sure am," I replied.

"Walk?" Aunt Ellen said, her ears practically standing up. She was my mother's sister and I had no doubt Mom had instructed her to report immediately about any potential developments in my life.

"Just a walk," I said.

"I don't go on shift until midmorning that day," Butch explained. "I was telling Lucy how when I first joined the police I always tried to take time for a stroll along the beach before work whenever I could. It got me in a good place to face whatever the day had coming."

"And," I added, "that habit, like most good habits, has

fallen away. I told him a marsh walk would be just as good, and to make sure he actually does it, he has to take me with him. I'd better get to work. Glasses need to be refreshed. Crab cakes delivered. That's if Theodore leaves any for anyone else." I plunged back into the crowd.

"You three," Bertie said, approaching us with a shake of her head once she'd made her way across the room after greeting her guests. "I can't believe you did all this without my noticing."

"It wasn't easy." Ronald handed her a glass of wine.

"I should have suspected something was up," Bertie said with a laugh, "judging by today's tie." Ronald glanced down. As the children's librarian he liked to dress up for the kids. His tie was covered with pictures of brightly colored birthday balloons. "Oh," he said, "I didn't even realize."

"Your subconscious at work. Oh, my goodness, will you look at that!" Bertie had spotted the cake. Josie stood beside it, beaming proudly.

In the momentary hush as everyone stopped talking to admire the gorgeous confection, I could hear the wind howling around the curved lighthouse walls, and the steady patter of rain hitting the windows.

"Gonna be a big one," Butch said as he twisted the cap off a bottle of beer.

"I hate to say it," Connor said, "but we should probably suggest people start making their way home once they've had cake."

"Yeah," Butch said. "We don't want anyone caught out in this if it gets any worse."

The library's located about ten miles outside of the town of Nags Head. That's ten dark and lonely miles, as the road runs through the Cape Hatteras National Seashore along the edge of the Atlantic Ocean.

"Speech," Ronald shouted.

"Speech, speech," the crowd chorused. A blushing Bertie was pushed to the front of the room. Her eyes sparkled with unshed tears and her voice broke as she began to speak.

"Thank you, friends, so much for coming. You have no idea how much this means to me. And thank you most of all to the world's best staff—Ronald, Charlene, and Lucy—for this."

Everyone cheered. Ronald took a deep bow.

Charles, who hadn't quite forgiven me for spoiling his fun earlier, leaped onto the shelf beside Bertie. She laughed. "And thank you, Charles. That storm's building, and fast. I hate to say it, but let's dig into this cake so we can get all of you safely home."

When Bertie finished to many cheers, Josie pulled out a knife and began cutting the cake. Bertie got the first piece, and everyone cheered again. I placed slices onto plates and a beaming Bertie handed them around.

While we did that, Butch exchanged a word with Ronald and Charlene, and they nodded. Ronald put the caps back on the wine bottles, and Charlene began tidying up crumpled napkins and dirty paper plates. Connor spoke quietly to Bertie.

Soon, all that remained of the gorgeous cake was the bottom layer. Gradually the library began to empty as everyone gave Josie their compliments and said their good nights. Ronald, Charlene, and I finished tidying up with the help of Aunt Ellen and Josie.

Every time the door opened, rain streamed in and the wind caused the pages of magazines on the rack to shudder. Charles kept himself far away from the door, and I was glad I didn't have to venture out into the wild night. I live here, in the lighthouse, in a delightful, cozy little apartment on the fourth floor. My lighthouse aerie.

Josie packed the last of the cake into small boxes, distributed them among the stragglers, and then she and Aunt Ellen gave me kisses and said good night. Ronald and Charlene, clutching their cake boxes while unfurling umbrellas, escorted Bertie to her car.

At the end of the night, only Butch and Connor remained.

The men eyed each other.

I looked from one to the other. *Oh dear.*

"Good night, Mr. Mayor," Butch said.

"Night, Officer Greenblatt," Connor said.

Neither of them made a move.

"Guess it's time to be going," Connor said.

"Yup," Butch said. "Nice party, Lucy."

Charles sat on the shelf, his head moving from one man to the other as if he were at a tennis match.

"Do you want . . . ?"

"Can I see you . . . ?"

"Good night, gentlemen," I said.

They looked at me. Then they looked at each other. Charles watched them both.

"I'll follow you, Connor," Butch said. "Make sure you get to town safely in that little car of yours. Can't have the mayor going off the road in the dark."

"No need to do that," Connor said. "I've been driving these roads as long as you have."

I crossed the room and opened the door. I peered outside. The night was a wet black void. "Neither of you will get to town if you don't leave now. If anything, that wind is picking up."

"Once I've seen Connor off, I can come back and . . . uh . . . make sure you stay safe here, if you'd like, Lucy," Butch said.

"I don't think that's a particularly good idea," Connor said. "Suppose there's an emergency and you get called to come into work."

"Out. Both of you," I said.

They moved at the same time, squeezing through the doorway, apologizing all over themselves, calling good night to me.

I shut the door behind them and gave the lock a satisfying twist.

Charles jumped off the shelf and headed toward the stairs.

Excellent idea, I thought.

I followed him upstairs with a warm, contented glow.

Chapter 2

Rain lashed the walls of the Bodie Island Lighthouse, and the tall old building swayed in the wind. I put on warm fleecy pajamas covered in cartoon characters, plugged the kettle in for a pot of hot tea, and filled Charles's food bowl. We told library visitors not to feed the cat, but we had absolutely no hope of anyone paying any mind. At the party, I'd seen Mrs. Fitzgerald taking a slice of smoked salmon off her plate and surreptitiously slipping it under her chair.

I dithered over the music selection on my iPad. I like a pounding rock anthem as much as the next person, but tonight I was in the mood for something soft and quiet, so I could enjoy the sounds of the storm and get lost in the world of my book. I eventually settled on a playlist of piano concertos. Ronald and I had used Charlene as a distraction to keep Bertie in her office while party preparations were under way. Ronald had decided on a jazz selection for the night's music, and brought some CDs from home. While Charlene had been busy keeping Bertie occupied, he'd taken the opportunity to hide Charlene's collection of CDs. Our academic librarian's passion in life was rap and hip-hop, and she was convinced that with sufficient exposure to it, all the rest of the world would join her in her love. That we hadn't told her to go away and take her passion with her was testament to how much everyone liked her. I'll never forget the look on Eunice Fitzgerald's face the time Charlene cornered our library board chair and stuffed EarPods into her ears and told her to listen to Jay-Z's newest recording.

With a chuckle at the memory, I found my book and settled into the deep comfortable window alcove to read. I'd been busy taking care of our guests so I hadn't had anything to eat, and I enjoyed my cake now with a cup of steaming black tea. The cake was as delicious as it was beautiful. Josie was truly a wonder in more ways than one. My cousin was beautiful, talented, hard-working, and just plain all-around nice. Charles, also beautiful and talented but definitely not hard-working, finished his own dinner and jumped onto my bed.

The warm glow from the success of the party, not to mention the attentions of two highly desirable men, lingered, and I let out a contented sigh, happy with my world and my new life on the Outer Banks. The heavy draperies were pulled back and the deep black of the night was broken only when the great first-order Fresnel lens high above me burst on in the two point five seconds on, two point five seconds off, two point five seconds on, and twenty-two point five seconds off pattern it would maintain throughout the night.

On nights like this, I truly came to understand the

power and importance of a lighthouse. It must be bad enough to be out at sea on a dark and stormy night with modern satellite guidance systems and the entire Eastern seaboard lit up, but in the days when the only glow from shore might be the dim and dirty light of a tallow candle or the dying flames from a damp cooking fire?

I shivered in delight and turned back to my book. Charles had moved off the bed and was now purring softly on my lap in the comfy, pillow-covered window alcove tucked into the four-foot-thick stone walls. I was reading *Kidnapped* by Robert Louis Stevenson in preparation for the next meeting of my classic-novel reading group. By coincidence I was at the part where the brig *Covenant*, bearing the kidnapped young David Balfour and the rescued Jacobite hero Alan Breck Stewart, is about to be destroyed on the storm-tossed rocks off the western isles of Scotland.

I stroked Charles's fur and he rolled over with a contented stretch.

Poor David had been tossed into the cold sea and had barely managed to stagger onto the deserted shore, more dead than alive, when I again looked out the window. To the north the lights of Nags Head were a yellow smudge on the horizon, but where this stretch of the coast ran along the Cape Hatteras National Seashore, all was as dark as could be. No car lights lit up the strip of highway, and nothing moved out at sea. Ships had headed for safer waters long ago. I had candles and matches and bottles of water at hand in case the electricity went out. My cell phone was fully charged, although getting a signal inside these stone walls was a matter of luck at the best of times. To conduct a proper conversation, I had to open the window and lean as far out as I could reach, protected (hopefully) by a grate of iron bars.

Knowing I wouldn't get a chance to head outside this evening, I'd taken a late lunch break and gone to Coquina Beach to enjoy a short walk. I'm from Boston, and thus no stranger to the sea, but I love this stretch of the coast more than any place in the world. A storm warning had been issued; the wind had been strong, the waves high, and the sky to the south a mass of boiling black and gray clouds, so I hadn't walked for long. The beach had been almost deserted. No family groups remained, but a handful of storm lovers had been out. A young woman had stood on the edge of the water, her feet in the pounding surf, her head back and eyes closed, arms held out almost in benediction. The wind had whipped her long, loose dress around her legs. Close by, a man had been surveying the shoreline with binoculars. He'd worn a Red Sox ball cap low over his eyes and Bermuda shorts over thin and very hairy legs with prominent knees. He'd glanced at me as I passed, and I had felt the binoculars following me down the shore. I didn't walk for much longer after that, but went back to work to carry on with the party preparations.

The light above me went into its twenty-two-point-five-second dormancy, and I was about to turn my attention back to the book when a white flash caught my eye. I grabbed my binoculars. I love to sit here watching the activity out at sea. Gray battleships, huge tankers, mammoth cruise ships, luxury yachts, commercial and sport fishing boats, and sailboats of varying sizes all pass by my lighthouse aerie. Tonight, however, I wouldn't have expected any activity, certainly not close to shore. I adjusted the glasses and scanned the black void that I knew was the sea. There it was again: a light rolled and jerked, as if being tossed by the waves. I estimated that it couldn't have been more than twenty or thirty yards offshore.

From this distance, it was impossible to tell if the light was attached to a boat. It might have been on a dinghy that had come loose from its moorings and drifted away. As I began to lower the binoculars, again intending to return to my book, another light caught my attention. This one, I estimated, was on shore. It was followed by a second light and then two more until there were four lights, maybe twenty feet apart. They bobbed up and down, but I was pretty sure they were on the beach, not in the water. At first I thought of campers and bonfires. But the rain was relentless; no open fire would last long. And no sensible person would want to be sitting around it in any event. It couldn't be a camper because that beach was for day-use only.

I wasn't sure what I was seeing. My eyes were having trouble focusing through the binoculars, alternating between the pitch-dark of the storm and the sudden flash of light from the thousand-watt bulb above me.

As I watched, the light on the water began to approach the lights on the shore. It had to be a boat; it was moving against the force of the wind.

I leaped to my feet and grabbed a flashlight. I ran out the door and dashed up the twisting iron stairs. Two flights up, another window faced out to sea. I was higher, but the view wasn't better. A narrow walkway wound around the top of the building, making a complete circle of the lighthouse tower at its narrowest point. On a bright sunny day, the view from up there is one of the best along the coast.

I'm not afraid of heights, but not entirely comfortable with them either. When I'd gone out on the exposed walkway to take in the scenery, I'd kept my back flat against the solid stone walls. The door to the viewing platform was kept locked at night, the key somewhere downstairs in the library director's office.

I pressed against the window, binoculars in place. I hadn't shut my apartment door behind me, and Charles leaped onto the window ledge. He stood on his back legs and pawed at the glass.

"I can't see anything," I said to him. Opaque sheets of rain blew across my line of sight. As I tried to peer around the raindrops, a calm spot blew in and I could see. The light was dipping and weaving, there one second, gone the next, as waves tossed it about. It had almost reached the shore and was heading straight for the four bobbing lights. Those lights looked exactly like boats resting comfortably in harbor. But no harbor was there.

Ghost ships? The thought flashed unbidden into my mind. Louise Jane McKaughnan, the self-appointed source of all knowledge on the paranormal legends of the Outer Banks, had plenty of stories about ancient shipwrecks and long-dead sailors still struggling to save themselves.

Whether the lights were from a supernatural presence or not, there was a vessel out to sea and it was in distress.

I ran downstairs to my apartment. I grabbed the landline phone off the kitchen counter and was pleased to hear a steady dial tone. The lines were still up.

I dialed 911. "This is Lucy Richardson at the Bodie Island Lighthouse Library. There's a boat in trouble just south of Coquina Beach."

"Can you see it?" replied a calm, steady voice.

"I'm not entirely sure what I'm seeing. It's too dark to be sure that it's a boat, but there definitely is a light. And it's heading for shore, tacking against the wind."

"I'll report it to the coast guard," the operator said. "Thank you for your call, Ms. Richardson."

"Good night," I said. I hung up, feeling totally useless.

This was a dangerous stretch of coast, so dangerous that it was sometimes called the Graveyard of the Atlantic. Thousands of ships have been wrecked along the Outer Banks. The boat I saw, if it was a boat and not just an abandoned dinghy, was not far from the wreck of the *Laura Barnes*. The wooden schooner had come ashore in heavy fog in 1921, and its rotting remains were now, of all things, a tourist attraction.

I went back to the window, and resumed my post. The rain had lessened fractionally but I didn't see either the bobbing light or any of the four on land again.

It was a long time later when I switched off my own lamp, drew the curtains, and crawled into bed. Charles settled beside me and began to purr. Before falling asleep, I gave a thought to the men and women who go down to the sea in ships.

Chapter 3

When I woke, the first thing I did was grab my binoculars and pull back the draperies. The sun was a brilliant yellow ball hovering over the flat, watery horizon, and the sky was as blue and cloudless as it is in the tourist brochures. For a moment, I thought I must have dreamed the whole thing, inspired by my late-night reading of Stevenson's classic novel.

Then I saw it. A boat was on the beach, lying on its side like a tourist who'd fallen asleep in the sun and would soon wake to a serious sunburn. I adjusted the binoculars and saw that, rather than dozing in the sun, the boat was badly damaged with a hole in its side, and it had cast pieces of flotsam and jetsam across the sand. It was a motorboat, probably a twenty-footer, either a genuine antique or a carefully crafted replica, made of sleek golden wood.

Several cars were parked along the highway, and a small group of people milled around the wreck.

I picked up my phone and dialed Butch.

"Mornin', Lucy," he said in his deep Outer Banks accent.

"Hi, Butch," I said. "Are you working today?"

"Yeah. I just got in. I'm still in the station, reading last night's reports. It was a busy shift. Great party, by the way. What's up?"

"A boat's been wrecked off Coquina Beach. I saw it floundering last night after I'd come upstairs. I called to report it. Do you know if anyone was on it? Are they okay?"

"Give me a sec and I'll check," he said.

Charles meowed and gave me a serious glare. The first thing I do in the mornings is feed him. He was not looking happy at having been overlooked today.

"Found it," Butch said. "Coast guard got a call of a boat in distress. They arrived to find it coming apart in the surf. Two people had made it to shore, and the Guard called the police to pick them up and take them into town."

I let out a sigh of relief. "I'm so glad. I was watching from my window, but couldn't be sure what was going on."

"The owner's named William Williamson. How's that for a pretentious name?" Butch chuckled. "Address in Nags Head."

"I'm surprised he's local," I said. "He can't know much about the sea. What sort of idiot would go out on a night like that in a small boat? Or in any sort of boat, for that matter?"

"One with more money than brains. According to the report, the boat was almost new." Butch snorted with laughter.

"What is it?"

"This is a police report, Lucy, so I shouldn't really be telling you. But Mr. Williamson gives his age as sixty-two. His companion of last night was a woman, aged thirty-two."

"You've got a dirty mind," I said. "She might be his daughter."

"Might be, although the name is different. But I'd say as well as more money than brains, he might not be above a little showing off. Guess that didn't work out so well for him. Book club still on for tomorrow night?"

"Of course," I said. "Have you read the book?"

"It was hard to get into at first, all the strange words and the accents. But once I got over that, I really liked it. Quite an adventure story."

"Good. See you tomorrow."

"Right. Um, how about we go out for a drink after the meeting?"

I hesitated. I like Butch. Butch likes me. He's smart and handsome, big and manly, masculine in a self-deprecating way (when not being a cop) that I find totally charming. But I don't know if I want it to go any farther than friendship and I don't want to start giving signals he might misinterpret. Then there was Connor, for whom I also have feelings, to complicate things.

As I said, Butch's smart: he caught my hesitation. "Maybe Josie and Grace would like to come too. And anyone else we might round up."

"I'd like that," I said.

"See you tomorrow."

I hung up, realizing I'd said nothing to Butch, or to the 911 operator last night, about the mysterious lights on the shore. I wasn't sure what I'd seen. It didn't matter now. Aside from the loss of the boat, all had turned out okay.

I got ready for work, after filling Charles's food bowl of course.

It was late September, and the tourist season was coming to an end. A few patrons browsed the shelves, but the library was quiet as people took advantage of one of the last beach- and pool-worthy days. All summer the place had been a madhouse. Bertie and the board had obtained a loan for a complete set of Jane Austen first editions for the summer months. Despite having temporarily lost two of the precious volumes, the exhibit had been successful beyond our wildest dreams. Austen-philes had come from as far away as Texas and Quebec to see it.

The books, and the accompanying notebook of Miss Austen's, had been carefully packed up and returned to their owner, and the library staff had breathed a collective sigh of relief.

Tuesday morning, I worked on the circulation desk. The library was back to normal. The banner had been taken down, the last of the crumbs swept up, the trash taken out. When we'd gathered before opening, we'd taken the time to congratulate ourselves on a successful surprise party, and Bertie had told us she'd been truly touched, not only that we'd gone to the trouble to have the party, but by the number of friends who'd come out on a bad night to celebrate with her.

Now she was in her office, completing the staff performance reviews. Ronald was upstairs in the children's library, and Charlene's head was buried in a stack of old shipping logs someone had salvaged from his great-grandfather's estate.

The door swung open and a woman came in. She was a tiny little thing, fine boned, about five foot two, and not weighing much more than a hundred pounds soaking wet. She was almost invisible behind the stack of books in her arms. I jumped to my feet to give her a hand. Once the books were deposited on the returns cart, we exchanged a hug. Charles leaped onto the cart and asked for a scratch. Our visitor obliged.

"You missed a great party last night," I said.

Stephanie grimaced. Her skin was pale, her arms dotted with freckles, her curly hair a flaming red, and her eyes a deep, expressive gray. "Couldn't be helped. That storm was something else."

"It sure was. Everything okay?"

"Fine."

"Did your mom get through all those?" I asked, pointing to the books.

"She did. I swear she might have engineered that accident herself, just to be able to spend all the time she wants reading." Tears filled my friend's eyes and I gave her another hug.

"Why are you crying? She's going to be okay, isn't she?"

"Her accident brought home to me that my mom's mortal. I don't think I'd ever accepted it before. Someday I'll lose her."

"It'll be a long time before that happens."

She grinned and wiped at her eyes. "You're right,

Lucy. I'm not usually the emotional sort. I guess it's all hit me at once."

"I thought I heard your voice, Stephanie." Bertie came into the room, carrying an empty coffee cup. She also gave the younger woman a big hug. "How's your mom today?"

"She's in good spirits this morning. The physiotherapist is at the house to take her through her exercises, so I took the chance to do some shopping and get more books."

"And how are you doing, honey?"

"I'm fine," Stephanie said. The bags beneath her wide gray eyes and the lines of strain around her mouth put the lie to her words. "I'm also enjoying the chance to catch up on my reading. Mom and I have always had totally different tastes. Nothing I love more than a good bodice-ripper. . . ."

"Nothing wrong with that," Bertie and I chorused.

Stephanie laughed. "I finished the Susanna Kearsley over the weekend, and I couldn't find anything I fancied in the house, so I ended up reading that one." She nodded to the book at the top of the returns cart. *Treasure Island* by Robert Louis Stevenson.

Bertie's eyes lit up. She pounced on Stephanie's words as quickly as Charles had moved when a little girl's long braid had come loose in preschool play group. "If you liked that one, you'll love *Kidnapped*. Lucy, do we have a copy around?"

We didn't, because they'd all been taken out by book club members. "I finished it," I said. "Why don't I run up and get my copy for Steph."

"Excellent," Bertie said.

"I don't . . ." Stephanie began.

I dashed up the stairs. I hadn't finished the book last night, but I'd read it several times before. I remembered it well enough to lead the club's discussion.

I grabbed the book and ran back down, taking the steps two at a time. "Here you go." I thrust the tattered paperback into Stephanie's hands.

"Thanks," she said.

"I've an excellent idea!" Bertie exclaimed as if she'd thought of it at that very moment. "Lucy's book club just happens to be meeting tomorrow to discuss *Kidnapped*. Why don't you join them?"

"I can't leave . . ."

"Nonsense. You missed the party last night. You need to get out sometime. I'll sit with your mother. I'd love nothing more than a nice long chat without one of us having to rush off hither and yon. What time does the club meet, Lucy?"

As if she didn't know. "Seven."

"Perfect. I'll be at your house at quarter of. Lucy often goes out with Josie and some of the others after. Isn't that right, Lucy?"

"Right," I lied. Butch's suggestion of a drink in town was not part of our normal routine.

"I won't expect you back until eleven or even later," Bertie said.

Stephanie gave Bertie a soft smile. "Thanks. I'd better get off then. Looks like I have some reading to do."

When the door had shut behind Stephanie, I turned to Bertie. "That's nice of you."

"Stephanie keeps up a brave front, but it's never easy caring for an invalid. As much as I love Pat, she can't be easy to live with at the best of times. She might joke about enjoying her reading, but she's got to be desperately bored. Stephanie needs the break, I'm sure. All her life, it's been just the two of them. Stephanie and Pat."

"Where's Stephanie's dad?"

"He's never been in the picture. Pat never talks about him. She must have been quite young when she had Stephanie. I suspect she had to drop out of school. She hasn't had things easy, what with not much money, no husband, and a child to raise on her own. She's estranged from her own family. I don't know the story there, but it might have something to do with Stephanie not having an obvious fatherly presence. It makes me so mad. Pat's had a difficult life, but she's always worked hard, never complained, and she raised a wonderful daughter. Now that Stephanie's got her law degree and has a good job, Pat should've finally been able to relax and get some enjoyment out of life, but then this accident had to happen to her. I can't think she has much, if anything, in the way of benefits from her job at the restaurant."

Stephanie was a lawyer in Raleigh. The firm had given her a leave of absence to care for her mother, and I knew she was doing what work she could remotely, but she was probably taking a financial hit all the same. It would be hard enough for anyone, and she probably still had student loans to pay off.

I was glad Butch had suggested that a group of us go out after book club. It would do Stephanie some good.

* * *

"I loved it!" Stephanie exclaimed as she burst through the library doors shortly before seven o'clock the next evening. "Sold into slavery. Sword fights on a sailing ship. Dueling bagpipes. A dark, brooding Scottish hero on the run!" She looked great in a black T-shirt under a knitted shrug and skinny jeans tucked into knee-high black leather boots with killer heels.

I laughed. "*Kidnapped* is all that, for sure. A good, fun, rollicking adventure."

I'd set out chairs in the third floor meeting room and laid out glasses, napkins, lemonade, and sweet tea. Josie always brought a box of "leftovers" from her bakery, so I made sure to leave some room on the table. Josie's Cozy Bakery was so popular that it never had much in the way of leftovers, so I suspected she did extra baking for us. I always insisted on paying for the treats over her protests.

Josie and her friend Grace arrived after Stephanie, and then the regulars began trooping in. CeeCee Watson, wife of the police detective, bounded up the stairs while Butch gave me a wink before asking Mrs. Fitzgerald, library board chair, if he could assist her. Mrs. Peterson came with two of her five daughters, who hadn't gotten out of the house fast enough after supper and were corralled into coming with her. Ronald had told me earlier that Louise Jane called to say she was going to Elizabeth City for the day and might not make it back in time. My hopes were high, but they were soon shattered when Louise Jane came walking through the door, smiling her barracuda smile at me. She made no secret of the fact that she wanted a job at the library. My job. And to see me heading back to Boston lickety-split to boot.

"Good evening, Louise Jane," I said in the excessively polite tone I'd learned while watching my mother greet unwelcome guests.

"Something wrong with your voice?" Louise Jane said. "You haven't been smoking again, have you, Lucy?"

"I've never smoked," I said to her retreating back.

I waited at the door a few moments longer. I peered into the gathering dusk, waiting for one last club member. No headlights were coming down the long driveway, no rumbling car engine getting close. I told myself I wasn't at all disappointed, plastered a smile on my face, and went upstairs to talk about *Kidnapped*.

The disappointment I wasn't feeling didn't last for long. Everyone had helped themselves to drinks and Josie's baking—tonight she'd brought her hugely popular pecan tarts as well as a new treat of reverse-chocolate-chip cookies—and had found seats, when the bell at the front door rang. My heart sped up.

"I'll get it," Grace said.

She was soon back, followed by Connor McNeil and two people I didn't know. I got to my feet, followed by Butch and Theodore.

"Sorry we're late," Connor said. He was dressed for book club in jeans and a black leather jacket. His dark hair, curling slightly in the damp, was wind-tossed. "I brought a couple of guests. Hope that's okay, Lucy." He gave me his soft grin. The one I thought of as his private smile. Or maybe that was just my imagination, and he smiled at everyone like that. I smiled back, thinking that the room had gotten very warm all of a sudden. "Of course it is. All are welcome."

The man who'd come with Connor was in his late fifties, early sixties maybe, on the short side, but fit and handsome with large gray eyes and a mane of silver-and-black hair. He wore a brown sport coat, ironed Dockers, and hand-sewn Italian loafers without socks. A thick gold band circled his wrist, keeping his gold Rolex in place. The woman was around my age, early thirties, with glowing skin and shiny blond hair pulled back into a tight, high ponytail. Her long legs and bare arms were well tanned, and she wore white capris, a white-and-blue-striped T-shirt, and flat sandals. She was pretty, but not beautiful, and her broad smile looked genuine.

"I'm Marlene," she said to the room. "This is so great! A book club in a lighthouse! When Connor told Will about it, I said we absolutely had to come! I'm afraid I haven't read the book though. Not yet, anyway, but I saw the movie *Kidnapped* when I was a kid. Is the book the same?"

"There have been several movie versions," Mrs. Fitzgerald sniffed. "To which one might you be referring?" Mrs. Fitzgerald took books, and book club, seriously.

"Gee," Marlene said, "I don't know. A bunch of English guys were in it."

"And this," Connor said, gesturing to the man with him, "is William Williamson."

"Call me Will."

Butch and I couldn't help exchanging a glance, before we looked quickly away as if caught plotting to raid the cookie jar.

"Are you here on vacation, Mr. Williamson?" Mrs. Fitzgerald asked.

"No, ma'am. I've been away for a long time, but now I've come home. I'm renting a place over on Sea Spray Court while lookin' for the right house to buy."

"Will's a Nags Head boy," Connor said. "He was friends with my dad, back in the day."

"Yup. I went into the oil business. Not a lot of oil in North Carolina so I lived in Alaska all these years. Couldn't wait to get back to where the water's warm, and here I am at last."

"And with your daughter," Mrs. Fitzgerald said. "Isn't that nice?"

Marlene let out a peal of laughter. The rest of us shifted uncomfortably in our seats.

"We seem to be out of chairs," Butch said. "Why don't you take mine, sir? I don't mind standing. Why, I might stand right here by the buffet table." Marlene gave him a huge smile. Butch did look pretty good, dressed super casual in faded jeans, a white T-shirt under a University of North Carolina Tar Heels sweatshirt. His hair was too short to ever get mussed, but the dark stubble on his strong jaw was growing in thick and fast.

"That's mighty kind of you," Will said. He sat beside Stephanie, and they exchanged greetings. I looked at them together and blinked. Same gray eyes, same bump in the center of the nose, same slightly pointed chin. But her hair was red, like her mother's, and she had pale skin and lots of freckles, whereas his hair still had traces of black running through the gray. I thought no more about it. Outer Banks family lines twisted all over themselves and went back a long, long way.

"You're our guest," Josie said to Marlene. "Please, take my chair."

She laughed again and said, "I just love these Southern manners." Marlene might laugh too often and too loudly, and seemed to speak every sentence with an exclamation mark, but I liked her already. Her enthusiasm was infectious. I glanced around the room. Everyone was smiling.

Not quite everyone. Louise Jane ostentatiously checked her watch. "If we could continue . . ."

"Sure, sure," Will said. "Don't let us interrupt. I'm sorry to say I haven't read the book either. Not much cause for reading old books in the oil business. You'd think that we'd have time, out on those rigs all winter, but let me tell you . . ."

"Be quiet, honey," Marlene said. "You can talk about your days on the rigs later."

Connor caught my eye and shrugged, as if to say "I couldn't stop them from coming, now could I?"

I borrowed Mrs. Fitzgerald's copy of the book and held it up. The cover illustration was of the *Covenant* floundering in the storm. I opened my mouth to make an opening statement.

"Will you look at that, honey?" Marlene said. "That could've been us last night!"

"A shipwreck?" Butch asked, playing the innocent. He'd recognized the name William Williamson right away, as had I.

"Sure was. We went out last night in Will's boat. It was just awful! Wasn't it, honey?"

"You were out in that storm?" Josie said. "Was that . . . uh . . . wise?"

"Oh, Will's an excellent sailor. He kinda forgot about differences between the Arctic Ocean and the Atlantic. No harm done, was there?"

"Forgot about the differences between common sense and a darned fool, sounds like," Josie whispered to me. I kept my face impassive. That they could have been killed, and that the coast guard rescuing them were putting themselves in danger, seemed not to matter to Marlene.

"We don't need to talk about that," Will said.

"But these nice people are interested. There we were, out at sea, in the wind, the rain! I was starting to get worried, I can tell you. Although I have total trust in Will, of course."

"Of course," Josie said.

As I listened to Marlene dally on, I chewed my lip to keep myself from glancing at Butch. I was so totally trying not to look at him it was becoming difficult. I suspected he was in the same situation.

"We'd gone down toward Cape Hatteras, but I guess we sorta lost track of the time—didn't we, honey? Well, then it got real dark and the storm hit us, just like that. Wham!" She clapped her hands together, and I jumped. "We knew we were almost at Nags Head, 'cause we could see this lighthouse."

"It was those blasted lights on the shore," Will muttered. "Led me astray."

I straightened.

"Will said we were passing the mouth of a small harbor," Marlene continued. "We could get refuge there. He must have just seen some cars though, 'cause when we got closer we hit the bottom right hard. Wham! And those lights Will saw just up and disappeared. Poof!"

"There are no small boat harbors along this stretch," Butch said. "Didn't you know that?"

Will wasn't looking all too comfortable as Marlene told the story. She might be an innocent, but he was nothing but an idiot. And he knew it. "We forgot the map," Marlene said. "And then we couldn't figure out how to read that satellite thingy, could we, honey?"

"Navigation was supposed to be your job," he mumbled.

She let out another peal of laughter, unconcerned. "Oopsie."

"How's the boat?" CeeCee asked.

"A total wreck!" Marlene said. "We were lucky, weren't we, honey? The boat was going down fast. I've never seen so much water. I was starting to get worried, 'cause I'm not a good swimmer, but then the coast guard arrived and saved us."

Will huffed. "We were perfectly safe at all times, Marlene. You're making something out of nothing. Although those lights I saw were mighty strange."

Louise Jane had moved to the edge of her seat, paying rapt attention. Rather than encouraging us to get on with the meeting, her interest had intensified as Will and Marlene told the story. "These lights. Were they moving?"

"Yes, they were. As if they were on the water and bobbing up and down. Like this." Will illustrated with a motion of his hands.

"That's incredible," Louise Jane said. "You know what I'm getting at, don't you, Mrs. Fitzgerald?"

"Of course I do. But I can't credit it."

"What?" Stephanie asked.

"Y'all know how Nags Head got its name?"

Most of us nodded.

"I don't," Marlene said. "It's a mighty strange name for a town. 'Course all the towns round here have strange names. Like Duck." She laughed. No one else joined in.

Louise Jane cleared her throat. She was a born storyteller and loved nothing more than relating the history and legends of the Outer Banks. "In the old days, before the lighthouse was built and electricity came to town, folks would try to lure ships onto the shore. Cause them to wreck deliberately."

"Why would anyone do that?" Marlene asked.

"To salvage the remains. Grab whatever washed up on shore. Those people were known as wreckers. They tied lanterns around horses' necks—old horses are called *nags*—and walked them along the roughest part of the shoreline or where the currents are the worst. From out at sea, at night, the lights looked like boats moored peacefully in harbor. The unlucky ships would sail straight into the trap."

"Did that actually work?" Stephanie asked. "You didn't get to be a captain or pilot of a ship in those days by being a fool."

"They'd have charts and know these waters," Grace said.

"Not well enough," Louise Jane said. "Remember—this is the Graveyard of the Atlantic."

"You're not suggesting that Monday night someone was trying to play at luring boats to their doom," CeeCee said. "No one is so dumb as to fall for that."

I broke into a coughing fit. The situation Will and Marlene had been in that night wasn't funny, truly it wasn't, but this conversation was almost surreal. Will, apparently, *was* dumb enough to fall for it.

Butch grabbed a cookie and stuffed it into his mouth. What had he said to me on the phone the morning after the storm? *More money than brains.*

Connor gave us both a curious glance.

"Playing," Louise Jane said softly, drawing her audience in. "No one was playing. There are stories, plenty of them, in this part of the world. Lost sailors crying out, trying to reach shore through all eternity. Men, women, and children swimming without ceasing. Even ships themselves sailing on regardless of broken masts and tattered sails, constantly re-creating the moment of their doom."

Silence hung over the room. Outside the light flashed.

"Did anyone else just feel a chill?" CeeCee said, wrapping her arms around herself. Marlene's mouth hung open. Will eyed the dark spaces in the corners. Dallas Peterson, age ten, edged slightly closer to her mother. Charity, her fourteen-year-old sister, dropped the look of total boredom and stared wide-eyed at Louise Jane.

"If you mean ghost ships," Stephanie said, breaking the quiet, "I don't believe in ghosts."

Mrs. Peterson tried to interrupt. "I don't believe this conversation is suitable . . ."

"Believe what you may," Louise Jane said. "It's a known fact that severe weather increases supernatural activity. Monday night would have been perfect. As Lucy knows, even this lighthouse, perhaps this very room, is full of unexplained phenomena."

"Cool," said Charity.

"Wow," said Dallas.

"I don't know anything of the sort," I protested. "I've never experienced anything here."

"So you say." Louise Jane smiled at me. I almost expected to her reach out, pat my hand, and say, "There, there."

"I've never heard of ghostly wreckers," she went on. "But it would be fitting, wouldn't it, if they were trapped here on Earth in punishment for their crimes. I'll call my grandmother. If anyone knows, she will."

"You mean we were lured astray by a ghost?" Marlene said.

"No," Connor said.

"I mean we have to consider the possibility," Louise Jane said. "Will, what do you think?"

"That's quite a story. I'm not going to dismiss it outright." Clearly, Will wanted to believe. It made his stupidity seem less foolish. "I saw some mighty strange things in Alaska in my time on the rigs. I can tell you stories that would make your hair turn color. Like when—"

"*Kidnapped* was written a hundred years after the events it describes," I said. "Does anyone want to comment on how that might have affected the story?"

The evening was not a success. I struggled mightily to keep the conversation on track, but it was an impossible task. I should have realized that any tale of doomed eighteenth-century ships and pitch-dark nights would cause Louise Jane to continually interrupt with Outer Banks stories. She was an amazing source of knowledge about the history of this coast, but it was impossible to tell what was true and what she was making up on the spur of the moment. I suspect that to Louise Jane it didn't matter, but it was one reason (among many) that Bertie didn't want her working in our library. Who knows what she would tell patrons, be they gullible tourists or serious historical researchers.

Marlene exclaimed in delight at every twist and turn of the book's plot, and Will kept remembering that it reminded him of the days of his youth on the rigs. Mrs. Peterson left early, dragging two (for once) reluctant girls behind her, when Louise Jane began to speculate what sort of death David and Alan would have faced were they captured.

At last I felt that we'd been here long enough, and I decided to wrap up the meeting. "So," I said. "What shall we read next?"

"Something American?" Grace asked. "We've read a lot of English stuff. I've loved them all, but it's time for a change."

"That's a good idea," I said.

"*Moby-Dick,*" Louise Jane said.

I tried to cut her off, but I wasn't fast enough.

"That would tie in well with *Kidnapped,*" Butch said. "Another tale of men at sea, battling the elements."

"I vote for that," Connor said. "I haven't read *Moby-Dick* since my school days, and I'd like to look at it with an adult perspective."

"Why are we always reading about men?" Josie said, getting to her feet to collect empty pastry boxes and crumpled napkins.

"You mean like when we read *Pride and Prejudice*

and *Tess of the D'Urbervilles*?" Butch said. "That sort of manly stuff?"

"Oh, all right," she said. "I'll grant you one point." She punched him lightly in the arm and he gave her a fond smile. Josie was unofficially engaged to Butch's older brother, Jake, and they were close friends.

"I'll walk you to your car, Eunice," Louise Jane said to Mrs. Fitzgerald. "We haven't had time to talk much about my suggestion for the haunted Outer Banks exhibit, and Halloween's fast approaching."

"An excellent idea," Mrs. Fitzgerald replied. "Lucy, I don't know why Bertie's dragging her feet on this one. The board has approved Louise Jane's project."

Louise Jane smirked. Bertie had concerns, but the board had leaped on the idea with great enthusiasm. Louise Jane could be very convincing. Not that the idea didn't have merit. Ghost stories can be a lot of fun and also educational if we use them to talk about how people lived in the past. But this was a library, and we didn't want any of our patrons coming away thinking that the building itself was haunted.

Which, according to Louise Jane, it was.

They left, Louise Jane's strong voice rising up, telling Mrs. Fitzgerald about her ideas for costuming the staff.

"Hope you enjoyed yourself tonight, Will," Connor said.

"Thanks for inviting us," he said, noncommittally. I'd caught him checking his watch several times. He'd slipped out at one point to "see if I have any important calls." Will Williamson seemed like a man who preferred to be the one doing all the talking.

"It was great!" Marlene gushed. "You were so sweet to ask us." She gave Connor a spontaneous hug. I thought she kept herself in his embrace for a fraction longer than was necessary. Will seemed to think so also, as he pulled roughly on her arm. "Let's go. I know I said we'd go out for a drink after, Connor, to talk about your campaign, but I'm wiped. Another time maybe."

Marlene wiggled her fingers at me, as Will pulled her away.

"Campaign?" I said once they'd left.

"I've been hoping for a nice donation, as well as Will's endorsement," Connor said. "He suggested we have dinner. I said I was busy tonight, and how about tomorrow? And then, unfortunately, I mentioned the book club. Marlene practically jumped up and down at that, and she insisted they had to come. She's rather a force of nature, isn't she?"

"I liked her," I said.

"I'm going too," Josie said. "I said I'd go out for a drink with y'all, but I'm beat. It was a heck of a day. Two employees called in sick, and if they aren't back tomorrow it's going to be another heck of a day."

"Me too," Grace said. "Another time."

Grace and Josie clattered down the stairs, leaving Connor, Butch, Stephanie, and me in an awkward situation. I knew that Stephanie needed the break, and Bertie wasn't expecting her home for another couple of hours. "Shall we go to Jake's?" I said, referring to Butch's brother's restaurant. "We don't have to eat. We can sit at the bar."

"I can always eat," Butch said. He wasn't kidding. He could put away a prodigious amount of groceries.

We laughed and the tension left the room. They helped me stack chairs and carry glasses and trash downstairs.

To my surprise Will and Marlene were still in the library. She was standing at the magazine rack, flipping through what was on offer. Will was tapping his watch. He rolled his eyes at Butch and Connor.

"We're closed now," I said to Marlene. "But you can borrow a magazine or two if you want. I'll make a note, and you can come in tomorrow and take out a library card."

She shrugged. "No, thanks. I've read all these. All the interesting ones anyway. Thanks again for inviting us, Connor. It was great."

"If you're quite finished," Will huffed.

Marlene laughed and took his arm. "You're such a bear sometimes."

They left, and Butch, Connor, and Steph followed. I came last and locked the door behind us.

Marlene threw back her head. We were a long way from town, the sky was clear with no moon, so the stars were a dense blanket of twinkling jewels. "Will you look at those stars, honey? Aren't they wonderful?"

"Nothing at all like the night sky I saw out on the rigs," Will said.

The light high above us flashed. A figure stepped out of the shadows at the side of the building. Marlene squealed. Stephanie and I sucked in our breath. Connor touched my arm, and Butch took a step toward the man. "Can I help you, buddy?" he said.

"Evenin', Greenblatt. Dr. McNeil." The new arrival sounded as though he was speaking around a mouthful of gravel. "Didn't mean to frighten you folks." He was an older man, well into his sixties probably and not going there easily. A mane of thick gray hair curled around his neck; he sported an unkempt gray beard and excessively bushy eyebrows. His oatmeal-colored fisherman's knit sweater had a generous number of holes and strands of unraveling yarn, and when he lifted his hand to rub his beard, I could see traces of dirt in the cracks and crevices.

"Late to be out for a walk, isn't it, Ralph? What brings you here?" Butch asked.

Ralph didn't reply. He stroked his beard and stared at Will Williamson.

"You again! Are you following me?" Will snapped.

"Might be. Saw your fancy car headin' out of town. Figured you and me still have unfinished business to conduct."

"You've been waiting here all night?" Will's bark of laughter was strained. "You really are an idiot."

The man didn't react to the insult. "Didn't want to interrupt these nice people's meeting."

"Hey, I remember you," Marlene said. "Nice to see you again. Thanks for your help the other night."

"He didn't help," Will snapped. He tightened his grip on Marlene's arm. "His fumbling incompetence made a dangerous situation worse. As usual. Let's go, honey."

"What are you talking about?" Butch asked.

Ralph wasn't a big man, but he was solid. He stood in the path, directly in front of Will, his feet wide apart and his hands planted on his hips.

I had not the slightest idea what was going on here.

"I hear you've laid a complaint," Ralph said.

"You hear right," Will said. "Now get out of my way before I have to take out a restraining order on you."

Ralph turned his head and spat. Then, unhurried, he stepped off the path. Will almost dragged Marlene to their car. They leaped in and sped way, going way too fast.

None of us said a word until the Navigator had disappeared between the trees.

"Want to tell us what that was about, Ralph?" Connor said.

Ralph rubbed at his beard. "His boat ran aground the other night off Coquina Beach."

"So we heard," Connor said.

"He's threatening to sue me and the coast guard crew that pulled him and his fancy lady out of the water."

"What?!" Butch said.

"Yup. Says he was doin' okay until we got in the way."

"That's ridiculous," Connor said.

"Don't be following him, Ralph," Butch said. "Whatever else happens, that cannot end well."

"Some folks," Ralph said, "need to stay on dry land, where they belong. They think they can master the sea with their big boats and fancy equipment. No one can do that. Night, folks. Ladies." He seemed to almost glide on the night air as he drifted away, back to a rusty old pickup truck.

I let out a long breath. "Who was that?"

"Ralph Harper. Fisherman, coast guard volunteer. There aren't many people around here who know this coast the way Ralph does. His family goes as far back as the first European settlers on the Outer Banks, and every one of the men fished."

"He's quite a legend," Butch said. "He talks about the sea as though it's a living thing. A vengeful creature too, sometimes."

Stephanie spoke for the first time. "Will Williamson doesn't seem like a very nice man. Let's go and get that drink."

Chapter 4

It seemed silly to take four cars, but the others had come by themselves, and I didn't want to make anyone drive the ten miles back to the lighthouse later in order to drop me off. I pulled into the rear of our little convoy, and we headed into the night. Two deer watched us pass from the row of pine trees lining the long driveway to the lighthouse. It was a Wednesday evening in late September. Only a scattering of cars were in the parking lot at Jake's. Inside, a few customers lingered over their meal in the dining room, but the bar area was empty. The four of us sat ourselves at a big round table by the windows, looking over the dark expanse of Roanoke Sound to Roanoke Island. Lights twinkled on the far shore and the fourth-order Fresnel lens of the lighthouse flashed its rhythm. Outside, lamps were lit along the wood railings, and the soft murmur of conversation came from tables on the deck.

"Hey, Butch, Connor. Whatchya havin'?" the bartender called to us.

I ordered a small glass of white wine, and Butch and Connor asked for beers. Stephanie ordered a double scotch on the rocks. I saw Butch—the cop—raise his eyebrows at that, but he said nothing.

Connor had taken the chair that put his back to the windows. "Don't look now," I said, "but isn't that Doug Whiteside having dinner on the deck?"

Butch had the seat in the corner, back to the wall as always. He glanced outside. "Yup."

"Who's that with him?" I asked.

"Jack Ambridge. He's on the police board. The other guy is Whiteside's campaign manager. I can't remember his name."

Connor grunted.

"Who's Doug Whiteside?" Stephanie asked.

"A mayoral candidate," Butch said.

Stephanie looked at Connor. "Didn't someone tell me that you're the mayor?"

"That's right," I said.

"And an excellent one too," Butch added.

"The election's coming up," Connor said. "Anyone is, of course, welcome to run; that's how democracy works."

"Ambridge," Butch said, "is always after the chief to find what he calls *efficiencies* in the police budget."

"Efficiencies," I snorted. "What some people call cutting essential services."

Stephanie lifted her hands. "I'm staying out of this. I don't know enough to comment. Although I'm sure," she added quickly, "you're an excellent mayor, Connor."

"Thanks," he said.

"I can tell you one thing," I said. "Anyone would make

a better mayor than Doug Whiteside. He's an opportunist, pure and simple. His sister was murdered a while ago, and he had the audacity to use her death as a springboard to launch his campaign. I wouldn't trust him farther than I'd . . . I'd . . ." I sputtered to a halt, unable to find a suitable idiom. "Don't talk to him, Steph, or he'll give you an ugly fridge magnet."

"I'll make no comment on Doug, his campaign, or his suitability for mayor," Connor said. "But I'll tell you privately that I don't trust Bill Hill. That guy has ambition written all over him. Everyone in politics has ambition. Nothing wrong with that. Unless it's taken to extremes. I wouldn't be surprised if Bill is already dreaming of a presidential campaign."

"You think he wants to be president?" Butch asked. "That's a stretch."

"Not for him. He's a political staffer. They can be every bit as ambitious as any candidate."

Our discussion of the unsuitability of Doug Whiteside for mayor and the possible ambitions of his campaign manager was interrupted by the welcome arrival of the waiter, bringing our drinks as well as a bowl of peanuts and the bar menu. We clinked glasses.

"The book club was great fun," Stephanie said. "Thanks for inviting me, Lucy."

"Thank Bertie," I said.

"Why?" Connor asked.

"My mom's recovering from a car accident," Stephanie said, taking a long drink. "Bertie offered to sit with her tonight so I could get out."

"Sorry to hear that," Connor said.

Butch said, "Is your mom going to be okay?"

"Yes, but it's going to be a long haul. She broke both legs, among other injuries."

"That's gotta be tough. I'm going to have a platter of wings. Anyone else?"

We all declined.

"Tough on Mom for sure," Stephanie said, once the waiter had taken the menus and left. "Life isn't fair sometimes."

"Stephanie lives in Raleigh," I said. "She's taken a leave of absence from her job to help her mom."

"What do you do?" Butch asked.

"I'm a defense attorney."

Perhaps only I noticed Butch stiffen. "Is that right?" he said slowly.

"I'm just an associate, but I'm with Berton, Baxter. They're an important firm and I was lucky to get in there."

"I've heard of them," Butch said.

Stephanie caught the tone in his voice. "You have some kind of problem?"

"Problem? Why should I have a problem with your boss getting that cop killer off by intimidating the only eyewitness?"

"Hardly intimidating. The witness was a flake. He didn't know what he saw. His story changed depending on who was asking."

I knew of the case. It had been big news over the summer. "Let's not . . ."

"His story changed when Chuck Baxter paid him to change it," Butch said.

"That's not true. I know Chuck. He's a good lawyer and a moral man."

Butch slapped his beer bottle down with enough force that the table shook and my wineglass jumped. I grabbed it. "A moral man? There are three little kids growing up without a mother, and for the rest of their lives they'll know the man who shot their mama in cold blood is walking the streets. Baxter should have been strung up along with that client of his." Butch got to his feet and threw money on the table.

"Convicting an innocent man wouldn't have helped those children." Stephanie's face was flushed. "Nor would it have done anything for the cause of justice." She gestured to the bartender to pour her another drink.

"I hope you're not driving tonight," Butch said.

"What are you? Some kind of cop?"

"Yes."

"Figures," she said. "You going to tell your buddies to follow me?"

"If you give me reason to."

"Why don't I drive Stephanie home?" I said.

"See that you do." Butch stormed out, barely avoiding knocking down the waiter coming out of the kitchen with a plate piled high with extra-hot chicken wings. "Everything okay here?" he asked us once the door had slammed shut behind Butch.

"Perfectly fine," Stephanie said. Her color was high and her eyes shone. I guess there's little a defense lawyer likes more than a good argument.

"Do you still want these?" the waiter asked.

"Might as well," Connor said. The platter was placed in the center of the table.

The waiter gave Stephanie her drink, and she took a hefty swallow.

"I should be used to arguments like that by now," she said. "I've heard it all before. For the record, we would have represented that man whether he was guilty or not, but it's true that the witness changed his story more than once. Without being paid off or intimidated. Anyway, tell me about Butch. Detective or uniform?"

"Uniform," Connor said. "His brother's Jake."

I spread my arms out. "Of this place."

"I suppose I'm *persona non grata* now."

"I doubt it," Connor said. "You caught Butch by surprise. He's not the sort to carry a grudge. We all know cops and defense lawyers can be on different sides sometimes."

"That's good to hear." Stephanie finished her drink. "This tastes so good. It's nice to be out with friends for a change rather than sitting at home with Mom. I love my mother beyond words, but . . ."

"I understand," I said. I patted her hand, and she gave me a grateful smile.

The waiter asked if we needed anything else and Stephanie ordered another drink.

Connor lifted one eyebrow at me. I gave him a nod. I'd take care of Stephanie.

"So," she said, "tell me more about Butch. Is he married?"

We didn't stay for much longer. I was getting uncomfortable as Stephanie continued drinking steadily, while Connor and I stuck to one drink each. The extra-hot wings sat in the middle of the table like an unwanted visitor.

Connor insisted on taking care of the bill, and then we walked out into the night. Stephanie tripped on her

four-inch heels coming down the stairs and was saved
from falling flat on her face only when Connor grabbed
her arm with a "steady there."

"I hope you meant it when you said you'd drive me
home, Lucy," she said.

"I did."

She hiccuped.

Connor helped Stephanie into the passenger seat of
my Yaris, and then he came around to my door to say
good night.

"It was certainly an . . . interesting evening," I said,
aware of just how close he was standing.

"Never a dull moment."

We said nothing for a few seconds. "Good night,"
Connor said at last. "You take care of yourself, Lucy."

"I will."

He leaned in and kissed me on the lips. It was a light
kiss, more of a peck, but my heart began to hammer
and blood flooded into my face. When he pulled away
his eyes were dark and intense. "Do you want me to
come with you? Help get Stephanie home?"

"I'm good. She'll be embarrassed enough tomorrow
as it is."

He stepped back, and I got into my car, started it up,
and pulled out of the space. When I reached the road, I
took a quick peek in the rearview mirror. Connor was
standing alone in the center of the empty lot. A bright
light shone down on him, and he lifted his hand. I pulled
into the traffic.

"Is it nice," Stephanie asked, "coming from a big
family?"

"No," I said. "I have three older brothers. All they ever did when we were kids was boss me around, and now that we're adults, their wives offer me the benefit of their words of wisdom."

"I wish I had brothers."

"Perhaps I spoke too soon. Sometimes it wasn't so bad. You can be sure no one bullied me in high school, and I had no shortage of girls who wanted to be my friend. Not because they particularly liked me, but because they hoped I'd invite them around to our house and they'd bump into whichever of my brothers was the object of their current crush. It did get tedious."

"You have a mom and a dad. Aunts and uncles. That must be nice."

"It is," I said. My parents were never what you'd call affectionate or even attentive, but I always knew they loved me, and I loved them very much. My mother's sister, Ellen, and her husband, Amos, had been second parents to me whenever I visited the Outer Banks, and sometimes I thought I belonged more with my cousins than with my own brothers. "You have a relationship with your mother that's very special, Steph. I envy that. We can't all have everything."

She sighed. "I know that. I just wish . . ." Her voice trailed off.

It was only ten minutes to Stephanie's mom's house. Bertie's car was parked on the street in front and the downstairs lights were on. Pat's battered old Neon was in the driveway. Despite Pat's serious injuries, her car had suffered only some body damage in the crash, and Stephanie had had the necessary repairs done.

"We're here," I said, switching the engine off.

"Home already? Why don't you come in for a drink, Lucy?"

"I hope you don't mind my saying so, but you've had enough," I said.

"I know I have. I also know that I'm going to be sorry in the morning, but right now I don't care. Believe it or not, I don't drink much. I guess things are getting to me."

"That's okay. I'll walk you in."

Bertie was standing at the open door as we came up the sand-covered path. The house was a couple of blocks from the beach, and having a lawn or garden was a lost cause for all but the most committed gardeners. The house was old and small and weather-beaten, but freshly painted and well maintained.

"Did you have a nice evening?" Bertie asked.

"Yup," Stephanie hiccuped.

"We've had a delightful visit," Bertie said. "It was so nice to have the time to really catch up."

The front door opened directly onto the living room. Photographs of Stephanie at all stages of her life, from screaming baby to newly minted lawyer, covered the tabletops. Pat was seated in a reclining chair, dressed in blue-and-yellow-striped pajamas. Her legs were propped up, covered in a blue blanket. She had the same pale skin and curly red hair as her daughter, although the fire color had faded and the hair was now more gray than auburn. Lines of fresh pain were etched into her face, but she gave us a bright smile. "Lucy, how nice of you to bring Stephanie home."

"It was my pleasure," I said, leaning down to give her a kiss.

"I'll be off now," Bertie said. "I'm sure you're ready for bed too, Pat."

"I am tired," Pat said. "But I'm not getting up to run a marathon tomorrow. Although my physiotherapist seems to think that should be my goal. I wasn't even going to try that when both legs worked perfectly."

"Who's my father?" Stephanie said abruptly.

I turned. Stephanie was standing with her back against the door. Her arms were crossed over her chest, a dark cloud filled her gray eyes, and her lips were a tight line. So this was what all the questions in the car about family had been leading up to. Poor Steph. I knew everything there was to know about my parents' families and my lineage. I knew where I came from. Steph didn't even know her father's name.

"I don't want . . . ," Pat said.

"It's time, Mom. Long past time. Do you understand that when . . . if . . . you go, I'll have no one. No one in the whole world I can call my own."

"I am not dying," Pat said. "I'll be fit as a fiddle soon enough. Maybe running marathons."

"Then what? Even you aren't going to live forever. Stuff happens to everyone. You could have been killed by that drunk."

"No matter what happens, Stephanie," Bertie said. "You will not be alone. You'll have me, for one."

"And me," I added. But I doubt Stephanie heard me.

"That's hardly the same. I'll have no one who looks like me, who shares my blood, my ancestry. Someone who knows my history. It's time, Mom. I deserve to know."

"We'll be off," Bertie said.

"No," Pat said. "Stay, please, Bertie. You too, Lucy. Stephanie's right. She does deserve to know. If she's sure she wants to. I have to confess that my brush with mortality has unnerved me too."

Bertie and I exchanged glances. She gave me a nod, and we sank into the couch.

"You said it didn't matter," Stephanie said, "and for a long time it didn't. We didn't need anyone else. But now, tonight, I guess I realized that it does matter." Tears spilled out of her eyes. She did not move to wipe them away.

Pat closed her own eyes with a deep sigh. "I was still in high school when I met him. My family life wasn't pleasant. I was an only child and my parents were cold and distant people, much older than my friends' parents. I won't make excuses, except to say that like so many girls who only wanted someone to love them, I mistook an older man's passing fancy for true love. He was married, had a young son, but he swore he would leave his wife for me." Pat laughed without humor. No one else said anything.

"Well, long story short, when I told him I was pregnant I expected him to be overjoyed at the news; instead he said he was leaving North Carolina. He'd accepted a job with an oil company and he was moving his family out of state."

I threw a quick glance at Stephanie. Those gray eyes. Pat's eyes were dark brown. A horrible feeling began to crawl up my spine.

"I suspect he'd been offered the job and was going to turn it down, but when I dropped my bombshell, he saw the opportunity to get the heck out of town. He wanted to be as far away from me as he could get."

"So he up and left," Stephanie said. "Did he ever meet me? See pictures?"

Pat shook her head. "No. His loss, I've always said. Foolishly, I wrote to him when you were born, thinking he'd change his mind and come back to me. He replied, only once, telling me not to contact him again or I'd be hearing from his lawyers. He said things, horrible things, about me, casting doubt on your paternity."

"How awful," Bertie said.

"I was young, and so naive. I was devastated at his betrayal. His as well as my own family's. When I told my parents I was pregnant they said they never wanted anything to do with me again."

Bertie shook her head. "They've missed so much."

"He was from a well-known local family and I heard word of him now and again over the years. He lived in Alaska, they said, and he became a big-shot executive in his company, making a lot of money. Do you remember, dear, the time I broke my arm? You were around ten, and I was working as a waitress at the Ocean Side Hotel restaurant. It was the beginning of the summer, when I'd make most of the money I'd need to see us through the year. It was a bad break." She glanced ruefully at the blanket over her legs, bulky in their casts. "I seem to make a habit of that. Anyway, I lost the whole season. I swallowed my pride and wrote to him, saying I was in desperate straits and needed financial help. I was so excited when I got a letter with an Alaska postmark. It said, and how well I still remember, that if I needed money I could ask your real father, if I knew who he was. I am sorry, dear. For many years I never talked about him because I was ashamed, but then I came to realize that he simply wasn't good enough to be so much as a shadow in your life. Can you forgive me?"

"Nothing to forgive. I never figured he was some saint." Stephanie appeared to have sobered up completely. "He never mattered to me all that much. You know that, Mom. But things are different now. I'm not entirely without legal resources, you know. There's such a thing as DNA testing these days. It's time he paid up."

"Let it go, honey. What good can it do now?"

"Revenge," Stephanie said, her voice as cold as the ocean waters flowing around Alaska. "Pure and simple. Revenge. What's his name?"

Pat hesitated.

"Mom. His name?"

"I heard that he'd divorced the wife he had when he was with me, and his second wife died some years ago. He recently retired, and has come back to the Outer Banks."

"Is that so?" Stephanie asked. "Saved me a trip to Alaska. What's the name?"

"You won't do anything rash, will you, dear?"

"Have you ever known me to do a rash act in all my life?" Stephanie said.

A trace of a smile touched Pat's lips. "There was that time in seventh grade when you punched that boy who tried to put his hand up your shirt."

"Even that wasn't rash," Stephanie said. "He had a reputation, and I was ready for him."

Pat let out a long sigh. Bertie and I sat immobile. Stephanie waited, saying nothing, just watching her mother. Finally, Pat said, "Will Williamson. I called him Willy. I said I was a stupid young girl."

The name came as no surprise to me, but Stephanie's mouth dropped open. "What?"

Alarmed, Bertie got to her feet. "Do you know him?"

"A man by that name was at the library tonight," I said, also standing up.

"I can't believe it," Steph said. "He sat right there, next to me, making a fool of himself while some simpering girl who's probably no older than me giggled and fussed over him."

"It's just a name," Bertie said. "Might not be the same person."

"Right age, recently back from Alaska. Oil company exec. It's him all right. Of all things."

"You said you wouldn't do anything rash," Pat said.

"And I won't." Stephanie turned to Bertie and me. "Thanks for being here. Secrets are better when shared. I trust you'll keep this to yourselves."

"Goes without saying," Bertie said. I nodded.

"It's late, Pat," Bertie said. "Can I help you get settled for the night?"

"I'll do it," Stephanie said.

"Thank you for coming, Bertie," Pat said. "It was fun to talk about the old days, wasn't it?"

"It was."

"I'm going to open that bottle of wine in the back of the fridge," Stephanie said, "and think long and hard about good-old-dad. Nothing rash, right? Lucy, you want to stay for a drink?"

"Not for me. I have work tomorrow."

We said our good nights. Bertie and Pat embraced for a long time. I wanted to give Stephanie a hug too, but a hard shell seemed to have settled over my friend. She had a heck of a lot to take in, I knew. The secret of her life had been uncovered, just like that.

I was worried about what she might do.

Chapter 5

After Butch had stormed out of Jake's last night, I thought he might have forgotten our plans for a morning hike. But I got up early anyway, and pulled on jeans, a loose sweater, and thick, practical boots. If Butch didn't come, I'd go by myself.

I pulled back the draperies and was pleased to see another clear, cloudless sky. The forecast was calling for rain in the afternoon, but that wouldn't interrupt our hike.

I love the marsh in the mornings. The sun is rising in the east, the birds are waking up and searching for breakfast, the turtles are looking for a sunny spot to spend the day, and even the plants seem to be eager to greet a new dawn.

Charles studied my preparations. He didn't look impressed as I laced up my boots. Hiking was not to Charles's taste, but I suspected that those birds out in the marsh were. I'd often find him sitting in the window, gazing longingly outside. I poured kibble into his bowl.

He jumped off the bed and strolled casually into the kitchen, fluffy tail high, as if to say he was only eating it to make me happy. I knew better.

When he'd dined to his heart's content, we went downstairs. Charles was a big cat. He was a Himalayan, with a dark brown and tan face, pointed ears, and thick tan fur. He spent his days among the books, resting on the shelves, greeting patrons, and accepting the adoring praise he considered his due. He was particularly loved by the children, and spent story time curled up on one little lap or another. I left him to check if any mice had gotten into the library during the night, and went outside.

I was locking the door behind me when I heard Butch's car turn into the parking lot. He soon joined me on the path leading to the marsh, also dressed for a good hike.

"Everything okay last night after I . . . uh, left?" he asked.

"We didn't stay much longer," I said.

"I'm sorry about storming out. I know Stephanie has a job to do, and someone has to represent those creeps. They're entitled to a defense, but it gets my goat sometimes. Did she say anything about me? Was she mad at me?"

"She said she's used to it. Cops and defense attorneys are natural adversaries, I guess."

He mumbled something noncommittal, then said, "She got home okay?"

"I drove her. I got the impression she's not used to drinking. She's having a difficult time looking after her mom. It's not nice to realize our parents won't be there for us forever."

A flock of Canada geese passed overhead in the classic V formation, honking loudly, heading south for the winter. We walked along the boardwalk in comfortable silence.

The space inside my head was anything but comfortable. I was torn in all directions about my feelings for Butch. I liked him a lot. He was a great guy, kind, intelligent, funny. In any other circumstances, I could have fallen head over heels for him. I knew he liked me, and I suspected he was waiting for me to make the next move. Josie kept dropping not-very-subtle hints.

But in these circumstances there was Connor. Also kind, also intelligent and funny. Also, I thought, waiting for me to indicate my feelings.

How's that for irony? Most women in my position would be absolutely delighted to meet one guy like Butch or Connor. I had the attentions of two, and I didn't know what to do.

Never again would I want to be in the situation I found myself in over the summer, when I had mistakenly made a date with both of them for the same night. Not just a common or garden date either, but the grand opening of Jake's Seafood Bar with Butch and the Mayor's Summer Ball with Connor.

The whole thing had been hideously embarrassing for all concerned. So embarrassing that the three of us stepped away from one another for a while. The men continued to come to the library and to the book club, and we did things in a group with Josie or other friends, but no more casual flirting or talk of dates. If I wasn't careful, I knew, I'd end up without either of them.

But I didn't want anyone to get hurt. Least of all me.

"How long's Stephanie staying for?" Butch asked suddenly.

"Until her mom can manage on her own. She's doing some of her work remotely, and has taken leave from the rest. She has to be taking a big financial hit, and Pat doesn't have much." I said nothing about what had been revealed last night. It was not my story to tell, and I was sworn to secrecy.

Sun sparkled on the marsh. The long grasses moved as small animals fled our approaching footsteps. Butch dug into his pocket and pulled out two granola bars. He handed one to me without a word. I accepted it, tore the wrapper off, tucked the trash away, and took a big bite. I'd have coffee and breakfast later before getting dressed for work.

"So," Butch said, "you think Stephanie might come to book club next time?"

"She might," I said. "She seemed to enjoy it. If you don't chase her away."

"I'll try to be behave myself. Although I can't imagine a defense attorney being afraid of a little argument."

The path wound through the long grasses of the marsh, heading for the warm shallow waters of the sound. A small boat dock sits at the edge where people can tie up their boats before taking a walk. The marsh is a popular spot, good for bird-watching and nature hikes, but this morning we were the only people in the area.

We were a few feet from the shoreline when I said, "Time to turn back."

"Hold on a sec. I think there's a boat at the dock."

"So?" I said. "Plenty of people tie up here to go for a walk or do some bird-watching."

"Yeah," Butch said, "but no one's around. Kids come out sometimes at night. Sometimes they get themselves into trouble. I want to check it out."

"Be careful," I said. I tiptoed behind him. Butch's broad back was so big, I couldn't see around him, but I made no move to see better. I figured that if a ten-foot-long alligator protested the interruption of his breakfast, he'd have Butch to contend with first. I had no doubt it would be a fair fight.

We were only a couple of feet from the water's edge when Butch stopped so abruptly I crashed into him. The impact was sorta like my Yaris coming into contact with a speeding freight train.

"What the . . . ?" I said.

"Whoa!" Butch stretched out his arms, holding me back.

"What is it?" I said, trying to peer around him despite my better instincts. "Is someone down there? Have they been doing something yucky?"

"Not yucky, no. Go back to the lighthouse, Lucy."

"Why?" I can be stubborn sometimes.

"Because I said so." The tone of his voice meant he was not kidding. If I didn't know better, I'd have said he'd gone into cop mode. Without another word to me, he pulled his phone out of his pocket and punched a button.

"This is Officer Butch Greenblatt with the Nags Head PD. I have a situation at the Bodie Island Lighthouse. I need officers, including a detective, and an ambulance."

He *had* gone into cop mode.

I stepped off the path and peered over the edge. A small flat-topped open fishing boat with a two-stroke outboard motor was tied up to the wooden pilings and bobbing gently in the calm waters of the sound. A large black crow, perched on the bow like the figurehead on a sailing ship of old, was telling me to go away.

A man lay in the bottom of the boat, a ball cap lying across his face as though he was taking a nap. I opened my mouth to ask him if he was okay. Nothing but a squeak came out as the cloud in my head cleared and I realized that this was a forever nap. The blade of a knife pierced the center of his chest. His arms were thrown out, and his gold Rolex caught the light of the morning sun. Most of his face was covered but, as well as the watch, I recognized the square chin, and short, stocky body of William Williamson.

Chapter 6

"Not again!" Bertie said as she ran through the front door of the library.

I looked up from my mug of hot tea. Charles was curled on my lap, his comforting bulk a welcome presence. He meowed at Bertie as if to say, "Yes! Again!"

Bertie must have come straight from her studio. She was dressed in sleek black yoga pants with a turquoise stripe down the leg and a matching sleeveless shirt. Bare feet were stuffed into flip-flops and the salt-and-pepper hair she wore to work fastened into a tight bun was caught in a loose ponytail.

"Butch called me," Bertie said. "I'd just finished a class. He said I had to get down here right away."

"What's going on?" Connor followed Bertie. "Lucy, are you all right? I was in a meeting with the chief when the call came in."

"I'm fine," I said. "But . . ." I swallowed. "Will Williamson. The man who was here last night. For book club. Remember?"

"Of course I remember," Connor said. "I brought him. What about him?"

"He's dead. Murdered. In a boat, down by the marsh."

Bertie plucked the empty mug out of my hands. "I'm going to make another pot. Connor, you stay with her."

Connor crouched down beside my chair. Charles shifted an inch to give him room, and he took my hands in his.

"I'm okay, really. It was a bit of a shock; that's all. Butch was there. He's taking care of everything."

"You were with Butch?" Connor pulled his hands away. Charles hissed.

"A morning hike. He was telling me how he used to go for a walk before day shift. He said it got his head in the right place to face the day. I said he should keep it up, and he asked me to join him this morning."

"I guess that's okay then."

"Why wouldn't it be?"

"No reason."

Bertie came back carrying a tray, the teapot, and two mugs. "All the activity seems to be down by the sound. The emergency vehicles aren't blocking our entrance this time. One can be grateful for small favors. Tea, Connor?"

"No, thanks." He pushed himself to his feet. His tie was askew and his hair mussed. "I'd better get back. The chief and I never finished our meeting." I clutched my mug. Charles swatted my hand.

"Can you stay with Lucy for a few minutes?" Bertie said. "I want to find out for myself what's happening."

"I'm okay," I said.

"No, you are not," she said. And she left.

"I really am fine," I said. "It was a bit of a shock; that's all. Nothing to do with the library, thank heavens."

"I wouldn't be so sure about that," Connor said. "Why do you suppose Will was out here in a boat, anyway?"

"I have no idea."

"No sign of anyone else? Marlene?"

"We didn't see another soul all morning. Obviously someone must have been with him. I can't imagine him doing that to himself." I shuddered at the memory of the knife.

"Someone's going to have to notify Marlene," Connor said. "Since I know her, I guess I should do it. The chief'll have to wait."

"I'll go with you."

"That's not necessary, Lucy."

"I think it is." I shifted Charles aside, put down my mug, and got to my feet. "You shouldn't have to go alone, and she knows me now too."

"Thanks."

"Thank you for coming in such a rush," I said. "You're a good friend to the library."

"I hope I'm more than that," he said.

He had not moved back when I stood up, and we were standing very close. I felt a gentle push of Charles's paw in the small of my back, almost as though he was nudging me forward. Connor lifted his hand.

Outside the front door, a police radio squawked and Connor and I leaped apart.

"I'm so sorry, Lucy," Butch said, coming into the library. He'd pinned a badge to his sweatshirt. "Not quite the nice start to the day that I was expecting. Hi, Connor. What brings you here?"

"Just checking everything's okay. Morning, Sam."

Detective Sam Watson had come with Butch. "I've told Ms. James that the library can go about its business as usual today. We'll restrict our activities to the far end of the parking lot and the western boardwalk."

"Glad to hear it," I said.

"Lucy," Watson said. "Butch tells me you were with him when you came across the body."

I swallowed. "Uh, yes."

"Did you see anything out of the ordinary this morning? Anyone around when you first came outside?"

I shook my head. "No. Not a soul. Most days bird-watchers and nature enthusiasts are here as soon as the sun's up, but not always. Wasn't the case this morning. We had the walk to ourselves."

"I told the detective that," Butch said.

Connor mumbled.

"You say something, Mr. Mayor?" Watson said.

"Nope."

"What about that boat? Have you seen it before?"

"No. I don't think so, anyway," I said. "I'm not one for boats, and it didn't seem any different from plenty of others you see around here."

"Did you look out your window before you came down?"

"Yes, I did. To check the weather. My window faces east, out to sea, not west to the sound."

"Butch tells me he knows the guy. His wallet was still in his pocket and the ID confirms the name. William Williamson. He came to your book club last night?"

"I brought him," Connor said. "I was about to go

around to his house and break the news to his . . . uh, partner."

"Tell me about Williamson."

"He's from an Outer Banks family, but the family moved away over the years. He lived in Alaska for a long time, but recently retired and came back. He's renting a house in Nags Head while looking for something to buy."

"How did he hook up with you?" Watson asked.

"He was friends with my dad when they were young. He recognized my name in some newspaper article and gave me a call a couple of days ago. Mom and Dad are away visiting friends in Colorado, so Williamson suggested he and I meet up."

"And you did?"

"Sure I did. Aside from the fact that I like most of my dad's old buddies and love hearing their stories, Williamson says he's moving back to OBX. That means a potential voter. Not to mention campaign contributor. He seems . . . seemed . . . to be well-off financially."

"Fair enough," Watson said. "So you brought them to your book club. That's an odd place to invite a guest. Heck, my wife's always after me to come along, but that's only because she thinks I need hobbies." He might have added "Over my dead body" under his breath, but I couldn't be sure.

Connor chuckled. "Believe me—Will had no interest whatsoever in our book club, but his girlfriend was keen. She said if she's going to be living here, she wants to make friends."

"Fair enough," Watson said again.

"I liked her," I said.

"I'm sure you did," Watson said. "What time did book club end?"

"The usual time. Around nine," Connor said.

"What did they do then?"

Connor, Butch, and I exchanged a glance.

"Okay. What happened?" Watson asked.

"Ralph Harper was waiting for Williamson," Butch said. "Williamson has threatened legal action against Ralph and the coast guard members who rescued him and Marlene, his girlfriend, the night of the big storm when their boat went aground."

"He was suing them for saving him?"

"Threatening to, anyway."

"So, what happened?"

"Nothing much. I told Ralph to back off, and he did. Williamson left before Ralph, but not much before. A minute. Two at the outside."

"After telling you not to mess with the power of the sea, I expect," Watson said. "I'll go around to talk to him."

"I have to add that Ralph was not belligerent," Butch said. "If anything, he sounded calm and reasonable. As he always is."

"We left immediately after them," Connor said. "I didn't see any sign of either Williamson's car or Ralph's on the road into Nags Head."

"We?"

"Butch, Lucy, Stephanie, and I went out for a drink after."

"Who the heck is Stephanie?" Watson said.

My heart dropped into my stomach. My stomach dropped even farther. Stephanie! With all the commotion,

I'd forgotten all about Stephanie and the shocking news she'd learned only last night. Will Williamson was her father. And now he was dead.

"Lucy?" Watson said. "Who's Stephanie?"

"A friend of Lucy's," Butch put in. "From Raleigh, she said. I didn't think much of her."

"She . . . uh. . . . She's, uh . . . She's visiting her mom, who's a friend of Bertie," I said.

"Does this Stephanie have a last name?"

"I didn't get it," Butch said.

"Stanton," I said. "Same as her mom. She has her mom's name and not her father's because . . ." A gaping chasm opened in front of me. I managed to stop myself before I fell over the cliff and blurted everything out.

"What relevance does that have?" Watson asked. I didn't like the look in his eyes. He was too darn perceptive.

"None," I said, trying to sound nonchalant. "None at all. Why until last night she didn't even know . . ."

I practically jumped out of my skin as the entire returns shelf fell over. Books flew everywhere. The shelf, just a cart on wheels, crashed into the circulation desk, and *The Joy of Cooking*, easily three inches thick, hit the back of the computer monitor. The monitor wobbled, and Connor, who was standing closest, leaped for it. He reached it in time, but his foot slipped on a magazine and his legs spilled out from under him. He fell to the floor in a heap, where he lay wide-eyed and startled, among scattered books and magazines.

At the sound of the crashing cart, Watson and Butch had whirled around. Watson was reaching into his jacket, and Butch's hand lunged for his hip.

"Don't shoot," Connor said plaintively.

Butch reached down, grabbed Connor's hand, and pulled him to his feet.

Only I saw Charles slip out from under the overturned cart, carrying a small blue-and-white ball in his mouth. He tossed the ball to one side, leaped up onto the arm of my chair, and gave me a self-satisfied smirk. I gave him a hearty pat. *Extra kibble for you tonight, buddy.*

"What on earth is going on in here?" Bertie surveyed the chaos from the doorway.

"We're finishing up now, Ms. James," Watson said. "You can have your library back. Mr. Mayor, do you have the address of the place the deceased was renting?"

"I've been there," Connor said. "If you're going now, I'd like to go with you. It would be better if someone Marlene knows, even minimally, is there when you break the news."

Watson nodded. "You said they aren't married. What's the woman's surname?"

"I don't think I got it," Connor said.

"I'm coming too," I said, preparing for an argument.

To my surprise, Watson said, "That's probably a good idea."

"If you can wait a minute," Bertie said. "I want to talk to Lucy privately. We won't be long." She stood by the open door, and made a gesture as though she were ushering tardy dinner guests out.

"One minute," Watson said sternly. "Or we'll leave without her."

The men left. Bertie slammed the door behind them. "Quick," she said. "I heard one of the police officers say the dead man is named Williamson. Is that right?"

"Yes. I saw him. Most of his face was covered by a cap, but it was the same guy who came to book club last night. Butch confirmed it."

"Stephanie's father?"

"It must be. I noticed a strong family resemblance between them last night, but thought nothing of it. As soon as Pat said he was back from Alaska, I knew it had to be the same man. How awful. Poor Stephanie finally found her father, and now he's dead."

"Sounds like no loss to anyone," Bertie said. "Have you told the police this?"

I thought of Charles and the book cart. "No. Should I?"

Bertie let out a long sigh. "I don't see how we can't, honey."

"But it doesn't have anything to do with Stephanie or Pat. Pat told us in complete confidence. She's kept that secret for thirty years. We can't blurt it out the first chance we get."

"When it comes to the law, we might have to. I don't like it either. I'd suggest you say nothing, but if you're directly asked if there's a relationship between Stephanie or Pat and this man Williamson, you can't lie."

"His death has nothing to do with Stephanie." I studied Bertie's face. "It doesn't. You must know that."

"Honey, I don't know what I know. But you can be sure that if I'm thinking it's a heck of a coincidence that Williamson was murdered hours after Stephanie found out he's the man who got her mother pregnant and abandoned them to a life of poverty and hard work, you can be sure Watson will think so too."

"Her learning about him had nothing to do with it. An earlier attempt was made on his life."

"When? Do the police know this?"

"Monday night. I don't think they know, but I saw the lights."

"What lights? What are you talking about, Lucy?"

"Someone deliberately misled his boat in the storm, caused it to crash onto the shore. I saw it. The boat was wrecked. Will and Marlene were lucky to survive."

"We're leaving, Ms. Richardson. Now!" Watson bellowed.

"You have to go," Bertie said. "I'm heading to Pat's, and I'll break the news to her and Stephanie. It's up to Pat and Stephanie to decide if they want to go to the police with what they know about Williamson. But I have to tell them that lights or no lights, you and I can't keep this secret for long."

Chapter 7

Detective Watson and Connor McNeil were standing in the parking lot beside their cars, each of them tapping away at their iPhones. When I came running up, Watson suggested we all drive into Nags Head together, but Connor said he had to get back to his office as soon as he'd seen Marlene. I leaped into Connor's car before Watson could object.

If I was stuck with Watson for more than a minute, who knows what secrets I'd spill.

Bertie was right, and I knew it. All I could do was hope I wouldn't be asked a direct question about Stephanie. Not until she had the chance to go to the cops herself.

I should call and let her know what had happened, but I wouldn't be able to do that until I got some time to myself. Stephanie had met Will only once. If I was to keep her confidence as long as possible, I couldn't let on that she had any particular reason to need to know that he had died. Thank heavens for Bertie. She'd sort it all out.

"What did Bertie want?" Connor said.

"Nothing," I squeaked. I cleared my throat. "I mean, nothing."

"You're a dreadful liar, Lucy."

"So my mother always said." I slid down in my seat. Connor drove a comfortable BMW sports car. At the moment I wasn't feeling at all comfortable. My mother told me I gave out a physical signal when I lied, but she would never tell me precisely what that signal might be.

I could only hope that Detective Watson hadn't picked up on it.

"Do you want to talk about it?" Connor asked.

"What do you do when someone tells you something in deepest confidence, but then you discover that that secret might influence an important legal matter?"

"I guess it depends on how important the matter is. And how much influence the secret has on it," he said. "I'm sure you know that not informing the authorities about information relevant to a police investigation amounts to withholding evidence. Which is a felony, particularly in a murder case."

"Who said anything about murder?"

He smiled. "Regardless of the situation, you'll do the right thing, Lucy. I'm here to support you, if you need it."

I felt the weight lift off my shoulders, if only a fraction. "Thank you, Connor."

The house Will and Marlene had rented was typical Nags Head beach style. Four stories tall, long and thin, painted a pale peach. Huge windows with baby blue trim were on every level, as well as a jumble of balconies and outdoor staircases. On the second and third levels small balconies faced the street, occupied by chairs painted to match the color of the window trim. The fourth floor had dormer windows nestled into steep-peaked gables. In place of a front garden, a concrete pad for cars filled the space in front of the double garage that dominated the lower level.

Watson had parked in the street and he was already standing on the top step, pressing the doorbell, when Connor and I arrived. We climbed the steps to stand next to him. Watson alternately leaned on the bell and hammered on the door.

"She might not be in. Do you have her phone number, Connor?" Watson asked.

Connor shook his head. "Only his. Did Will have his phone with him when he was found?"

"Yes."

"No use then," Connor said.

"You two stay here. I'm going around back. If she's outside she might not hear the door." He was halfway down the steps when we heard footsteps and a muffled female voice said, "Who is it?"

"Marlene? It's Connor McNeil. We met yesterday. I'm with Detective Watson of the Nags Head Police. We need to speak with you."

The door flew open, and Marlene blinked at us through sleepy eyes. She was dressed in a short white silk nightgown trimmed with pink lace and her feet were bare, showing bright red toenails. The skin on her left cheek still carried the impression of a pillow, her hair was a rat's nest, and her face was clean of makeup. "What's the matter? What's going on?"

"May we come in?" Watson said.

She saw Connor and me standing slightly behind him. "Will isn't here. I don't know where he's gone. I'm still in bed."

"It's you I'm here to see, Marlene," Watson said.

She said nothing to that but stepped back, and we entered the house. "Would you like a coffee or something?"

"That would be nice. Thank you," Watson said.

Marlene led the way upstairs to the main level, which was completely open plan. The kitchen was the type of modern kitchen that's so high-tech, it looked as though no one ever cooked anything in it. There were gleaming steel appliances, a marble backsplash, granite countertops, a spotless hardwood floor, red walls, and red accents. Four red leather stools were lined up to the counter separating the kitchen from the living area. A couple of empty wine bottles and a box of crumpled and discarded beer cans were on the floor in a corner, and several dirty glasses were in the sink.

The rich red hardwood flooring extended into the rest of the room, where the furniture consisted of solid wood tables and plush red-and-white couches and chairs. A giant TV filled the wall over the fireplace, and gossip and fashion magazines were stacked on the side tables. The paintings were standard Outer Banks rental: beach scenes of colorful umbrellas and pristine sand, children playing in the surf, sailing boats resting in harbor. The far side of the room, looking east out to sea, was a wall of glass.

"Why don't you have a seat?" Watson said. "Lucy can make the coffee."

I was tempted to protest, but I decided discretion

was the better part of valor. I had invited myself to come along, after all.

Marlene threw me a look full of questions. I tried to give her an encouraging smile. She slowly lowered herself to perch on the edge of the couch and watched Watson with wide eyes. The detective strolled across the room and stood at the floor-to-ceiling windows, looking out. The curtains were pulled back and sunlight streamed into the room. Curious, I followed him, wanting a peek at the view. French doors opened onto a spacious deck with lounge chairs, a dining table with seating for eight, and a grilling area so elaborate it was more of an outdoor kitchen. The deck overlooked a swimming pool, blue water sparkling in the sun; the grass and sand of the dunes; and the ocean beyond. People walked or jogged along the beach and fishermen were setting themselves up for the day.

"Nice," I said. The house must easily be worth one and a half to two million bucks. Judging by the size and the fact that it was a vacation rental, it probably had six or seven bedrooms and a matching number of bathrooms. Two kitchens maybe, in addition to the outdoor one.

A lot of space for two people. And a lot of money, even at the end of the tourist season.

"Coffee, Lucy?" Watson said.

I scurried back to the kitchen. Connor had taken a seat in a chair next to Marlene.

"Are you going to tell me what this is about?" she asked. Her face had gone pale beneath her tan. "Has something happened to Will?"

Watson turned to face into the room. "First, may I ask your name?"

"Marlene Bergen."

"Your permanent address?"

She waved a hand, indicating her surroundings. "Until Will buys a place, anyway. He's looking at real estate, but he's very particular."

"I am sorry, but we have bad news, Ms. Bergen," Watson said.

"Will? Is he hurt? Has he been in an accident?" She jumped to her feet. "I'll get dressed so you can take me to the hospital."

I'd started rummaging through the cupboards, most of them as vast an expanse of empty white as Alaskan ice fields, searching for coffee, but I soon gave up, as I doubted anyone wanted a hot drink anyway.

"I'm sorry, Marlene," Connor said. "But Will's dead."

"Don't be silly," she said with a strangled laugh. "He's not dead. He's as healthy as a horse. When I had that cold a couple of weeks ago, he didn't catch as much as a sniffle. He said he never gets sick."

"Sit down, Marlene, please," Connor said. She dropped onto the couch.

I sat beside her and took her hand in mine. Her long fingernails were painted the same color as her toes. "It's true, Marlene."

She turned large round eyes to me. Then she gave her whole body a shake, pulled her hand away, and stood up once again. "In that case, I guess I have some calls to make. Thank you for coming to tell me, Detective. Connor . . . uh . . ."

"Lucy."

"Where have they taken him?" she said. "I suppose you want me to call and make the arrangements."

"You're not interested in hearing how he died?" Watson asked.

"I assume the old fool got himself drunk and crashed the car. It was bound to happen sometime. Heavens, I hope he didn't hurt anyone else!"

"Was Mr. Williamson in the habit of driving after drinking?" Watson asked.

"All the time. Said he could handle it." She lowered her voice into a surprisingly good imitation of Will. "'Man learned how to drink out in the rigs, don'tcha know. Ha-ha.'" She resumed her own voice. "Silly old bugger."

Watson gave me a nod. I realized that he was asking me to tell her.

"Marlene," I said, getting to my feet also. I placed a hand on her shoulder, trying to be comforting. "Will wasn't in any sort of accident. He was murdered."

"You can't be serious?"

"I'm afraid she's very serious," Connor said.

"Sit down, please," Watson said.

Marlene slowly did so. I sat beside her, but didn't take her hand again.

"I've been told you and Mr. Williamson were at the book club at the Lighthouse Library yesterday evening," Watson said. "Is that correct?"

"He"—Marlene nodded toward Connor—"invited us. It was fun. Lucy was there too."

"What did you do after that?"

"We went to the Ocean Side Hotel for dinner and a couple of drinks."

"Did anyone join you?"

She shook her head.

"A man by the name of Ralph Harper spoke to Mr.

Williamson at the library as you were leaving. Did you see him again?"

"No."

"Are you sure?"

"Of course I'm sure."

"What did you do after your dinner?"

"We drove home. I mean back here. I watched TV for a bit and went to bed."

"What time was that?" Watson asked.

"Midnight, maybe a little after."

"Mr. Williamson? What did he do?"

"He got a phone call, shortly after we got home. He went out right after that. I . . . didn't see him come to bed. I don't think he did." Marlene's eyes began to fill with tears. "Silly old fool."

"Who was this phone call from?"

"He didn't say. He just said he was going out. I figured he wanted a drink."

"Was he in the habit of going out for another drink after the two of you came home?"

"Sometimes. He drank a lot, Will did. Sometimes he stayed in and drank in front of the TV or his computer, but he usually liked to find a bar. Losers drink alone, he always said."

"But you stayed in?"

"I'd had enough and I was tired."

"You don't know where he went or who he was meeting? Or even if he was meeting anyone?"

"Nope." She stood up again. I popped to my feet as well, feeling somewhat like a jack-in-the-box. "Do you want me to identify the body? It's not too icky, is it? I should get dressed."

"I'll take care of that," Connor said. "The identification, I mean. And no, it's not icky."

She gave him a big smile. "That is so sweet of you."

"Did Mr. Williamson take his car when he went out?" Watson asked.

"Probably. It was late, and Will didn't like to walk if he didn't have to."

"Can we check if it's in the garage?"

"Sure. Come on." Marlene led the way across the living room and down the steps. A door to the garage was beside the front entrance. She opened it, flicked on a light switch, and we all crowded around to peer inside. I don't think I've ever seen a cleaner or emptier garage. Even the concrete floor looked as though it was polished daily. There was none of the detritus of living: no old suitcases, no gardening tools, no boxes or chests gathering dust. My mom was a fastidious housekeeper (okay, she hired a maid who was a fastidious housekeeper) but even our garage contained the occasional spiderweb and dead fly.

Only one space was occupied in this garage: a tiny, spotlessly clean, bright yellow Smart car. "Is that Mr. Williamson's vehicle?" Watson asked, a note of disbelief in his voice.

"Last night he was driving a Lincoln Navigator," Connor said.

"That one's mine," Marlene said. "I needed a little runabout, so Will bought it for me. Cute, isn't it?"

"Very cute," Watson said dryly. He pulled out his notebook. "I'll need a contact number for you, Ms. Bergen. And I'll have to ask you not to leave Dare County until further notice."

"I'm not going anywhere. The rent's paid up on this place until the end of the year."

I couldn't help glancing at Connor. I've never before had to be the one to break the news to someone that their loved one has died, and I guess different people react in different ways. Marlene didn't seem to be too dreadfully upset. I tried to think charitable thoughts. Maybe she was waiting until she was alone to break down.

"Are you and Mr. Williamson married?" Watson asked.

"Nope."

"Who would be his next of kin then?"

"His wife died a couple of years ago. He has one son. I guess I should call him. His name's Michael."

Watson handed her a square of paper. "I'll leave you to get dressed and make what phone calls you need to. I will be back to take a full statement from you later, but you can call me at that number if you think of anything."

"Okay," she said.

"Can you think of any reason anyone might want Mr. Williamson dead?" Watson asked.

"Gosh, no. Will was such a sweetie. Everyone loved him."

I doubted that, and the expression on Watson's face indicated he agreed with me.

"Do you want me to stay for a while?" I blurted out without thinking. If the man in my life—not that I had one—died suddenly, I wouldn't want to be all alone.

"Why would you do that?" she said in simple curiosity.

"I . . . uh . . . well, I thought you might not want to be left on your own. You have a lot to . . . uh . . . process."

"I'm fine. Oh, one thing, Detective. You won't be . . . like, freezing his bank account or anything, will you?"

"Why do you ask?"

"He gave me a credit card of my own, but it's on his bank. Good thing the rent's paid up on this place."

Watson walked away, shaking his head. Connor followed. I gave Marlene one last look. "What?" she said. "I have to live, don't I?"

We went outside. Marlene shut the door behind us. I dug in my bag for my sunglasses. A man and a woman, each one leaner and fitter than the other, ran past, not sparing us a glance. An elderly couple walking three miniature dachshunds shuffled down the road. "Morning," the woman called to us in that cheerful way retired people have toward people who are clearly late for work.

"You think that phone call might have been from Ralph Harper?" Connor asked.

"If so, I can't see Williamson going out at night to meet with him," Watson said. "But I'll ask. I want to pay a call on Ralph anyway. When I can track him down. This time of day, he'll be out on the water."

"He captains a charter fishing boat," Connor explained to me. "Out of Pirate's Cove."

I wasn't thinking about Ralph or about Williamson's phone call. "Was that weird or what?" I asked Watson.

"What do you mean?"

"Marlene didn't seem all that upset."

"She might be the sort to do her grieving in private," he said slowly. "But I don't see it. All in all, I'd much rather someone not pretend to be mourning when they aren't, than putting on a show because they think I expect one."

"She seemed more concerned," I said, "about the potential death of his bank account than the man himself."

"You see it here a lot," Watson said, gesturing to the street of million-dollar vacation homes. "Old guy with money to burn wants a sexy young woman on his arm. Sexy young woman wants a rich guy on hers. It's just a business deal."

"Does being a police officer make you such a cynic?" I said.

When he smiled, and that was a rare occurrence indeed, Detective Watson could be quite handsome. He did so now. "You thought they were in love? How innocent you are, Lucy."

"I'm not innocent," I protested, although I had to admit that I was. I'd been born into a wealthy family, given an excellent education, gone on to have a career I loved and was good at. I turned and looked at Connor. Why, I even believed in love.

And, I realized as though a bolt of lightning had streaked out of the cloudless sky and smacked me straight in the forehead, that the man standing right here beside me was the one. I'd let time tell me if he was the one I wanted to grow old along beside, but right here, right now, Connor was the man I wanted to be with.

"Will you look at that?" Watson laughed. "She's been struck dumb." His phone rang and he pulled it out of his pocket. "Be right there," he said, hanging up. "Two pieces of news. A Lincoln Navigator registered to William Williamson has been located at a marina in Wanchese. When the cruiser pulled up to check it out, the marina manager came out of the office, impressed at how quickly the police had arrived. Seems he'd only just put down his phone, having called in the theft of a boat.

"I'm heading over there now. Connor, Lucy, try to think of anything that might have happened out of the ordinary last night at your book club. Give me a call if you come up with anything."

With that he got into his car. He pulled out of the driveway and sped away as the tires kicked up sand. The dog walkers and the runners had disappeared. Connor and I were alone. I wanted to tell this wonderful, handsome, smart, marvelous man that I loved him.

Instead I said, "I guess I'd better get back to work."

And he said, "I can't keep the budget committee waiting any longer. I'll drop you off."

Chapter 8

"Penny for your thoughts," Connor said.

Blood rushed into my face. "I . . . I . . ." I stuttered.

"I'll admit, I was also taken aback by Marlene's apparent indifference to the news of Will's death, but Sam has a good point. If Will was nothing to her but a meal ticket, she's going to be more concerned about losing that ticket than anything else. I wonder how Marlene and Will's son get on. She didn't mention any other kids from his marriages."

"She said he had only the one son."

We came to a stoplight, and Connor glanced at me.

I dragged my thoughts away from admiration of his gorgeous blue eyes, the color of the open ocean on a sunny day. You can be sure that the wives of my three older brothers have ensured that I know everything there is to know regarding the laws of inheritance in Massachusetts, but I don't know anything about North Carolina. If Stephanie could prove Will was her biological father, might she be in line to inherit something? She might well be. Plenty of wills are open-ended about children and grandchildren. *Present and future heirs of my body,* and such stuffy legal language.

For a moment, I hoped so. If anyone deserved an unexpected windfall it was Stephanie and Pat Stanton. Then, with a shock, I realized that might not be such a good thing. Not if it gave the police a reason to suspect Stephanie of causing Will's premature demise.

Connor turned at Whalebone Junction, and the BMW picked up speed as Highway 12 opened up, heading to the remote seaside villages of Cape Hatteras and the end of the road at Ocracoke Island.

"It's been a good summer," he said, changing the subject. "The merchants should all be pleased."

I mumbled agreement. "It gets pretty quiet here in the winter, I guess."

"Gives us a chance to catch our breath," he said with a laugh. "And restock the stores."

I've been coming to the Outer Banks my whole life, but I've never spent a winter here. My mom and her sister, Ellen, Josie's mother, were born and raised in Nags Head. Mom moved to Boston when she married my dad, but Ellen stayed and convinced her own husband, my uncle Amos, to open a law practice here rather than return to his native Louisiana. Mom brought my siblings and me down here every summer when we were young. She stopped coming once I was old enough to travel on my own, but I continued to visit for at least a couple of weeks every year. Those long glorious summers on the Outer Banks, wrapped in the loving embrace of Ellen and Amos's chaotic family, were the best times of my life.

When I broke off with my long-long-long-standing boyfriend, Richard Eric Lewiston III, son of my father's law partner, and impulsively quit my job, where else would I go but to my favorite place in all the world and into the welcoming arms of my beloved aunt?

And so, here I was, making a new life for myself on the Outer Banks. I turned and looked at Connor. I'd first met Connor the summer I was fourteen and he was fifteen. A walk along the beach. A stolen kiss. We'd gone our separate ways after that, but neither of us had totally forgotten the other. He'd gone to Duke and UNC, became a dentist, and was now the mayor of Nags Head. I'd gotten a master of library science from Simmons, and had worked in the libraries at Harvard.

"So, Dr. McNeil," I said now, "do you have any thoughts on who might have killed Will?"

"Not a one, but I scarcely knew the man."

"What about that Ralph guy we met last night?"

"I've known Ralph Harper a long time. He's pretty much a fixture around here. Him and his *Old Man and the Sea* persona. He wouldn't care if Will threatened to sue him, but to imply that Ralph had made a mistake on the water? Yeah, that would get him mad. Mad enough to kill? No. I don't see it. Ralph's a gentle soul, never been in any trouble. That I know of anyway.

"Where the body was found is puzzling. It's unlikely to be a random sort of attack, if he or his killer went to the bother of stealing a boat." The car slowed and turned into the long driveway. Emergency vehicles were still at the far end of the parking lot, near the boardwalk, and I could see Officer Franklin standing guard beside the yellow police tape.

Farther away, a smaller collection of cars was pulled up near the path to the lighthouse. As well as Bertie's I recognized Ronald and Charlene's, but there were several I didn't know.

I checked my watch and was startled to see how late it was. "Oh, my gosh. It's after ten. I'm late for work."

"I think they'll forgive you this one time," Connor said. He pulled up to the side of the lot, making no move to take a parking spot. "But the budget committee might not forgive me. I hope you don't mind if I don't come in."

"I'm good," I said. I gave him a smile. He smiled back but I got the feeling his mind was already sorting through numbers and balance sheets, moving on to that budget meeting. This morning, I'd had the most amazing, incredible, wonderful, burst of insight. I wanted to shout it to the world, or at least to Connor.

But the world didn't seem all that interested. And I didn't know if Connor even was.

"Have a nice day." I got out of the car and went to work.

Inside, everyone stopped what they were doing as I came in. What they were doing, I guessed, was speculating about the murder. The main room was packed. Nags Head is a small community, and news travels mighty fast. I wasn't surprised to see Louise Jane as well as several members of our library board here.

"Oh, good." Diane Uppiton, board member, turned away from Bertie when she saw me. "Now we can find out what's going on. Have they made an arrest?"

"I hope so. We have to move into damage control immediately," said Curtis Gardner, another board member. Unlike what one might reasonably expect, not all the members of the board are enthusiastic supporters of the library. Diane's goal in life was to see us closed down, and Curtis's goal in life was to keep Diane happy and thus continuing to fund his taste for fast cars and quality bourbon. I hadn't seen his Corvette outside, so he must have come with Diane. Diane was the widow of Jonathan Uppiton, late chair of the board. Fortunately for Diane, at the time of Jonathan's death the couple were separated, very acrimoniously, but not yet divorced. Jonathan hadn't changed his will, so Diane inherited everything.

Everything, unfortunately for us, except his deep love of the Bodie Island Lighthouse Library.

"Damage control?" Bertie said. "Don't be melodramatic, Curtis. I told you, over and over, this has nothing to do with the library. Now, if you'll excuse us, some of us have work to do."

"It may seem to have nothing to do with the library," Louise Jane said, "but the spirits can wander, you know. Those Civil War soldiers that protect the lighthouse would have no trouble going out into the marsh. Would they, Lucy?"

"Why are you asking me?" I said.

"You're the one who lives here."

"Enough," Bertie said. "Lucy, run upstairs and get changed out of your hiking clothes. Charlene, watch the desk until Lucy gets back. I will be in my office if anyone needs me. On *library* business." She turned and walked away.

"See you later, Louise Jane," Charlene said.

Louise Jane harrumphed. She didn't care to be reminded that she didn't actually work here. Diane and Curtis headed for the exit, and Louise Jane suddenly perked up. "Have you a moment, Diane? I've got some great ideas for my Halloween exhibit. Mrs. Fitzgerald thinks they're great, but I want to be sure they meet with your approval."

"I don't . . ." Diane began. Diane had not the slightest interest in the running of the library.

"I'd suggest we pull up a couple of chairs, but we don't seem to be wanted here. Why don't we go into town and grab a coffee?"

Diane did, however, have an interest in impressing on us all her importance. "Yes, that's an excellent idea. We can let these people . . . uh . . . work." The corner of her lip turned up at the very idea.

I ran upstairs to my apartment. Before I jumped in the shower, I made a phone call. "Hi, Stephanie, it's Lucy. Did you or Pat hear from Bertie today?"

"She came around to the house, earlier, to tell us that Will Williamson was found dead this morning. Mom's pretty upset about it."

"How do you feel?"

"Me? I simply don't know, Lucy. I should hate the man for the way he treated Mom, for not caring about me. I wish I'd had the chance to tell him what I thought about him. But on the other hand, I can't help thinking that I've lost my father. I'm sad. And I'm surprised that I'm sad. Does that make any sense?"

"It makes perfect sense. I can't talk for long. I'm late for work as it is. Do you want to have dinner tonight or something?"

"I'm okay, Lucy, but thanks for asking. Mom and I are going to stay in tonight. Another time, maybe."

"You take care," I said.

"I will."

* * *

The morning was busy. Something about police activity and folks needing an excuse to find out what was going on, so they pretended to have been intending to come to the library anyway.

I was on the circulation desk at noon, when Theodore came down the back stairs from the rare-book room. He'd rushed in about a half hour before, saying he desperately needed to consult an old atlas.

"Find what you needed?" I said.

"Jolly good," he replied. He was wearing a tweed jacket, much too warm for the day.

"Open your coat, please," I said.

"Really, Lucy, I resent your implications."

When I first began working here, Bertie had warned me about Theodore. He loved books, the older and rarer the better, but he didn't always worry about how they came into his possession. Taking books from the library without checking them out, and then hunting them down, was almost a game Theodore and Jonathan Uppiton had played.

Bertie, on the other hand, refused to play.

"Coat," I repeated.

He did as I asked. I could see no mysterious lumps or excessively full pockets. "Thanks," I said.

He let out a martyred sigh, and then he leaned over the desk and lowered his voice. "What do you know about the untimely and tragic death of Will Williamson?"

"Nothing."

"I heard you discovered the body."

"No. Butch did," I said, telling the perfect truth.

"I hear the recently departed was at book club the other night. I was sorry I had to miss it. Did he have any interesting insights to offer?"

"About *Kidnapped*, you mean? Not a thing. He only came because his girlfriend wanted to."

"His girlfriend? That is interesting. A friend of literature, is she?"

"I guess," I said, wondering what Theodore was getting at.

"You don't suppose his demise had anything to do with the book club meeting, do you, Lucy?"

"Of course not," I said. "How could it? None of us had met Will before last night."

"You will keep me in the loop, won't you, my dear?"

"There is no loop in which to be kept."

He touched the side of his nose and gave me what he thought of as a conspiratorial wink.

I winked back. *Let him have his fun.*

On his way out, Theodore held the door for Detective Watson, who was coming in. "I need to talk to you, Lucy," Watson said. Theodore's ears twitched and instead of leaving he snatched up the nearest piece of reading material. I doubted he was all that interested in the most recent issue of *Martha Stewart Living*, which was waiting to be returned to the magazine shelf.

"I can't talk right now," I said. "Charlene's gone to lunch. When she gets back she can look after the desk for me."

Watson gave me a long look. Then he turned around and let out an authoritative shout. "Folks, the library's closing. Now."

Heads popped around shelves, and patrons put down books. Theodore looked up from the magazine.

"If you would be on your way, ladies and gentlemen. Thank you," Watson said.

"Hey!" I protested. "You said we didn't have to close today."

He loomed over me, close enough that I leaned back in my chair. He dropped his voice. "I also said that I wanted to talk to you, Lucy. As you cannot leave your work, your work will have to leave you. I don't want half of Nags Head listening in." He looked pointedly at Theodore.

"Okay, okay," I said. "I'll call Bertie to look after the desk."

"Excellent idea," Watson said. He put on his crowd-control voice again. "Never mind, folks. Go back to your business."

The patrons shrugged and exchanged curious glances. "What's goin' on out there, Sam?" a man said.

"Police business," Watson replied.

I picked up the phone and told Bertie what was happening. She said she'd be right out.

"You can tell me, Sammy my boy," the man said. He gave Watson a wink. "It'll go no farther."

"No farther than the nearest bar," Watson said. "Surprised to see you in a library, Eddie. Regular visitor, are you?"

"Figured it was time to check the place out. Meet some nice-lookin' ladies." He smiled at me. I gave him a not very sympathetic smile in return. At seventy years old, with bad hips and a dire shortage of both teeth and hair, Eddie really shouldn't have been trying to flirt with me.

Bertie said we could use her office. She didn't need to add "again." Charles attempted to follow us, but Watson was faster, and the door was slammed shut in the cat's disappointed face.

I settled myself in the single visitor's chair and primly folded my hands in my lap and my legs at the ankles. I was wearing a teal sweater and a black knee-length skirt over opaque tights. Very prim and proper and librarian-ish. "How can I help you, Detective?"

"First, Lucy, you can tell me about the relationship between Stephanie Stanton and Will Williamson." Watson had not taken the seat behind Bertie's desk.

"Who?" I croaked. "I mean, who?"

"Please don't play dumb with me, Lucy. Earlier, when the name of your friend came up, you led me to believe you know something about her that I might want to know."

"I never said—"

"You didn't have to. We were interrupted, and I didn't get the chance to ask further. I'm asking you now."

I took a deep breath. I felt absolutely awful about it, but I had no choice except to spill the beans. "Stephanie is Will's illegitimate daughter."

Watson's face was impassive. I might have told him that they both liked cream in their coffee. "Is this common knowledge?"

"No."

"Why do you know?"

I tried to come up with some reason that wouldn't cast suspicion on Stephanie. I simply couldn't think fast enough under the cool, unblinking stare of Detective Sam Watson. Something about Watson always made me hear the sound of cell doors clanging shut behind me. "I was there when Pat, her mom, told her. Stephanie didn't know who her father was until . . . recently."

"How recently?"

"Uh . . . last night?"

"Why not until last night?"

I let out a long sigh. "Will was married when he had an affair with Pat Stanton, Stephanie's mother. He deserted Pat the moment he found out she was pregnant. He refused to acknowledge paternity, left North Carolina, and never had the slightest thing to do with them. Pat raised Stephanie on her own and never mentioned the rat who'd fathered her. She did a darn fine job, too. Stephanie's a lawyer. And," I added, "a wonderful person."

"All the more reason for me to wonder what happened last night, of all nights, to cause Stephanie's mother to reveal a secret she's held for, what, thirty years?"

"Pat was recently in a serious car accident. She was badly injured. She's going to be okay, but it'll be a long, hard process. That made Stephanie aware of her mother's mortality. Look, it was my bright idea to take Stephanie out last night after book club. Let her have some fun, I thought. She had too much to drink at Jake's, and when she got home, she wanted to know about her father. So Pat told her."

"You're sure Stephanie hadn't known his identity before?"

"Yes, I'm positive. But that doesn't have anything to do with anything. She wanted to know. That's all. Wouldn't you want to know something like that?"

He didn't bother to comment. "You went with Stephanie to her mother's house after you left the restaurant?"

"Yes. She had . . . a drink or two, so I thought she shouldn't drive. I took her home, and came in to say hi to Pat."

"When did you leave their house?"

"I can't have been there more than fifteen minutes or so. Bertie offered to help Pat get ready for bed but Stephanie said she'd do it."

"Bertie? Bertie James was there also?"

"She'd spent the evening with Pat so Stephanie could come to book club. They're good friends."

Watson shook his head. "So Ms. James also heard this story about Williamson?"

"Yes."

"Ms. James didn't think to inform me of this?"

"Why should she?" I protested. "Nothing that happened last night between Pat and Stephanie, or Bertie and me, had anything to do with the death of Will Williamson. We just happened to be talking about him, that's all. Gee, you might as well be asking your wife. She was talking to the man at book club too, you know."

"I have," Watson said.

"Oh."

"Is there anything else about Stephanie Stanton you're keeping from me, Lucy?"

I shook my head. "She lives in Raleigh now, but she's come home to care for her mom after the accident. She's a defense attorney."

"Is that so? Thanks for your time, Lucy. I shouldn't have to mention that if you think of anything else that might be relevant to this case, you'll be in touch." He turned and opened the door. Charles was sitting in the hall, waiting patiently. I knew from CeeCee that her husband was not a cat person. Watson looked down. Charles looked up. His expression indicated that he was no fonder of the good detective than Watson was of him.

I jumped to my feet. "What are you going to do now?"

"Go on a Caribbean cruise," he said dryly. "What do you think I'm going to do, Lucy? I intend to continue with a murder investigation."

He walked away. I ran after him. Charles strolled along behind us.

When we got to the main room, Bertie was politely telling the old guy who'd been asking Watson about the case that if he wanted to take out a book, he needed to apply for a library card. Theodore had left.

Watson pulled his phone out of his pocket as he walked out of the library. Everyone stopped whatever they were doing to watch him go.

Bertie gave me a questioning look. I shook my head, and mouthed, "Stephanie."

"Go," she said.

I galloped upstairs to get my purse and car keys.

By the time I got outside, Watson and his car were nowhere in sight. I leaped into my Yaris and tore out of the parking lot. Once I reached the highway, I realized that excessive speed was probably not a good idea. Watson was sure to guess that I'd be following him, and he wouldn't be above asking the traffic cops to keep an eye out for me.

I eased my foot off the gas and proceeded into town at a statelier pace, keeping a sharp eye for cruisers waiting to pounce.

I made it to Pat's house without incident. Sure enough, Watson's car was on the street, so I parked behind it and got out of my car. Watson obviously hadn't broken any speed limits either, as he was still standing in the doorway while Stephanie asked him what he wanted. Pat's Neon and Stephanie's Corolla were in the driveway, so Steph must have hitched a ride to Jake's to pick up her car earlier.

She glanced over Watson's shoulder and spotted me parking on the street and hurrying up the path.

"Ms. Richardson." Watson rolled his eyes. "Isn't this a surprise? Imagine meeting you here."

"Your visit reminded me," I said. "I have the book Stephanie asked to borrow the other day."

"What book?" Stephanie said.

"The library makes home deliveries?" Watson said. "Isn't that nice?"

I opened my mouth to tell him I was entitled to visit the home of my friend, but snapped it shut when he said, "You're here now, you might as well stay. Ms. Stanton?"

"Stephanie, who's there? What's happening?" Pat called.

"It's the police, Mom. And Lucy."

"Let them in, dear."

Stephanie stepped back, and Watson and I entered. Pat was in the same chair she'd been sitting in yesterday, with a glass of tea and a stack of books resting on the table next to her and a book open on her lap. Sunlight streamed into the room, and something delicious simmered in the kitchen. Tomato soup perhaps. At the scent of food, my stomach reminded me that I'd had nothing to eat since that granola bar with Butch hours ago.

Watson asked Pat and Stephanie their names. They didn't look at each other or at me. They knew why we were here. Stephanie remained standing, and she did not offer Detective Watson a seat.

"Are you acquainted with a man by the name of William Williamson?" Watson asked.

"Yes," Pat said. "Although that was a long time ago, and we have had no contact for many years. I heard he was found dead this morning. I assume you're here about that?" She'd lost a lot of weight since her accident, and her deep brown eyes, so unlike her daughter's, were eagle-sharp in a face outlined by prominent bones.

"How did you hear?" Watson asked.

"A friend stopped by to tell me. Everyone's talking about it."

He nodded, acknowledging her point. "Do either of you want to tell me about your relationship with Mr. Williamson?"

Stephanie glanced at me. I gave her what I hoped was an apologetic smile. It was all my fault that the police had come here. I'd had no choice, but I doubted Stephanie would be in the mood to forgive me. "Because you're here, Detective," she said. "I assume you've been told that William Williamson was my father. That was in the biological sense only. I never knew him, and he was never in my life or in my mother's life after I was born."

"When did you find this out?"

Stephanie gave me a look. "I assume you know that also. Thanks, Lucy."

"I didn't . . ."

"If it matters," Watson said, "Ms. Richardson spoke to me only when I asked. She's aware of her legal obligation to help the police in cases such as this."

"I'm a lawyer," Stephanie said. "I assume you know that too."

"I do. Now, please answer my question."

"My mother told me the details of my parentage for the first time last night."

"The time?"

"Eleven, or thereabouts."

"Why last night? Why never before?"

"Please, Detective," Pat said. "This is extremely painful. I've kept this secret for many years."

"It's okay, Mom. We have nothing to hide and you have nothing at all to be ashamed of." Stephanie turned back to Watson. In the sort of clipped tones she'd probably use in court, she told him that her mother had come close to death, and if Pat had died, she would have never known who her father was. "So I asked her. And she told me."

"Had you met Mr. Williamson prior to this revelation by your mother?"

"He came to Lucy's book club last night." Stephanie let out a choked laugh. "There he was, my own dad, sitting down beside me and saying 'nice to meet you' in a totally bored and disinterested voice, and neither of us even knew. Other than that, I've never laid eyes on him."

Watson glanced around the living room. The house was small, the decor decades out-of-date, the old and well-worn furniture looked like the kind that was cheap even when it had been new. "Were you aware that Mr. Williamson was a wealthy man?"

"I guessed so. He looked prosperous enough—nice clothes, big flashy gold watch. He had a girlfriend about my age, the sort of giggly blond airhead who wouldn't have given him the time of day if he didn't have money to spend on her."

"Did you think you might be in line for an inheritance?"

Stephanie's back stiffed and she clenched her fists. She faced him, a tiny ball of fury, struggling to keep her redheaded temper under control.

"That is a preposterous suggestion," Pat said.

"Is it?" Watson said. "What did you do last night, after Lucy and Bertie James left here?"

"I helped my mom get into bed, and then I sat in front of the TV and drank. It was very late when I went to my own bed. I didn't check the time."

"Ms. Stanton?"

"As my daughter told you, I went to bed."

"Did you get up during the night?"

"I did not. I have, you might have noticed"—she grimaced toward her legs, propped up and covered in blankets—"mobility issues."

"Did your daughter leave the house at any time?"

"No," Stephanie said.

"No," Pat said.

"Would you have known if she had, Ms. Stanton?" The two women couldn't help exchanging glances.

"Ms. Stanton?" Watson said.

Pat said nothing. Watson let the silence linger.

"My mother's in some pain from her injuries, so she takes a sleeping pill to help her sleep," Stephanie said at last.

"Do you have anyone who can account for your movements last night?" Watson said. "After, say, eleven o'clock?"

"No," Stephanie replied.

"In that case, I'm going to have to ask you to come down to the station with me," Watson said.

"No!" I said. "That's ridiculous. I can vouch for Stephanie. She had a drink or two at Jake's last night. She wouldn't have been driving. When I left she said she was going to open a bottle of wine."

"Drunk, was she?" Watson asked.

"Lucy, you're not helping here," Stephanie said. "I can't leave my mother, Detective. You will have to wait until I can call someone to stay with her."

"Lucy can do that," Watson said.

"Hey!" I protested. "I mean, I don't mind looking after Pat, but I . . . have to get back to work."

"You left your work quickly enough to come here, and uninvited," Watson pointed out. "Let's go, Ms. Stanton."

"Am I under arrest?" Steph asked.

"Not at this time."

"Lucy," Pat said, "bring my chair." The wheelchair was in the corner of the room, where it had been yesterday.

"It's okay, Mom. I'll go down to the station and answer the detective's questions. He has to spend his time doing something, even though he should be out searching for a killer."

Watson kept his face impassive.

"As for you, Lucy," Stephanie said. "You might as well do something helpful."

"I . . ."

Stephanie headed for the door. Watson followed.

"I'll call my uncle. Amos O'Malley," I shouted after them. "He's a criminal lawyer. He'll help."

Stephanie looked over her shoulder at me. "Thanks."

And they left. Watson shut the door behind him.

"I am so, so sorry," I said to Pat. "I didn't know what to do. I had to tell Watson what I knew."

"Of course you did, dear," Pat said. "Don't give it another thought. Stephanie will set everything straight, and that will be that. I suppose I should be grateful that no one can suspect I crept out of the house in the dead of night, drove into town, and murdered a man in cold blood. Believe me—there were times when I wanted to do precisely that, but those times are long gone. When I heard he was back in town, I surprised myself when I realized I had absolutely no desire to see him."

Here was Pat, her daughter dragged off to the police station to be interrogated about the murder of her former lover, trying to make *me* feel better. If it was possible, I felt worse.

I was the one who talked Stephanie into coming out for a drink. I was the one with the face so readable, Watson knew I knew something. I dropped into a chair. "This is all my fault."

"Don't be ridiculous. It's all the fault of the person who killed Will Williamson. And we both know that person was not my daughter. Stephanie was making our lunch when you came to the door. I'll have it now, once you've called Amos."

I fumbled for my phone.

"I'd like you to join me, if you haven't had your own lunch. In the meantime, I'm going to call Bertie and let her know what's happening. I have the number of a nursing service here, in case Stephanie is . . . delayed." Finally, her voice broke. Pat burst into tears.

The nursing service arrived a couple of hours later, and I drove back to the library, feeling about as lousy as I ever had. Uncle Amos had been in his office when I called, and said he'd go to the police station immediately. In his day, my uncle had been one of the top defense attorneys in the state. He was now easing into retirement, spending most of his time doing less exciting legal stuff, but he was ready to leap back into the fray if needed.

I hoped he would not be needed this time. Not by Stephanie. But I was glad she'd have him on her side, in case worse came to worst.

Bertie was still on the circulation desk when I got back. She took one look at my face and said, "Tea." She picked up the phone, and a minute later Ronald came jogging down the stairs.

"The YA book club will coming in soon, Bertie, so I can't take the desk for long."

"We won't be long."

I said, "Where's Charlene?"

"She's gone to Manteo for a meeting. With the municipal election coming up, they're thinking of putting together a display with information about the history of voting rights, particularly for women, and she's helping them out. Now, let's get that tea."

We went to the staff break room. Bertie told me to

sit down and switched the kettle on. I have never developed a taste for iced tea and prefer it piping hot. She took a full pitcher out of the small fridge and poured herself a glass while waiting for the water to boil. "What happened, honey?"

I buried my head in my hands. "Oh, Bertie. It's all my fault."

"Did you kill Will Williamson?"

I looked up, shocked at the question. "Of course not."

"Then it's not your fault."

"Well, not that part anyway." Charles had leaped up onto the table, and I gave him a pat. Bertie made my tea and put a steaming cup in front of me before sitting down.

"I told Watson about Will and Pat and Stephanie. I know you were right and that I had to, but I sure didn't want to and now she's in trouble. Watson's taken Steph to the police station."

"Has he arrested her?"

"He didn't say so, at least not when I was there."

"That's good then."

"Amos is with her."

"Even better."

I sipped at my tea. I was trying to cut back on sugar, but Bertie had put an extra spoonful in. I appreciated it. "I still feel bad."

"That's natural enough, honey. Pat thought she was doing the right thing by keeping the truth from Stephanie, but secrets have a way of multiplying when they're kept secret. Bad things fester in the dark. I have faith in Sam Watson. He's a good man and a good detective. He'll get to the bottom of it."

"This is another blow to Pat and Steph, another crisis

they sure don't need. Someone from the nursing home care service is with Pat now and that has to be costing a lot, particularly if Stephanie has to keep going down to the police station. Never mind that Stephanie's losing even more time from her work and—"

"I'm going to call Pat's and my circle of friends. We'll start doing shifts at Pat's house. I'll set up a roster that Stephanie can call upon if she needs to."

"That'll be great. You can put me down too."

Bertie smiled at me.

"But right now, I think I can be put to better use," I said.

"How?"

"Stephanie didn't kill Will. You and I know that because we know Stephanie. But even more to the point, I know it because I saw those lights on Monday night, the lights someone put out to trick Will into crashing onto the shore. Marlene saw them too. Even if no one believes us, I know what I saw. Will and Marlene weren't hurt, but they may well have died, and I'm going to bet that was the intention of whoever did it. Those lights prove that Will's death wasn't a random attack or a mugging gone wrong. It means someone had to know, first, that he'd be out in his boat that day, and second, that he's such a bad sailor he could be fooled by a trick."

Bertie nodded.

"That someone was determined enough to come back another night to try to kill Will a different way. This time they succeeded. Will Williamson wasn't a nice man when he was young, and I'm going to assume he never got much better. That means he had enemies.

Marlene says everyone loved him, but I doubt that very much. I can't say I loved him on first meeting." I thought about the incident with Ralph. If my theory about the lights was right, then Ralph probably wouldn't have killed Will either. I made a mental note to tell Watson that. "I'm going to find out what I can about who might have had it in for Will. Don't try to stop me, Bertie; I'm determined to do this. I need to do what I can to help Stephanie."

"Stop you?" Bertie said. "I think it's a great idea. As long as you promise me that whatever you uncover, you'll take to Watson immediately."

"I promise," I said.

"Where do you plan to start?"

I drained my teacup and got to my feet. "Marlene. She's obviously the best person to tell me what Will's been up to since he came back to Nags Head. I'm going to act on the assumption that there's a reason he was killed here, on the Outer Banks, and not in Alaska or wherever he was living before." I glanced at the clock on the wall. "It's almost four now. I'll head over there when the library closes."

"Go now," Bertie said. "I'll take the desk for the rest of the day."

"Are you sure? I don't mean to skip out on work."

"Take whatever time you need. We can consider this case library business. Pat has done so much for the library over the years that it's time for us to return the favor."

I gave Bertie a hug, feeling tears welling up behind my eyes.

When we got back to the main room, the kids were arriving for the YA book club. Some of these teenagers were old enough to drive, but most were being dropped off by parents. The parents were taking the opportunity to gossip about the murder. Ronald, today sporting a tie inspired by the TV show *The Big Bang Theory*, was going to great pains to inform them that no one had died in the marsh, although the body had been found there.

"Is that true?" I whispered to him. "Have the police found out where he was killed?"

"I have absolutely no idea. We don't need any more talk of this property being a magnet for murder." He turned back to the teens. "Time to begin! Let's head upstairs, everyone."

Their footsteps clattered on the iron stairs. I had to grin at the range of their attire. Everything from preppy skirts hiked up to the thigh (and beyond), to baggy jeans that left less to the imagination than one might like, to solid black Goth clothes and makeup.

A boy ran past me, one hand struggling to hold up his pants and the other gripping a paperback with a lurid cover of vampire fangs and dripping blood. When Ronald had begun the YA group, he had to argue with parents who wanted the kids reading classics, or at least books the parents thought they should be reading. He pointed out that Young Adult books today had a lot to say about the world in which these kids were growing up, and he wanted the kids to use the books as a springboard to discuss things about their own lives.

As always, Ronald—charming, gentle Ronald—won the parents over. His YA book club was a huge success. Although, I wondered as I saw Charity, the eldest Peterson girl, give the pants-clutching boy an elbow to the ribs with a giggle and toss of her hair, if some of the kids had joined for reasons other than personal improvement and the opportunity to engage in discussion about the state of the world.

Judging by the look on Mrs. Peterson's face as she watched her daughter, she was thinking the same thing. Poor overprotective Mrs. Peterson was in for a rough few years.

Chapter 9

I decided not to call ahead to ask Marlene if I could come over, thinking it would be better to catch her off guard. I had no idea what I hoped to accomplish by paying her a visit. It was unlikely she'd either drop to her knees in front of me to tearfully confess, or gasp and say something like, "Now that you mention it, I saw the butler slipping a knife into his pocket." I'm a perfectly dreadful judge of character and likely to not notice if a confession was written across the guilty party's face.

But I drove into town, knowing that I had to try. I might be able to uncover something to take to Detective Watson.

Although when (if?) I did learn something, I might be better off telling Butch first. Watson never seemed overly fond of me.

Thinking of Butch the cop made me think of Butch the man. Oh dear. Now that I realized I was in love with Connor, what was I to do about Butch? Could I continue going out for drinks or enjoying early-morning walks with him? Would I be breaking his heart? Would he be angry at me? Would he say he never wanted to see me again?

Would he even care?

Why is life so complicated? All I want is for everyone to be happy.

I pulled up in front of Marlene's rental house and reminded myself that right now my complications were pretty minor compared to the mess Stephanie was finding herself in.

Marlene answered the door before the last chime had died away. "Oh," she said. "I was expecting someone else." She was dressed in a tight blue T-shirt and white short-shorts that showed off her long, gorgeous, deeply tanned legs. I felt dreadfully dowdy in my librarian uniform.

"Sorry," I said. "I was passing and thought I'd drop in and check that you're okay."

She smiled. "That's sweet of you, Lucy, but I'm fine. Would you like to come in? I've just opened a bottle of chilled white wine."

"Thanks," I said, following her into the house and up the stairs. Wow, this detecting stuff was easy.

As we walked past the kitchen, Marlene grabbed a glass from the cupboard. Red-and-white-striped cushions were laid out on the lounge chairs on the deck, and a frosty silver cooler rested on the table beside a stack of fashion magazines.

Marlene handed me the glass and dropped into her chair. "Help yourself."

I poured a dribble of the wine, although I didn't particularly want a drink at four in the afternoon. If I had a full glass, I'd be ready for bed by six, but I wanted to keep this meeting friendly and casual. I glanced around, searching for somewhere comfortable to sit. The only seats with cushions on them were loungers, and I didn't fancy trying to balance on the bare slats of the aluminum furniture. I lowered myself gingerly and tucked my legs up, feeling somewhat silly stretched out in the sun wearing tights and pumps. Marlene had not put up any umbrellas, so I had no protection from the hot sun.

A yellow beach towel was draped over the balcony railing. The blue waters of the pool sparkled and out at sea, waves roared ashore. Farther down the beach, brilliantly colored kites danced on the wind.

"Isn't this perfect?" Marlene said with a contented sigh.

"It is that. Where are you from?"

"North Dakota. Where the winters are long and cold and the only water is what fills the bathtub and the kitchen sink." She shuddered, not entirely for show. "I'm never going back there. You're lucky to live here. Do you like it?"

"I love it." I wasn't here to talk about myself. "Are you going to be able to . . . uh . . . stay on?"

"I sure the heck hope so." She took a long drink, and then she gestured to her own body, spread out and soaking up the sun. "I know you're thinking that I didn't exactly pull out the widow's weeds. But heck, Will and I weren't married, so I'm not a widow. He was an okay guy, and he could be a lot of fun to be around. He sure knew how to spoil a girl. I'm sorry he's dead, if that matters, but I intend to go on living. I don't believe in hypocrisy. I had enough of that in North Dakota. As for staying on here . . . the rent's paid for a couple more months, and I checked my credit card. It's still good. I transferred some cash into my own account, just to be sure. Does that make me sound mercenary?"

"Uh . . ."

"I don't care if it does. A girl's gotta look after herself, right? Ain't no one else going to do it for me, is there? That guy Will met the other night, who brought us to your library? The mayor? I heard he's a doctor too, must have some money. Do you know if he's single?"

"No!"

Marlene's eyebrows rose. "Like that, is it? Okay, I know when to back off."

"I didn't mean . . ."

"You sure did."

Marlene was obviously a lot better at reading people than I was. I finished my dribble of wine. Marlene waved her hand. "Help yourself to another."

I checked the label as I poured. Way out of my price range. I kicked off my shoes, and settled back in my chair. The sun was as delicious on my bare arms as the excellent wine was on my tongue. I wanted to strip off my tights so I could tan my legs too.

"I have a bathing suit I can lend you if you want to go for a swim," she said.

Tempting as that offer was, I reminded myself why I was here. "No, thanks. I won't stay long. Has Detective Watson been back?"

"He sent a female cop around with a bunch more questions. She fingerprinted me. She said it was for elimination purposes," Marlene grimaced, "but it made me feel like a common criminal. I can't help them, and I told her so. I don't know who phoned Will last night, or why he went out, or who he was meeting. He might not have been planning to meet anyone. He didn't talk to me much, not about stuff like what he was thinking. He talked a lot about the old days, when he was young. I didn't care, so never paid much attention."

I wondered what it would be like to live with a man you didn't love, didn't pretend to love, and who didn't love you in return.

For many years, my parents' marriage had not been a good one. Aunt Ellen told me they fell head over heels for each other when they met, her a high school girl, him a college student. Obviously things changed; I'm the youngest of their four children and for as long as I can remember my parents had barely tolerated each other. They went to social occasions together, putting on a show of beaming happily at each other and exchanging not so secret little glances, but otherwise he went to work, played golf, or sat in his den and drank expensive whiskey and smoked big cigars, while she fluttered about with her charities and social (i.e., gossip) circles. Not long ago, Mom had caught him having an affair. It looked for a while as though the sham of a marriage would finally be over, but somehow both of them dug deep and came out of it stronger. They'd gone on an extended European vacation, their first together in decades, and by all accounts had enjoyed spending time in each other's company.

It was what I'd seen in my parents' marriage that had caused me to flee when Richard Eric Lewiston III, who everyone called Ricky, had done the long-expected thing and proposed to me. I realized that if I married Ricky,

I'd be committing myself to the same loveless life as my mother. And Ricky and I hadn't even had that mad head-over-heels phase that might have made the dull years worthwhile.

"That cop took Will's computer," Marlene said. "I'm going to have to buy myself one now. I can't just use my phone all the time. Do you know a good place?"

"They took his computer? Did they say why?"

She shrugged. "Checking his e-mails to see if he'd been in contact with someone who was threatening him, I guess. Will really liked his computer. He spent a lot of time on the Internet. I told her, that cop, that. He played a lot of games." She laughed. "Sometimes, I'd hear him laughing and cheering, and sometimes he'd be yelling like the blazes at the darn thing."

"Last night you told the book club you'd seen strange lights from shore when you were out in the storm on Monday." I asked Marlene, "Did you tell the police that?"

"Why would I?"

"Don't you think they'd find that important?"

"I told her about wrecking the boat, but she didn't seem interested." Marlene's eyes opened wide. "Gosh, I sure hope the boat was insured. It was worth a lot."

"Was it new?"

"No, it was old. An antique, like. Worth a lot of money. Will bought it when we first got here to the Outer Banks. He said he'd been dreaming of having his own boat for thirty years. He used to go out on the water with his dad when he was a kid. He said that was when he learned everything he needed to know about operating a boat." She shook her head. Her glossy ponytail bounced. "Will wasn't good at learning new things. Or at letting people tell him what to do."

"Did you tell the coast guard people who rescued you about the lights?"

"Nah. What was the point? They were sure mad at Will and he got mad right back. Lots of waving and shouting. He threatened to sue them."

"Why?"

"He said he'd been managing fine until they interfered and caused him to go off course. That was just Will's way. Nothing was ever Will's fault. He never would have taken them to court or anything. I learned not to interfere when Will was on his high horse. That old guy laughed at Will, which made Will all the madder. Will didn't like to be laughed at. Didn't matter much anyway. In all that fuss and bother, no one paid any attention to little old me."

I was sorry to hear that. If Marlene told Watson about the lights now, he'd assume she was only repeating the story Will had come up with, inspired by Louise Jane's tale, to make himself look like not quite the total fool he was.

"Did Will regularly threaten to sue people?"

"All the time," she sighed. "It did get tedious sometimes."

"He must have had enemies then?"

"Nah. No one took Will's threats seriously. That made him all the madder."

"How long were you together?" The hot sun and the cold wine were doing their magic on my head. I had to fight to keep my eyes open, to stop myself sinking into the chair and drifting off to sleep.

I doubt Sherlock Holmes ever fell asleep while questioning a suspect.

Was Marlene a suspect? I didn't know. I liked her. I liked her cheerfulness, bouncy nature, and wide-open honesty. But I was well aware that didn't mean she wasn't putting on an act, and had nothing but a heart of pure coal.

"I met him about two months ago," she said. "He was driving back from Alaska. He wanted to take his time, see the country. Visit all those places he'd never had time to go when he was working all the time. He came into the restaurant in Vegas where I was waitressing. We hit it off right away. I quit my job and left town with him."

"You just packed up and left? With a man you didn't know?" Maybe I *am* an innocent, like Watson had said.

"Sure. The job was useless. I'd been trying to get on at a better place, where I'd get decent tips, but there are more attractive women in Vegas than there are jobs. And let's say I know I'm not tops on that scale."

I mumbled something.

"It sounded like fun, and I had nothing to stay in Vegas for. Come on, Lucy, you met Will. Not hard to look at, was he?"

"I guess not."

"Although he was a bit too much on the short side for my taste. I had to give up wearing high heels because Will didn't like me to be taller than him. But best of all, he was rich. What's not to like?" She laughed and took another swig of her wine. She stretched languorously and wiggled her red-tipped toes. "Isn't this the life? Better than wearing my feet out working in a miserable diner in Vegas and sharing a mouse-infested apartment with three other girls, I can tell you." Her voice turned hard. "And I can tell you, Lucy, I'm not going back to that life."

Then she giggled again. "I've shocked you, haven't I?"

"I . . . uh . . ."

"I sure have. You're so sweet, Lucy. I like you. I hope I can stay on in the Outer Banks and we can become good friends."

"I'd like that," I said. And I meant it. Who am I to judge a woman for trying to get ahead in life?

Unless it involved murder. I had to remember why I was here. "Has anything else strange or unusual happened to you and Will since you got here? Like the lights, I mean?"

Her face turned serious, and she appeared to give the question some thought. "Not that I know of. Other than that guy who ran into the back of our car in the parking lot of the supermarket with his grocery cart and threatened Will."

"What happened?"

"Will was backing out, and some old guy wasn't watching where he was going. The car and his cart bumped. His eggs broke or something. They got into a shouting match." She stifled a yawn.

"Isn't it up to the driver of the car to watch for pedestrians?" I asked.

"Will said the man had deliberately run into us, wanting an insurance settlement or something. Typical Will." She shrugged.

"Sure is hot," I said, changing the subject.

"Bathing suit offer still stands."

"No, thanks. Sounds like Will got into trouble wherever he went. Did he ever mention anyone who might have followed him from Alaska?"

"Gee, Lucy, you're sounding like a cop or something."

"I don't mean to. I'm just speculating. You have to be wondering too, Marlene. Why would someone kill Will?"

"I guess you librarians read a lot, don't you? I figure there's no mystery about it. He was out at night, drinking, probably flashing his money around. Someone tried to roll him; Will fought back and he got the worst of it. They had to dump the body somewhere. Poor Will. I can so see him refusing to hand over twenty bucks and getting himself killed for it." She grimaced and wiped at her face. She hadn't taken her sunglasses off since I'd arrived, so I couldn't tell if she'd been crying.

Even Marlene hadn't connected the dots between the mysterious lights and the death of Will. Maybe I did read too many mystery novels. I'd like to think it was a common mugging gone wrong, but that was unlikely. Will's expensive watch hadn't been taken, and Watson had said Will still had his phone and wallet on him.

"You said Will has a son. Have you called him?"

"Yeah. He's on his way. I thought you were him at the door."

As if summoned by her very words, the doorbell rang. Marlene jumped up and hurried to answer it. I struggled to my feet. My glass was empty. With a regretful glance at the bottle, I put it down on the table.

When Marlene returned, she was followed by a man dressed in an ironed blue shirt, open at the collar, and pressed gray slacks. He crossed the room in a few quick steps and came out onto the balcony, hand outstretched. "Hi, I'm Mike Williamson. Marlene didn't tell me she had company." He was around my age, good-looking, with thick black curls, a strong jaw, sharp cheekbones, and gray eyes. Those eyes again. There could be no doubt that this was Will's son. Stephanie's half brother.

I accepted his handshake. His grip was strong, and he held my hand for a moment longer than was polite. At first I thought I'd seen him someplace before, but I decided it was the resemblance to his father. "I'm Lucy," I said, pulling my hand back, feeling my cheeks flush.

"Great to meet you, Lucy. You're not leaving on my account, I hope." He turned to Marlene. "Tell her to stay, Mar."

I studied the interaction between Marlene and Mike. They seemed friendly enough. I remembered that Mike's mom and Will were divorced and that Will's second wife had died. No reason the young man should have anything against his father's girlfriend, who was the same age as Mike.

"I'll get another bottle," Marlene said. She skipped into the house as I tried to say, "No more for me."

Mike kept his eyes fixed on my face, and the edges of his mouth curled up. A dimple appeared in his right cheek. I shifted, uncomfortable under his gaze. "I'm sorry for your loss."

"Thanks. Poor old Dad. My folks split up when I was in grade school. After that, my mom moved back to Raleigh and took me with her, so I didn't see my dad much. He and I weren't close, but it's still a shock." He took a breath. "It's nice that Marlene's friends are here to support her."

"I don't know that Marlene needs much in the way of support," I said.

She came out carrying a bottle of Prosecco and a fresh glass for Mike. "I thought bubbly would be nice," she said. I didn't think Italian sparkling wine was entirely appropriate, but who was I to object? Once she'd served Mike, she made a move to refill my glass. I stopped her. "I've had enough. Thanks. I'm driving."

"Come on," Marlene said. "Let's have a toast to poor Will."

"Not for me."

She gave me a pout of disappointment but didn't press it. "More for the rest of us. To Will. He was a good sport." She lifted her glass in a toast and then drank deeply, as did Mike.

When they'd finished, she asked him, "Have you spoken to the police yet?"

"Just on the phone. I've got an appointment at the station at six with the detective in charge of the case. Better go light on this for now." He gestured to his wineglass.

"So, Lucy," Mike said as we all took seats. Rather than laying myself out on the lounge chair, I perched on the edge, my feet on the floor. I had been getting far too comfortable. "Do you live here or are you on holiday?"

"Lucy works at the library," Marlene said.

Mike's eyebrows lifted. "A librarian. You sure don't look it."

I didn't bother to ask him what a librarian looked like. "Marlene and I've been wondering who might have had it in for your dad. Be mad enough to kill him, I mean. Do you have any ideas? The police will want to know."

Mike shrugged. "I didn't know him well, as I said. He and Marlene stopped off at my place for a couple of days on their way here. First time I've seen him in years. He might have had a ton of enemies, but I wouldn't know about it."

I got to my feet. "Well, I'd better be off. Thanks for the wine, Marlene."

She leaped up and gave me a hearty hug. "It was so great of you to come over. Let's go out for a drink one night soon. Dinner, maybe. I bet you know all the fun places."

"Sure. We can do that."

"Great idea," Mike said, although I hadn't noticed him being invited. "I'd like to get to know Lucy better."

"How long are you planning to be here?" I asked.

"I might not leave," he said, giving me a meaningful look. "Not if I have something to stay for."

I blushed and stumbled on the top step.

"Have you booked a hotel yet?" Marlene said.

"Hotel? Oh no, Mar, I'm not spending money on a hotel. This place will suit me fine."

"You can't . . ."

"Sure I can," he said. "It's plenty big enough for two. I don't imagine you'll be staying much longer anyway, now that the bank account's been closed."

Chapter 10

So things weren't quite as friendly between Michael and Marlene as first impressions indicated. I wished I'd thought to ask her if Will had recently changed his will, although that might have been *waaay* too nosy, even for me. He could have left his money to anyone he wanted, from a new girlfriend to a shelter for homeless cats, but if he didn't have a will, or hadn't changed it recently, then chances were that everything he had would go to Mike.

And, judging by his last comment, Mike was not inclined to share with Marlene.

I wondered how Mike would feel if he found out he had to share his inheritance with Stephanie. He probably wouldn't be overjoyed, although he might like to discover he had a long-lost sister. Most of my only-child friends said they wished they had siblings. I, on the other hand, often wished I didn't have three older brothers.

I glanced at my watch. Five thirty. Mike said he had

an appointment with the police at six, so there was no point in my going around to talk to Sam Watson. I wanted to call Bertie, but I didn't want to sit in their driveway while Marlene and Mike peeked out the windows, wondering what I was up to, so I drove around the corner and parked there.

"Any news?" I asked my boss when she answered the phone.

"Pat called a few minutes ago. Stephanie's at home."

I let out a long sigh. "Thank heavens. Did she say what happened?"

"The police are interested in Stephanie's whereabouts last night after you and I left around eleven. Stephanie has no alibi, but as Amos pointed out to Detective Watson, that means nothing. It was the middle of the night. Most people who don't have a bed partner, and even a good many of those who do, don't have alibis for the early hours."

"Good point."

"Pat didn't say it right out, but she implied that the police are trying to find someone who saw Stephanie or her car on the streets after we left."

"They're wasting their time," I said. "Besides, Steph's car was left behind at Jake's when I drove her home."

"Yes, but Pat's car's drivable. Easy enough for her to take that one. Sam Watson told Stephanie not to leave Dare County. Amos countered that she's a respected member of the legal profession employed by a prominent firm in Raleigh. Her home and all her contacts are in this state, so Watson said okay, but she's not to leave North Carolina."

"I guess that's better."

"Marginally."

"Do you need me back at work?" I asked.

"No. Do you have something in mind?"

"If an incident from Will's wayward youth has reared its ugly head," I said firmly, "I know precisely where to go to find out about it."

"See you tomorrow then," Bertie said, hanging up.

Aunt Ellen and Uncle Amos own a beautiful little house set back from the beach. They moved out of the big rambling home in which they raised their family and entertained my brothers and me and bought this small one that's delightfully perfect, although surrounded by giant rental homes like Will and Marlene's. When I drove up, I was pleased to see Uncle Amos's car in the driveway.

My aunt answered the door and enveloped me in a big hug. "What brings you here, honey? Not that it's not always a joy to see you."

"Not a joyful visit, I'm afraid. I want to talk to you about the Will Williamson situation."

"Now, Lucy, you know I can't say much about that." Amos stood at the top of the stairs. "Stephanie has retained me, so I am bound by client privilege."

"I know that," I said. "It's Aunt Ellen I'm here to see."

"Me? Good heavens, what do I know about any of this?"

"Perhaps more than you are aware." As we spoke we instinctively walked up the stairs. Like Marlene's house, the main floor was completely open. It was a good deal smaller and decorated with a personal touch that bordered on the chaotic, but the view was every bit as good as Marlene's. A pile of vegetables sat on the granite countertop, waiting to be chopped, and a pot of water bubbled on the stove. "Oh, I'm sorry. I've interrupted your dinner preparations."

"Take a seat, honey," Ellen said. "I can cook and talk at the same time."

"She can even chew gum and walk," Amos said, and I laughed, comfortable in this home, among these people.

Without asking what I wanted, my aunt put the kettle on, and I smiled to myself.

While Aunt Ellen prepared pasta sauce and Uncle Amos listened without interrupting, I explained about the mysterious lights. Aunt Ellen looked doubtful, but Amos's ears almost visibly pricked up. "That is interesting. Stephanie said nothing to me or Watson about it."

"That's because I seem to be the only person who thinks it relevant."

"I think it highly relevant," he said. "Now, tell us what you want Ellen to do?"

"We can't go to Alaska, digging into Will's past," I said. "But I'm thinking that doesn't matter. There's got to be a reason he was killed so soon after returning to the Outer Banks. It's entirely possible someone remembered an old grudge."

Ellen and Amos exchanged glances.

"He's about your age, Aunt Ellen. Did you know him back when?"

She nodded slowly. "He was at school same time I was, although a few years ahead."

"Do you remember anything about him?"

"I didn't remember him at all until I read about his

death in the paper. The article mentioned his age and said he'd lived here for many years. I dug out the old yearbooks and looked him up. He was a fine-looking young man."

"We know he married, but he had an affair with Pat Stanton, and he ran out on her as soon as she got pregnant. It's entirely possible other women or girls were in the same situation and never forgave him. Maybe even a husband or boyfriend wanting revenge after all these years." *Revenge*. Someone had said that word recently.

Stephanie. Stephanie had said it was time to get revenge on William Williamson.

I shoved the thought aside.

"You've thought of something," Amos said.

"Nothing!"

He gave me a look that must have turned many a fresh-faced young prosecutor to quivering jelly. "If you say so."

"I see what you're getting at, honey." Aunt Ellen poured spaghetti noodles into the boiling stockpot. "I'll ask around. I'm still in touch with plenty of people from my long-ago youth. Time to get the gossip mill in gear."

"That," Uncle Amos said, "will not be difficult."

"Now," Ellen said. "You'll stay for dinner, Lucy."

It was not a question, but I shook my head. "Thanks, but no. I have another call to make."

"Where?" Amos asked.

"You probably don't wanna know."

I drove the few blocks to the police station. The sun was setting over the sound and the sky was streaked with soft shades of gray and pink. I was hoping Watson would be finished with Mike, but if he wasn't I would wait.

"I'm sorry," said the officer behind the reception desk. "Detective Watson has left for the day. Do you want to see someone else?"

"No," I said. "I'll come back tomorrow."

"Lucy, what brings you here?" Butch crossed the room. He'd changed out of the clothes he'd worn to go hiking (was that only twelve hours ago?) and was wearing his uniform.

"I have some information for Detective Watson, but they tell me he's not here."

"Can I help you?"

I hesitated.

"Let's grab a drink and maybe a bite to eat and you can tell me."

"Aren't you working?"

"I'm just coming off shift. Your timing's excellent. How about the fishing pier?"

"Sure. I'll meet you there."

"Great," he said. "Give me ten minutes to change."

I knew I should have refused. I didn't want to encourage Butch, but I needed to run my ideas past someone.

I reached the restaurant first. I checked my phone, hoping I'd missed a beep to tell me I had an incoming call or text from Connor. Nothing. I swallowed my disappointment and went inside. The restaurant was almost full, but I was shown to a couple of brightly colored stools pulled up to the long counter overlooking the beach. I hopped onto a yellow seat and put my purse on the blue stool next to me to save Butch's spot. My drowsiness of earlier had passed, but I didn't want to risk having another drink. I ordered a glass of tea. I knew better than to ask for hot tea in any restaurant in the South. It was dark now, the ocean a black void. Surf pounded the shore in waves of white foam and the lights from the bar illuminated a narrow stretch of pale sand. In the shadows below the deck, a couple sat close together, murmuring softly.

Butch soon arrived, getting appreciative glances from a group of college-age women seated nearby. As usual, he seemed oblivious to their admiration. He ordered a beer. "Want anything to eat, Lucy?"

"No, I had something already," I lied. I was starving, but eating dinner together would seem too much as though we were on a date.

"How's Stephanie?" he asked.

"Okay, I guess. Despite being manhandled by the police."

"I doubt very much she was manhandled," Butch said.

"Sorry. I was being defensive."

His beer arrived, and he sipped it as he looked out to sea. "I hear she was released."

"Of course she was released. She didn't kill that man. Watson's clutching at straws."

"He's being thorough. Have you seen her?"

"Seen who?"

"Stephanie."

"Not this afternoon."

"I guess she's called in some high-powered legal help. That lot always helps their own."

"She's retained my uncle Amos in case she needs him."

"Really? That's good news."

"You think so?"

He shifted in his seat. Drank more beer. Didn't look at me. "Sure. Amos is a straight shooter. He'll do a good job of representing her. If . . . uh . . . he has to."

"Yes."

"Are you going around to her place tonight?"

"Why do you ask?"

"I thought you might need me to go along."

"Why would you think that?"

He shrugged his big shoulders. Judging by the number of beer bottles and wineglasses on their table, the young women seated near us were well on their way to vacation nirvana. One of them caught my eye and gave me an exaggerated thumbs-up with one hand while pointing at Butch with the other. Her friends collapsed into giggles.

"What are you looking at?" Butch said, twisting in his seat.

The girls squealed and buried their heads in their hands.

"That lot's gonna be trouble for some poor cop tonight," he said to me.

I was maybe ten years older than them. They made me feel as though I should have a walker and hearing aid ready at hand. "I spoke to Marlene earlier."

"Who?"

"Will's girlfriend. Remember, she was at book club?"

"Oh, yeah. Her. What about her?"

"She told me Will went around regularly making enemies of people and threatening to sue them. We saw that ourselves, didn't we, with Ralph? She had another story I found interesting." I related the tale of the supermarket cart versus car incident. "The police were called, so the name of the other guy must be on file. Maybe he offed Will?"

"Because his eggs got broken?"

When he put it like that, it did sound pretty ridiculous. "You never know," I said weakly.

"That's true enough. I learned my first week on this job not to assume something's too minor for some idiot to go totally nuts over. It's worth looking up."

"Thanks. What happened at the marina, by the way? I heard something about Will's car being located and a boat stolen. Is that true?"

"Yup. His Navigator was found parked on the street near a marina in Wanchese. A small boat was stolen from there last night. The very boat we found Williamson in this morning."

The image of Will's body flashed before my eyes. I swallowed.

Butch touched my arm. "You okay, Lucy?" His warm hazel eyes were full of concern.

I shook the memory away and tried to smile. "I'm good. What happens now?"

"Fingerprint techs and forensics have gone over the vehicle and the boat with a fine-tooth comb. If there's something to be found, it'll be found. Williamson's prints are all over the car, as you would expect, and Marlene's too. Plenty of others, which is natural enough as the SUV has a lot of miles on it. We have to locate the boat owners to eliminate their prints, but they're

out of town and the marina doesn't have cell numbers
for them. We can't find anyone who saw Williamson on
Roanoke Island last night or observed someone take
that boat."

"Have you wondered how the killer got back to wherever he'd come from? Someone had to have been with
Williamson either before or after he was dead to pilot
that boat and tie it to the dock. Where did they go after
that? It's a heck of a long walk back to town on a very
dark and lonely road."

His eyes twinkled. "Don't tell Watson I said so, but
you're good at thinking these things through, Lucy.
One of our working theories is that the murder was so
carefully planned and premeditated the killer had a
vehicle concealed close by to use to get away from the
scene. The other is that the killer had an accomplice,
someone they phoned to pick them up after the deed,
shall we say, was done."

"That would be a risk, wouldn't it? A parked car, an
isolated location, late at night. If a police patrol came
by they'd make a note of it."

"Murdering a man's a risk, Lucy. Everything else is
secondary to that. It's often those minor details that
help us catch the guy. Right now, Watson's biggest question is why Williamson would have been at a marina,
and that one in particular, late at night, and decide to
go for a boat ride."

"Maybe he had some business to conduct concerning
his boat that got wrecked on Monday."

"What sort of insurance adjuster meets a client in
the middle of the night? Even that doesn't wash. The

boat Williamson rented—and destroyed—was out of a marina in Kill Devil Hills."

"Rented? That boat was rented? Marlene told me he bought it right after they got here. She's hoping to get the insurance money."

Butch grinned. "He wouldn't be the first guy to want a woman to think he's a big-time spender. I wouldn't read much into that, Lucy. He probably wanted to be sure he'd enjoy boating before taking the plunge and buying. An antique motorboat of that size is a heck of a big investment, not to mention the cost of insurance and maintenance."

"My head's spinning." I hopped off the stool. "I'm going home. It's been one heck of a day."

He drained his bottle. "Yeah, that it has. If you talk to Stephanie, say hi for me, will you?"

"Okay."

The Croatan Highway runs through the towns of Kitty Hawk, Kill Devil Hills, and Nags Head. It ends at Whalebone Junction, where the majority of the traffic veers right to cross the bridge to Roanoke Island and points west. To the south, Highway 12 travels along what's at places barely more than a strip of sand in the Cape Hatteras National Seashore. In the daytime, the road's busy with tourists, but at night it's quiet. I always loved leaving the bright lights and heavy traffic of Nags Head behind me and heading into the dark. I loved it even more when the light of the lighthouse came into view, a glowing beacon against the dark. The parking lot was empty when I arrived at the library. My colleagues had gone home for the day, and the police vehicles were no longer at the edges of the marsh.

I parked my car and walked slowly up the path. I took a few moments to breathe in the fresh sea air and admire the quiet of the night, before letting myself in. As expected, Charles waited to greet me. He leaped up onto the cart of books to be reshelved, and I gave the top of his head a good scratch. He purred and rubbed against my hand.

"Tough day," I said out loud. "I'm glad it's over." I love the library at all times, but never more than at night, when I'm here alone. The quiet, the peace, the soft lights, the rows of books, all of them full of wonders. If there's a place that speaks louder of civilization than a library at night, I don't know of it.

Charles leaped down and swatted at my ankles with an impatient meow. The benefits of civilization are sometimes lost on Charles. Until he hears the sound of the can opener, that is.

I made my way up the curving iron stairs to my lighthouse aerie, where I busied myself with the usual end of the day chores. I fed Charles, put on my pajamas and a thick fluffy robe, heated up a microwavable pasta dinner (sparing a thought for Aunt Ellen's justifiably famous spaghetti sauce), and sat down to eat.

Only then did I allow myself to recall the events of the day. The more I thought about it, the more I was convinced I was on the right track. Either Will had made himself an enemy in the month he'd been back on the Outer Banks, or someone had been holding a grudge for an awful long time. I imagined Aunt Ellen, burning up the phone lines, getting the old-timers' gossip mill swinging into overtime.

I'd learned a few interesting things from Butch, but

my friend wasn't a detective and all he'd be likely to know would be station gossip. I wished I could talk to Sam Watson, get some updates on the case. We could meet for a drink, kick back, and try out our various theories on each other. *As if!* I had his home number because CeeCee was in my book club, but the man himself was highly unlikely to take my call, and even more unlikely to answer my questions.

I washed up my few dishes and settled into the window seat to read. After about a half hour, when I had scarcely turned the page, I picked up the phone.

"Stephanie, it's Lucy. Do you have time to talk?"

"If I must." Her voice was cool, the words clipped.

"I know you're mad at me for telling Watson what you learned last night, but you have to understand that I didn't want to. I didn't see that I had any choice. You're a lawyer; you must realize that I can't withhold evidence in a murder case."

"The fact that Will Williamson had an affair with my mother a long time ago is not evidence in his murder."

"You know that. I know that. Sam Watson does not. Sorry to bother you, Steph. I wanted you to know that I'm sorry, and if I can do anything to help, all you have to do is ask. Good night." I reached for the button to end the call.

"Wait," she said. "Don't go."

"I'm here."

She took a deep breath. "I apologize, Lucy. I needed someone to be mad at, and you were a convenient target. I can't be mad at my mom, can I? I want to be mad at Will Williamson, but somehow I can't even manage that. He was my father and, to my surprise, I'm still finding that means something. The person I should be mad at is me. I said you and Bertie could stay and hear what Mom had to say because I wanted your support. If I'd known what was going to happen I would never have put you in the position of having to break a confidence. Do you accept my apology?"

Tears welled up in my eyes. "If we could see the future, we'd all do a lot of things differently."

"True enough. Thanks for calling Amos. I've heard of him, of course. He's almost legendary in the legal profession. I'm honored that he's going to represent me if I need it."

"Did Watson say anything about any theories they might have? Any evidence?"

"He's a smart one—I'll give him that. He doesn't let anything slip that he doesn't intend to. I have no idea what he's thinking. He tried to get me to say that I'd gone out last night after Mom went to bed. But, because I hadn't, I didn't confess to it. Oh, that friend of yours was there for a while."

"What friend?"

"The big cop."

"Butch?"

"Do you think he's been trying to dig up the dirt on me?"

"Gosh, no. Butch doesn't deal in dirt. He's a great guy."

"If you say so. What's the story with him and you anyway?"

"No story. We're friends."

"Yeah, I figured that. Just thought I'd check. Is he married or anything?"

"No."

"Probably has a string of girlfriends though."

"Not that I know of. Why are you asking so much about Butch?"

"No reason. I guess I like to know who I'm dealing with, is all. It's the lawyer in me. I could go for your Connor, you know, but I don't want to step on your toes."

"Connor! He's not mine."

"No? You can't tell me you don't wish he was. It's written all over your face, Lucy, when you look at him."

"Aaaahh," was all I could say. Stephanie could tell I was in love with Connor before even I knew. Was it that obvious to everyone else?

Was it that obvious to Connor? He'd never said anything. Maybe because he didn't . . . uh . . . return the sentiment. I wanted to die.

Stephanie laughed. "I feel a lot better having someone to talk to. Thanks for calling, Lucy."

"You'll let me know if anything happens, or you need any help?"

"I will. Let's go out for dinner one night soon. You can invite Connor." She laughed again and hung up.

I put down the phone, feeling a lot better. I was glad I'd called my friend. I was glad we were friends again. I liked the idea of inviting Connor to join us for dinner; maybe we could ask Josie and Grace too. A fun night out with a group of friends.

I probably shouldn't invite Butch though. No telling what sort of argument he and Steph might get into.

I went back to my book and got a few pages read before the phone rang. My heart sped into overdrive when I saw the name of the caller on the display. Connor. "Hello."

"Hi, Lucy. It's Connor."

"Oh, Connor. Hi." Yes, I can sound completely inane at times.

"I know it's late, and I hope I'm not bothering you. I tried your cell, but it's out of range so that means you're at the library, right?"

"Yes." I glanced at my cell phone. No bars at all tonight.

"I know you had a tough day, so I wanted to check in, ask if you're okay."

"I'm . . . okay. I've been talking to Stephanie. Watson let her go."

"I heard she'd been brought in for questioning. But she wasn't charged, was she?"

"No, thank heavens for that. Connor, you're the one who knows . . . knew Will the best. Do you have any idea who might have killed him?"

"I didn't know him at all, Lucy. We'd only met a couple of times, and only briefly."

"You said he'd been a friend of your dad in their youth. Do you think maybe your dad might remember something about him? Perhaps he can think of someone who's been carrying a grudge all these years."

"Lucy, you're not getting involved in the police investigation, are you?"

"Me? Perish the thought."

"A nonanswer, if I've ever heard one. But I get your point. I can ask my dad, sure. There isn't much he'd rather do than talk about the good old days."

"Thanks, Connor."

"If Dad does know something, I'm taking it straight to Sam. Not to you. You shouldn't have anything to do with this."

"Okay," I said.

"Because . . . because I don't think I could bear it, if anything happened to you. Good night, Lucy."

"Good night, Connor." We hung up. I held the phone for a long time, as his last sentence tumbled over and over itself in my mind. Charles crawled onto my lap, and presented himself for a belly scratch.

Chapter 11

Despite what Bertie had said, I didn't think I could continue my investigation (what others might call snooping) and leave my colleagues to cover my job.

Besides, I'd come to a dead end. Aunt Ellen would call me if she learned anything important. Stephanie promised to keep in touch. No point in going around to question Marlene again this morning: she didn't look like the sort who got out of bed before noon. Watson was investigating Ralph's whereabouts on the night in question, as well as anyone else Will might have threatened to sue. And Connor wasn't going to tell me anything, even if his dad did know all the dark secrets of Will Williamson's past.

I decided it would be a good day to treat my coworkers, so I headed into Nags Head before the library opened for the day.

As could be expected, a line stretched to the doors of Josie's Cozy Bakery. In the height of tourist season, the line might well extend the length of the small strip mall.

While I waited, I busied myself by checking my phone.
The only missed call was last night from Connor. He told
my voice mail that he'd try the library number.

I played the message several times over.

"You look pleased with yourself this morning, Lucy,"
Alison, the clerk behind the counter, said when it was
my turn to place an order.

Did *everyone* know *everything* I was thinking?

I ordered a selection of pastries to take to the library
and a large drink for myself. Throwing caution to the
wind, I asked for a full-fat latte and avoided the more
healthy selections of bran and fruit muffins. "Is Josie
around?"

"Josie, Lucy's here!" Alison bellowed in a voice that
belied her tiny frame.

My cousin came out of the back, wiping floury hands
on her apron. The male customers broke into smiles. I
suspected that some of them came here only because they
hoped she'd put in an appearance. Josie had managed to
snag most of the good-looking genes from both sides of
her family. I got my paternal grandmother's uncontrol-
lable black curls and my mother's lack of height. As for
my father—well, he was financially comfortable.

Josie gave me a huge smile and a welcoming hug. I
loved her to bits.

"Everyone," she said, "is talking about that Will guy
we met at book club the other night. Incredible to think
we'd been talking to him just a couple of hours before
he was murdered."

"Incredible is the word. You say everyone's talking
about it. Anyone have any ideas?"

"Lots of them. Teenagers inspired by rap music or

video games to go on a killing spree, gangs from the big cities, maybe even a terrorist cell operating right here in Nags Head. There's a theory to suit every prejudice or political point of view." We were standing at the end of the counter, and I faced the entrance to the kitchen while Josie looked across the busy café to the door. "Speaking of which . . . don't look now."

I whirled around.

"I said don't look," Josie said.

"No one ever means that, do they?" Doug Whiteside, mayoral candidate, had come in, accompanied by his ever-present assistant, Bill or Bob or something. Doug smiled through a mouthful of overly white teeth at all and sundry, and exchanged greetings with anyone who looked like a potential voter. Bill or Bob or something handed out campaign fridge magnets.

"Slime bucket," Josie muttered under her breath.

We watched, while pretending not to, as the men reached the counter and placed their orders.

"Do you think he glues that smile on in the morning?" Josie whispered to me.

"It doesn't look entirely natural, does it?"

"When Connor talks to people, you can tell he does it because he likes them and he's interested in their concerns and opinions. With Doug it's all an act."

At that moment, the man himself spotted us. He came over, hand outstretched, smile firmly in place.

"Lucy, how nice to see you. And Josie too." Doug waved his hand at the busy bakery. "Looks like business is brisk. That's what we like to see."

Bill or Bob or something shoved a fridge magnet into my hand. He slapped another onto the metal trimming of the display case. Josie plucked it off. "Sorry, but we don't endorse one party or politician over another."

The campaign assistant glowered at her, but Doug said, "You're right to do so. I wouldn't want to alienate any of your customers, even if I am, as my slogan says, FOR Nags Head. Bill gets a mite enthusiastic sometimes. Can't help himself, can you, Billy?"

"I'm just so excited about your candidacy, Doug," Billy dutifully replied as he accepted a paper bag from the clerk. "Your mayoralty will be the best thing to happen to Nags Head for a good long time."

"We have to win that election first," Doug said, modestly.

"And that's why we can't stand and chat with these ladies, Doug. You have that meeting with the Ladies Guild this morning."

"Never a dull moment on the campaign trail," Doug said. "Catch you later, ladies."

He walked through the café, not taking the direct path to the door but winding his way past the tables. Billy handed out fridge magnets as they went.

I sipped at my piping hot latte and picked up the bakery box. "Do you think Connor needs to make up some sort of handout?"

Josie snorted. "Connor will win because he's the best choice for mayor. Not because he gives away junk." She threw the magnet into the trash. "I'll walk you to your car. I need some fresh air after that run-in with Doug Whiteside."

As we headed for the door, I heard someone say, "Mr. Williamson's death is going to be a blow to Doug." Two women were seated at a small table in the middle of the room, surrounded by papers, mugs, and crumb-covered plates. They'd been watching Doug and Billy make their way through the room.

The table next to the women was unoccupied, and I dropped onto a stool covered in a navy blue–and-white-striped fabric. The table itself had been reclaimed from a wooden tea chest. The serving area of Josie's bakery was all modern coffee culture, glass and steel and chrome, but the dining area was decorated in Outer Banks nautical. Josie gave me a questioning look, and I gestured for her to sit down.

"What do you mean?" the second woman at the next table asked.

My question exactly! I touched my lips with my finger and tried to unobtrusively point to the two women. Josie nodded in understanding and slipped quietly onto a stool. The women were in their forties. Judging by their one-inch pumps, business skirts, crisply ironed blouses, and small gold earrings, they were local people, not vacationers. I'd never seen either of them in the library.

"Doug's the development candidate," the first woman said. That was true. Connor maintained that Doug Whiteside was *too much* the development candidate. Meaning he was in the pay of the sort of developers not inclined to worry about the fragile ecosystem of the Outer Banks. Unfortunately, Connor had no proof, so he had to keep that thought to himself and his close friends. "Will Williamson made a lot of money in Alaska in the oil business. He wanted to invest that money here, and he knew Doug's the man who can create opportunities, rather than set up roadblocks."

I glanced at Josie. Her lovely face was set into serious

lines. By roadblocks, we assumed these women meant environmental impact reviews. Binders and folders were stacked on the table in front of them. Unfortunately they were closed, so I couldn't sneak a peek and see what business the two women were in.

"You're right about that, Joyce."

"Will's sudden—and so tragic—death worked out well for Connor McNeil, didn't it?" Joyce said.

"What do you mean?"

"Will was planning to make a hefty donation to Doug's campaign. A very hefty donation."

"How do you know that? I heard he was talking to Connor also."

Joyce tapped the side of her nose first, and then her binder with a long red fingernail. "Inside information. That's not going to happen now, is it?"

"Maybe his wife will carry on with the plans."

Joyce laughed. "His wife! Margaret Kramer, you can be so naive sometimes. I'm guessing you haven't seen that bimbo Will was shacked up with. Even if all his money that's not locked up in investments or trust funds goes to her, it will be spent on makeup and clothes. And finding a new man, I'll guess."

Margaret giggled. "I wouldn't mind meeting a new man myself. Although Ted probably wouldn't approve."

"It's not funny, Margaret. Even if the bimbo gives Doug the money he needs, she has no influence. Her involvement's more likely to turn off any insecure wife rather than attract supporters. Will, on the other hand, would have had a lot of street cred, seeing how he's a local boy made good and all, who came back home to spend his money right here."

Josie looked at me, eyes wide and lips pursed into a silent whistle. All around us people chatted and laughed, came and went. The espresso machines emitted clouds of fragrant steam, and the scent of baking bread and pastries wafted out of the back.

Joyce drained her mug and began gathering up her things. Margaret hurried to follow. Joyce said, "Connor's a big supporter of that library in the lighthouse."

"So?"

"Nothing." Her voice drifted off. I held my breath, waiting for the dramatic pause to break and for her to continue. "I wouldn't say this to anyone but you, Margaret, but it's a heck of a coincidence that Will was murdered at that very spot."

Margaret gasped so loudly she hid the sound of Josie pushing her chair back. I gave my cousin a quick shake of my head and gestured for her to be quiet.

"You don't think . . ."

"All I'm saying is connect the dots. Will would have been a huge help to Doug. Will's conveniently been taken out of the picture. It's not for me to say a certain someone didn't act to make that happen." She opened her sleek red leather briefcase and slipped her binder inside.

"That's creepy," Margaret said. "You've given me goose bumps. Although I can't see Connor McNeil doing anything like that. I might not like his politics, but he is a nice man."

"Politics," Joyce said as she closed the briefcase with a snap, "can make men do crazy things. Maybe he didn't have to do anything. A few words in the right ears . . ."

The women left. I buried my face in my takeaway cup as they passed our table.

"What the . . . ," Josie said.

"I don't believe it," I said. "That woman just about came right out and said that Connor killed Will."

"Surely no one else is thinking that?"

"I would have said no one at all is crazy enough to think that. Obviously, I would have been wrong."

"I bet she didn't come up with that theory all by herself," Josie said. "Do you think Doug's been planting the seeds?"

"I wouldn't put it past him," I said.

"Excuse me, Josie." Alison stood at our table. "I'm sorry to interrupt, but you're needed in the back. Something's wrong with the flour delivery."

"Gotta run," my cousin said to me. "Call Connor. Tell him what we heard. He needs to know."

Only an hour ago I'd decided not to get involved in the police investigation. Heading back to the library with my box of baked treats, I changed my mind. Stephanie had Uncle Amos on her side, and the police had no case against her. If those two horrid women were whispering that Will's death had benefited Connor, who else might be thinking that? Rumor and innuendo were powerful things. Suspicion alone, fanned by those who were not friends of Connor, could sink his campaign for reelection.

I made a left turn at Whalebone Junction and headed back toward town. I pulled into the parking lot of the police station. Before getting out, I made a quick call. It was almost nine o'clock, time for library opening. "Bertie. I'm going to be late. There's a few things I need to do about . . . that business we discussed yesterday."

"Stephanie?"

"She's fine. At least she was fine last night. We had a long talk and everything's good between us, but something else has come up."

"Take what time you need," she said. "But remember that tomorrow's Saturday, so Ronald has a full set of programs and Charlene has the day off."

"I'll remember." I hung up and glanced at the bakery box on the seat beside me. I grabbed it and got out of my car. In a bit of excellent timing, Detective Watson himself was heading out the door as I was going in.

"Good morning, Detective," I trilled. "I've been to Josie's and thought you might like a treat." I held up the box in evidence.

He glared at me. "Is that a bribe, Ms. Richardson?"

"What? Uh . . . no . . ."

"Glad to hear it," he said.

"Do you have a minute?"

"No."

I refused to let him intimidate me. "I have some information about the Will Williamson murder that I thought you'd be interested in."

"Here to confess, are you?"

"No!" I glanced around me, taking in the stern-faced detective, staring me down, the uniformed cops going in and out, all giving me *that* look, and the imposing building. I was surrounded by a mighty force of law and order. And totally intimidated.

Then Watson laughed. I didn't know he could do that. "Don't turn to a life of crime, Lucy," he said. "I've never seen a more expressive face. I can spare you a minute if it's important. If this isn't an official interview, why don't we grab a seat over there?"

He led the way. A couple of benches were grouped in a patch of rough grass struggling to survive in the sandy soil. A beech tree cast shade. We took seats. I opened the box and offered it. Watson plucked out a blueberry Danish. Just to keep things casual and friendly, I selected a white chocolate scone.

"Shoot," he said, taking a bite.

I told him what Josie and I had overheard. He chewed, his frown growing. "Never good when politics gets involved."

"You know Connor wouldn't do something like that, right?"

He raised an eyebrow. "If someone brings me their suspicions, I'll have to act on it. But rumor and muck spreading have no place in a police investigation."

"I'm not . . ."

"I know you're not telling me because you're enjoying the gossip. You're concerned about your friend, who's my friend also. Thanks for telling me. The more information I have, the better. Sometimes you never know what will turn out to be important." He popped the last bite of Danish into his mouth. "And thanks for this as well."

"Did Butch tell you what Marlene told me about Will? That he went around threatening to sue people all the time?"

"He did."

"And?"

"And, if you must know, I found the story of the shopping cart incident interesting, so I looked up the record of the call. The pedestrian was eighty-two years old. The responding officer said Williamson gave the man a hundred dollar bill and told him to go away, and the old guy was happy to do so. I doubt very much he decided later to get even and if he did, was able to lure Williamson onto a motorboat in the middle of the night."

"About the boat . . ."

"Enough, Lucy. When I have built a case you will be the first to know."

"You're not still suspecting Stephanie, I hope," I said.

"You're incorrigible. I'm not going to answer that, and you know it."

"At least one other attempt was made on Will Williamson's life. Before the fatal incident, I mean, before Stephanie knew he was her father. I witnessed it myself."

"Go ahead."

"Monday was the big storm. Remember?"

"I remember. That night Williamson wrecked the boat he'd rented and had to be rescued by Ralph Harper and the coast guard. And, before you ask, I have spoken to Ralph and that conversation is none of your business."

"What I'm about to tell you eliminates him as a suspect anyway."

At that, Watson actually looked interested in what I had to say.

"From my apartment I can see a long way out to sea. I saw that boat, Williamson's boat, lost in the storm. It was me who called nine-one-one to report it. But I saw something else. Lights where there shouldn't have been lights. Lights that made it look as though there was a small harbor or other port of refuge."

A cruiser tore out of the parking lot under lights and sirens. Watson watched it go. I was losing his attention.

"I saw it," I said.

He turned back to me. He started to stand up. "I asked CeeCee what had gone on at your book club the other night. She told me Louise Jane launched into that story of how Nags Head got its name. Sounds like the same story you've just told me."

"It's not a story. It happened. I saw the lights."

"Louise Jane can be highly convincing when she wants to be. Williamson wanted to be convinced, that way he could believe the wreck wasn't entirely his fault. You have the sequence of events mixed up in your mind, Lucy. Thanks again for your help. Mind if I . . ."

"Help yourself," I said. He grabbed a lemon Danish for the road and walked away.

I groaned. Watson thought I'd imagined seeing the lights, that the idea had been planted into my mind by Louise Jane McKaughnan and Will Williamson. I knew the detective didn't trust my instincts, but now he thought I was an overly impressionable bubblehead.

Why, oh why, hadn't I told the 911 dispatcher about those lights? Why hadn't I told Butch the following morning when I'd phoned him, or been the one to bring it up at book club before dratted Louise Jane opened her big mouth? Almost as bad as people thinking I was making the incident up was the idea that I could be so influenced by Louise Jane that I was imagining what I'd seen.

I peeked into the bakery box. The contents were rapidly diminishing, but a few delights remained. I'd make one more call before giving up.

Too bad if Marlene was still in bed.

She wasn't. When I arrived at her house, she was up and dressed and entertaining company.

Highly unexpected company.

"Lucy, what a delightful surprise." Theodore Kowalski jumped to his feet when I came into the room. He was dressed in his full English scholar getup of a brown Harris Tweed jacket and a paisley cravat. He peered at me through his plain glass spectacles.

"I hope I'm not interrupting anything," I said. I held out the box. "I thought you might like something for breakfast."

Marlene laughed. "Aren't you sweet? The neighbors haven't exactly been rushing over with condolences and casseroles." She wore her bathing suit with a floor-length rhinestone-trimmed turquoise wrap thrown over it. Her face was clear of makeup and her hair pulled back into a high ponytail. "Coffee?"

I put my box on the table next to two full mugs. "Thanks. Cream, no sugar. I didn't know you two were friends."

"Not friends, no," Marlene said, heading into the kitchen.

Theodore wiggled his eyebrows at me. He was trying to signal something but I had not the slightest idea what that might be. He studied the contents of the bakery box and finally selected a scone, plump with berries. He nibbled at it with his small browning teeth. I tried not to think of mice.

I took a seat and Marlene brought my coffee. "I wanted to pop in, check you're okay," I said.

"You did that yesterday," Marlene said. "I was okay then, and I'm okay now. But thanks anyway, Lucy."

Theodore cleared his throat. "Back to the matter at hand."

"Lucy's not interested," Marlene said.

"Lucy is a close friend. She won't mind if we continue our conversation, will you, dear?"

"Go ahead," I said. "Don't worry about me." I was curious as to what had brought Theodore here. I didn't see that he and Marlene would have a heck of a lot in common.

"Fifteen thousand dollars," Theodore said, causing me to choke on a mouthful of overly hot coffee, "is far less than had been arranged."

Marlene shrugged her thin shoulders. "If Will changed his mind, he had reason to. Will was a very astute businessman."

"The books are worth far more than that," Theodore said. Crumbs fell from his mouth and dusted the front of his jacket. "I made him an exceptionally good offer, wanting to help out a new and promising collector."

"Sorry," Marlene said. She crossed her legs and her robe fell back.

Theodore didn't even glance at the display. "I can only offer them at nineteen."

"For what?" I couldn't help myself. Books were Theodore's passion, but everyone knew he didn't have a lot of money. In order to buy one book, he usually had to sell another.

"Some old book," Marlene said.

"A set of Agatha Christies." Theodore sniffed. "Excellent quality. I'm asking less than they're worth in light of Ms. Bergen's recent tragic loss."

"See, Mr. Theodore," Marlene said. "I don't really

want your books. But I'm trying to be fair on account of that's what I know Will would want of me."

As I watched, horrified, a pulse began to beat in Theodore's neck. His face turned red and his eyes bulged. "Will agreed to my original price of twenty thousand. That's what we decided upon. And then, when I called to arrange to deliver the books and complete the transaction, he reneged and offered that insulting amount. And on top of that he stood me up when it came time to meet in person."

Marlene giggled. "Sorry about that. I insisted on taking him to Lucy's book club. I didn't know he'd said he'd meet with you."

"You and Will were at the library at the same time Theodore missed book club because he thought you were having a meeting?" I said.

"Will believed in being spontaneous," Marlene said with a shrug.

I did not say, *since when?* I didn't think one became a top executive with an oil company by blowing off meetings. Obviously, as important as this deal was to Theodore, it had been considerably less important to Will.

Out of nowhere, a chill crawled up my spine. I looked between Marlene and Theodore. She was glancing out the window, toying with the jeweled zipper on her robe. He was glaring at her with a look of pure anger such as I'd never seen on his face before.

Neither of them seemed to realize they'd just provided a motive for the death of Will. Had Theodore, enraged by Will's handling of their business deal, called Will late at night and demanded a meeting? Had Will gone to meet him, told Theodore he was dropping what he was offering for the books? Had a furious Theodore stabbed Will in a blind rage, dumped the body in a stolen boat, and then taken it to the marsh?

I'd once had the misfortune of seeing Theodore handling a rowboat. At the time I'd wondered how anyone brought up on the coast could be so useless on the water. I couldn't imagine him stealing a small boat and piloting it through the marsh at night. Still, I suppose desperate men can do desperate things.

No. I mentally shook my head. Theodore was eccentric, to be sure, and more than a little obsessed when it came to his beloved books, but he was no killer.

I might be convinced of his innocence, but not everyone knew him as well as I did. As if he was willingly digging himself deeper into a hole of suspicion, Theodore said in his haughtiest voice, "Miss Bergen. If Will thought I would sell those valuable books for a fraction of their true price, he was sadly mistaken. In recognition of your obvious grief, I will decrease my price slightly."

"Just a minute," I said. "I don't mean to be rude, but Will didn't strike me as a likely book collector." Anything but. He'd paid almost no attention to the discussion of *Kidnapped* at book club. He hadn't even known who Robert Louis Stevenson was. I knew that rare books could be a wise investment, but surely a buyer had to have *some interest* in collecting them? Otherwise why not buy mutual funds or oil company stock? I thought of my dad leaning over his computer, swearing at every dip in the stock market. "Where did Will and you meet, Theodore?"

Marlene laughed. "That was because of me. Will was in some boring old meeting with the real estate agents who were looking for a house for us, all money stuff, and he told me to stay in the waiting room. Well, my phone battery had died, and they didn't have a single interesting magazine in the room, so I picked up one about investments. I figured I'd look at property so I could give Will some good advice. I saw Theodore's ad. I don't know why anyone would buy a bunch of old books when they could buy jewelry . . ."

As Marlene chattered on, Teddy's face was turning ever redder, and I feared that soon I would be required to perform mouth-to-mouth resuscitation.

". . . but I showed the ad to Will 'cause he's always going on about how unreliable the stock market is these days and how smart investors are buying real things. I told him diamonds were real things, but he said that wasn't a good market either. Pooh." She pouted prettily.

"And quite right he was," Theodore said. "Rare books will do nothing but increase in value. Now, I am going to offer a small decrease on my original selling price, as an expression of my condolences on your loss. Nineteen thousand."

"Sixteen," Marlene said.

"Eighteen, and not a penny less."

"Sixteen and a half thou."

I felt as though I was in a Turkish bazaar.

"Not so fast," said a deep voice. Michael Williamson came into the room. He was dressed in Dockers ironed to a razor-sharp crease and a blue button-down shirt. His hair was damp, his face pink, and an aroma of liberally applied aftershave followed him. "I don't know who the heck you are, buddy."

Theodore leaped to his feet. He stuck out his hand.

"Theodore Kowalski, rare-book dealer and connoisseur."

Michael didn't offer his own hand, and Theodore's slowly dropped to his side. "Whatever. You seem to be laboring under a severe misunderstanding, Mr. Kowalski. Marlene here doesn't have sixteen thousand to buy your books or anything else. She doesn't have so much as sixteen bucks to her name."

Marlene jumped up. "Michael, go away."

"Why, so you can sell the farm out from underneath me? Get real, Marlene. Nothing you have here, except your clothes and a few trinkets of almost worthless jewelry, belongs to you. My father hasn't been so much as buried yet, and you're spending his money to feather your own nest."

"Will promised me . . ."

"That he'd leave everything to you? And you believed him? In that case, I have to wonder if you hurried his death along."

"Don't be ridiculous," she said. "For your information, Will was buying me those books as a gift. He was negotiating with Mr. Kowalski here on my behalf."

Michael snorted. "Because of your keen interest in twentieth-century American literature? I suggest you be on your way, buddy. If you sell those books to her for so much as a penny, or remove anything from this house in exchange, the police will be knocking on your door."

Theodore headed for the exit, rapidly. Michael thrust his hand out as the book collector passed. "Give me your card. When my dad's will's settled"—he gave Marlene a satisfied smirk—"I might be in touch." I doubted Michael had any more interest in book collecting than

Marlene did. He wanted to rub her nose in her dimin-
ished status in this family one more time.

"Certainly, certainly. Anytime." Theodore fumbled
in his pocket for his gold card case, flipped it open, and
pulled out one of the stiff little squares of paper. "Always
willing to do business with a gentleman."

Now it was Marlene's turn to snort.

I put my mug down and got to my feet as Theodore
made a break for the stairs. "I guess I'll be off too."

Mike turned to me with a smile. "No need to do that.
Looks like the coffee's fresh and someone brought pastries. Marlene, get me a cup, will you?"

I expected her to tell him to get his own darn coffee,
but to my surprise she went into the kitchen. Her robe
flowed behind her in a movement as graceful as a wave
rushing to shore.

"No, thanks," I said. "I have to get to work."

Mike took a step toward me. His gray eyes twinkled
and the edges of his mouth were turned up in a mischie-
vous grin. "Come on, play hooky for once. You don't want
to be stuck in some musty old library all day. It's a gorgeous day. Let's go down to the pool. Marlene'll have a
bathing suit you can wear." He ran his eyes down my body.
"You're about the same size. How about it, Marlene?"

She handed him his coffee. "I made the offer yesterday.
Stay, Lucy. I've got more Prosecco. I'll make mimosas."

Weird. I would have expected these two to be throwing
pillows at each other and tearing out hair, not inviting a
witness to that ugly scene to kick back and sip mimosas
in the sun. "Sorry—gotta run. Another time maybe."

"Whatever," Marlene said. "Speaking of Prosecco,
it's time to open a bottle. I've had enough coffee."

"I'll see you out," Mike said to me. "Stop by after work, why don't you, Lucy?"

"I . . . I . . . uh, I'm busy."

"Bring your friends. We can have a party. Might as well enjoy this house while we've got it."

"Not today," I said.

He stopped on the bottom step, turned, and put his hand on my arm. He was below me now, and looked up, deep into my eyes. "I'm saying that I want to see you again, Lucy. You don't have someone special in your life, do you?"

An image of Connor flashed behind my eyes. "No."

"I'm glad to hear that. I'll call you later, ask you to join me for dinner. I hope you'll say yes."

I slipped past him and continued down the steps. My face was burning. Mike was a nice-looking man, but I had enough complications in my life right now.

Chapter 12

My plan to thank my coworkers for filling in for me by treating them to a selection of Josie's pastries had come to naught. By the time I got back to the library, I didn't have any baked goods left for anyone.

I spent the rest of the day in a confused muddle. Neither Marlene nor Mike were exactly mourning Will, or even pretending to. Mike and his dad hadn't been close, but the man was his father. I'm not close to my father, and never have been. Still, I love my dad very much, and I know he loves me. I'd be devastated if he died.

I'd taken the chance during my afternoon coffee break to call Connor. His voice mail answered and I left a message for him to call me back, but as the clock ticked toward closing time, I hadn't heard from him. Mike had promised to call me, but he hadn't, and for that I was grateful. I didn't want to have dinner with him, and I'm never good at making excuses. Come to think of it, he hadn't asked me for my number. I suppose he could get it from Marlene, if he wanted to, but it made me think he wasn't all that interested in me anyway. Perhaps the casual flirting was only for show. I wondered if Mike was like his dad. He'd said he was divorced. Might that be because there'd been an equivalent to Pat in his past?

On Fridays, we close late. Darkness had fallen over the ocean to the east, and the clouds in the west were streaked with shades of deep indigo and purple when Connor came into the library. I got up from behind the front desk with a smile. My heart pounded as though it were a canvas sail and the wind had just caught it. "Hi. Did you get my message?" How nice—he'd come to see me in person rather than just call or text.

"Message? Oh, sorry, Lucy. Yes, I got your message. But you said it wasn't important so it slipped my mind."

That took the wind out of my canvas sails. I'd said it wasn't important, meaning the library wasn't on fire, or my car wasn't heading at full speed for the edge of a cliff. But it was still *important*. I'd thought (hoped?) I was important to him.

"Connor, so nice to see you." Bertie came out of the back. Her eyes were dancing with delight. Something was up. I looked at her suspiciously.

"You said it was important," Connor said. "You have an idea about something?"

"Not important, really," Bertie laughed, "but I knew a hint of mystery would get you down here. It was Charlene's idea. You're going to love it. Lucy, buzz Ronald and Charlene and ask them to come down, please." She giggled. Oh, yes. Something was definitely up.

Connor looked at me with a question. I shrugged to indicate I was as much in the dark as he was.

Charles wrapped himself around Connor's legs.

Ronald and Charlene clattered down the stairs, Ronald looking as confused as Connor and me, Charlene resembling nothing so much as a six-year-old on Christmas morning.

At that moment the door swung open. Curses, I'd been too slow to lock it. Louise Jane walked in. She was dressed in scruffy track pants, rubber boots, and a heavy rain jacket. She carried a flashlight, her pockets were bulging, and a backpack was slung across her shoulders. "Hi. I noticed the lights are still on and cars are outside. What's up?"

"A staff meeting," Bertie said.

"Good," Louise Jane said. "I'm glad you're all still here. Hi, Connor. Don't be alarmed, Lucy, if you see lights out in the marsh at night."

"Why would I be alarmed?" I said, forgetting that I always did a fine job of stepping straight into Louise Jane's carefully laid traps.

"I spent the day with my great-grandmother," she said.

"Is she . . . well?" Bertie asked. I swear our library director almost said, "Is she still alive?"

"Very well. The body is failing but the mind is as strong as ever. Almost as sharp as mine."

"Not good then," Charlene mumbled.

"What's that, Charlene, sweetie?" Louise Jane asked.

"Nothing."

"When I told my grandmother about the lights Will and Marlene had seen in the storm on Monday, Grandma said this was too deep for her, we needed Great-grandmama. That's why I haven't been able to come around before now. This is much too important for us to discuss on the phone so we had to make the trip out to the retirement home to talk in person, but Grandma was attending a bingo tournament in Elizabeth City. You'll be glad we were able to talk, Bertie."

"I'm sure I will," Bertie said.

Charles had unwound himself from Connor's legs and was making a careful inspection of Louise Jane's pink-and-purple rubber boots. The boots didn't have a speck of dirt on them, and I guessed they'd been bought specifically for this purpose. Whatever that purpose might be.

"There have been rumors, Great-grandmama said, over the years, about the ghosts of wreckers being active along the coast. But she's heard nothing, she said, for a long time. As the area got more and more developed the atmosphere changed and sometimes the spirit world is unable, or unwilling, to adapt."

"Imagine that," Charlene said. "Speaking of spirits, there's a nice cold bottle of chardonnay waiting for me at home. Spit it out, L.J."

"I understand your skepticism." Louise Jane sniffed. "It can be difficult for folks without any imagination to comprehend those of us who have the gift of a window to the spirit world. Isn't that right, Lucy?"

"Huh?"

"You've experienced so many things since coming here."

About all I'd experienced was Louise Jane trying to scare me to death. "I haven't . . ."

"You need to take care of her, Connor," Louise Jane said. "There are forces in this library that Lucy cannot understand. That even I cannot understand sometimes.

Forces that do not like people to be where they shouldn't be. Particularly at night."

"Lucy," Connor said, "is perfectly capable of looking after herself." He gave me a smile. That slow Southern grin.

"Louise Jane," Bertie said. "We are having a meeting here. If you have a point, get to it. Otherwise, the library is closed."

"Great-grandmama said it sounds as though the ghosts of the wreckers are back. If they're lighting lamps along the shore, that's awful dangerous. Why, look at what happened to poor Will and Marlene!"

I groaned. No one believed me about the lights I'd seen, and now Louise Jane was consulting her great-grandmother and interweaving ghost stories into Will and Marlene's experience. Any credibility I might have been hoping for was completely shot.

"You'd better notify the coast guard," Connor said. He kept his voice was deep and serious. Louise Jane glanced at Bertie and preened, and thus missed the wink Connor gave me.

So uninterested was Ronald in Louise Jane's spirit hunting, he'd gone to the window and pulled out his iPhone to check for messages. In contrast, Charles had jumped onto a shelf, the better to follow the conversation.

"Your open-mindedness does you credit, Dr. McNeil," Louise Jane said. "You can be sure you have my vote."

"Speaking of which," Bertie said. "Our meeting."

"Anyway, I wanted y'all to know that if you see lights in the marsh at night, it might be me."

Despite myself I had to ask. "What will you be doing in the marsh?"

"Asking the spirits to leave, of course. My great-grandmother realized it was time to pass some of her most potent spells onto her daughter. And from Grandma to me." She patted her pockets. "I've brought them tonight."

"If you're going to be prowling around the marsh, you're several hundred yards short," I said. "The wreckers worked on the coast."

"Try to keep up, Lucy dear. Have you learned nothing from all I've attempted to teach you? They can, and do, wander. You think it's a coincidence that poor Will Williamson was killed only two nights after the wreckers' attempt to lure him ashore in the storm?"

"I don't think it's a coincidence at all," I said firmly.

"Precisely. Foiled in their attempt to trick him, they tried more direct methods next. The spirits, Lucy, do not like to be thwarted. You might try to remember that next time you scorn my attempts to protect you from The Lady."

The Lady was the ghostly presence of a nineteenth-century woman who'd been confined to the lighthouse tower after her marriage to a mean old lighthouse keeper. That story may or may not be true, but her spirit existed in nothing more than Louise Jane's imagination, mixed with a healthy dose of spite and an attempt to scare me away.

"Seems to me," Charlene said, "that the big question is what brought Will out at night, placed him in that boat, and brought him into the marsh. Even if your spirits"—she coughed—"are active in the marsh, I doubt they phoned him up and persuaded him to go for a boat ride."

"Thank you for your opinion, Charlene. You can discuss that with the police and others with limited imagination. The whys of this affair are not my concern. Only the hows.

"Lucy, I want you to be on your guard these nights, being alone in the lighthouse. I'll try to follow my great-grandmother's instructions to the letter, but sometimes . . . well, we don't entirely know how the spirits might react when they're disturbed."

Despite myself, I peered into the shadows beneath the twisting iron stairs leading up into darkness.

Charles let out a huge yawn and the tension in the room broke. If Charles didn't think anything supernatural lived in the lighthouse, then nothing did.

"Have fun," Bertie said. "Now, if you'll excuse us, Louise Jane, we have library business to conduct."

"Pay me no mind. I'm going to sit over here and check my supplies. It's going to be a long night." She dumped the contents of her backpack onto the circulation desk. Among the granola bars, sandwiches, bags of nuts, and diet-soda cans, she had baggies full of dried herbs and something resembling twigs and bark. Despite my earnest effort to pay no attention, I snuck a peek. She caught me watching and grinned. I often thought of Louise Jane's smile as that of a shark or a barracuda. But, I now realized, it was more like a spider. Innocently spinning its web while I ventured closer and closer.

Bertie cleared her throat and Ronald put away his phone and joined us. "Now, where were we? Oh yes, Charlene's been in meetings with the people at the

Manteo library. With the local elections just over a month away, they want to do something to raise interest. As we all know, participation in municipal elections is nothing short of pathetic."

"Not just municipal," Ronald said. "People everywhere are forgetting the value of their vote."

"And," I said, "they're forgetting how hard the struggle for voting rights has been. For women and minorities in particular."

"That's exactly why the Manteo people want to run a series of special displays and features about the history of voting," Charlene said. "I've been helping them dig up local material. Old election posters, ballots, newspaper headlines, that sort of thing."

"I get it," I said. "You want us to do the same. Sure. I'd be happy to help."

"Oh, no," Charlene said with a laugh. "We're not going to do *the same*. We're going to decorate the outside of the lighthouse."

Ronald, Connor, and I exchanged glances. Louise Jane muttered as she sorted herbs. I sometimes wondered if Louise Jane did more with her spells than lay them down. Maybe there was something in those herbs that didn't repel spirits, but attracted them. To the consumer of the magic herbs anyway. I'd love to take one of those baggies to Butch and ask for a forensic analysis.

"I'm listening," Ronald said to Charlene.

"We're going to advertise the election by wrapping the entire lighthouse in red, white, and blue bunting," she said.

Connor roared with laughter. "That is the most outrageous thing I've ever heard. I love it."

"Is that even possible?" I said.

"Sure it is. We'll have people standing at all the windows to secure it. The fire department will provide a truck and a ladder. I've already asked them. It doesn't have to say anything, but will be a reminder to people that they need to vote. Not just another TV ad or their father nagging them to get out, but something really fun that will start a conversation."

"It'll be memorable," Connor said.

"When are we going to do this?" Ronald asked.

"Next Sunday," Charlene said. "When the library's closed. I've checked the weather report and it's supposed to be a nice day. No rain or high winds."

"Sunday!" Louise Jane shrieked. "You can't. What about my Halloween display? The board has approved my haunted Outer Banks idea. I was going to start putting it up next week. Has the board approved *this*?"

"Mrs. Fitzgerald thinks it's a delightful idea," Bertie said. "As the only expenditure we have is for the bunting itself, it doesn't have to be approved by the board."

"Red, white, and blue tape around the lighthouse!" Louise Jane wailed. "There's nothing haunted about that."

"No, but your exhibit will be inside."

"I'm going to decorate the outside."

"No," Bertie said, "you are not."

"The entrance at least," Louise Jane mumbled.

"That can still be done."

"I'll be on the phone tomorrow," Charlene said, "rounding up people to help. You don't have to come if you've got plans for your day off, Ronald and Lucy."

"I wouldn't miss it," I said.

"Count me in," Ronald said. "Nan too."

"And me," Connor said. "Charlene, you are a genius."

Charlene beamed and Charles meowed.

"I think that's been seconded," Connor said, giving the big cat a rub on the head.

Louise Jane wasn't finished yet. "Can't you leave it until November first?"

"No," Charlene said. "We can't. The idea is to get everyone talking about it, and thus interested in the election. That can't wait until a couple of days before."

"Seeing as how we're finished here," Bertie said, "I'm off home. Louise Jane, we're locking up."

Louise Jane stuffed her snacks and spells back into her bag. "After all I do for you people. Very well, you can count on me helping next Sunday as well."

"What a joy to hear," Charlene said.

Ronald stifled a laugh.

My coworkers followed Louise Jane out the door.

"You had something you wanted to talk to me about?" Connor said once they'd all left.

"I did. You may be aware of this already, but I overheard something earlier that you need to know."

"Sounds serious," he said. "The sort of serious that's better discussed over drinks. Or, even better, dinner. If you're free, that is?"

My tongue was suddenly too big for my mouth. I managed to say, "Yeah. Great. That would be nice. Okay."

Charles yawned.

"It's Friday night but getting late, so we might be able to get in at Jake's. You okay with that?"

"Perfect."

"Tonight, let me drive," he said. "I can bring you back

easily enough. Are you ready to go now, or do you have something you need to do first?"

"Now would be fine." I followed Connor outside. Before shutting the door I glanced back into the library to see Charles sitting on the circulation desk, watching. I swear he lifted a paw to wave me off.

Jake's was busy, but not overly so, and the waiter found us a table for two on the deck.

"Are you all right with Louise Jane prowling around outside in the dark?" Connor asked me once the wine had been ordered.

"I prefer knowing where she is," I said with a laugh. "To be honest, if a real ghost popped out of the cupboard and said boo, I wouldn't be scared in the least. I'd assume it was Louise Jane playing tricks and tell it to go away."

He smiled. He reached for my hand, but the waiter chose that moment to bring the drinks and Connor pulled back. I busied myself with my menu.

In the car, I'd told him what I'd overheard at Josie's, about him benefiting from Will's death. Connor had muttered under his breath.

"Is anyone else saying that?" I asked.

"Not that I'm aware of. But rumor spreads fast, and the dirtier it is, the faster it spreads."

"Specials today are Manhattan clam chowder to begin, and . . ." said the waiter.

I practically know Jake's menu by heart. I didn't have to think hard about what to order. "Shrimp and grits, please."

"You're becoming a true Southern woman," Connor said.

"If Southern means shrimp and grits, then I'm in. And a couple of hush puppies too, please."

Connor asked for a steak, medium rare. The waiter collected the menus and left.

"Did Will Williamson promise you a contribution toward your campaign?" I asked.

"Not in so many words. His talk was all about fond reminisces about his youth and wanting to maintain the spirit of the Outer Banks—the way it had been when he and my dad were growing up."

"Those women today said he was supporting Doug because he was in favor of more development."

"I've seen it before, Lucy. Men with money who enjoy playing both sides of the fence. It's like a game with them. See who they can get to flatter them the most. Sometimes it ends with no contribution at all. Just a suggestion that they need to think it over, but next election cycle they'll definitely make up their mind."

"Speaking of your dad . . ."

"I called him. They're having a great time in Colorado, but it's too bad those mountains get in the way and spoil the view."

I laughed as a warm glow filled me. The delicious wine, the beautiful star-filled night, the soft wind on my bare arms, the scents and sounds of the Outer Banks. The company . . .

"Dad didn't remember Will at all at first, but with some prodding on my part, it started to come back. Far from being great buddies, they were nothing more than casual acquaintances. They were in the same classes in school. Dad was on the football team, and Will wanted to be, so there was some jealousy there. Will was never in any trouble, not that Dad remembers."

"Anything about girls?"

"Dad said Will wasn't popular with girls, but he was the sort who talked the big talk. You know, bragging about exploits he never had, trying to blacken the reputation of girls who wouldn't go out with him. He and his wife came to their ten-year high school reunion. Dad remembers that because my mom hadn't been feeling well so she didn't go to the reunion. Will's wife sent a get-well-soon card around to the house the next day, and Dad thought that was a nice thing to do. Will had been to college somewhere, but Dad didn't remember where. He'd married right after college and they had one child. Not long after the reunion, Dad heard that Will had moved away. Never gave him another thought from that day until I called and asked about him."

"But Will seems to have remembered your dad?"

"That's common enough. People who move away cherish their memories; people who stay go on with their lives."

We leaned back to allow the waiter to put a huge platter of crisp golden hush puppies in the center of the table. "I told Jake you're here, Lucy, and he said you get a double serving on the house. Enjoy."

"Looks like I'm becoming known around here," I said.

"That you are."

The hush puppies were great, the shrimp and grits

even better. We didn't talk any more about Doug White-side or Will Williamson, but laughed together at Louise Jane's antics and Charlene's outrageous (and marvelous) idea for decorating the lighthouse.

"Ready to go?" Connor said at last.

The outdoor dining area had emptied without me even noticing. "Yes."

We drove back to the lighthouse in comfortable silence. I liked that about Connor: he had no need to fill every moment with chatter. Sometimes, it's enough simply to be together.

The sky was clear and a big white moon hung overhead. As we approached, the light from the thousand-watt bulb came into view, reliable in its rhythm, breaking the loneliness of the night.

"Do you find," Connor asked after he'd parked and we walked together up the path, "that light bothers you sometimes? Blinking on off all the time the way it does?"

"Never. Its regularity is extremely comforting. My draperies are heavy enough that they block the light when I'm in bed." Heat washed into my face. Fortunately the light went into its twenty-two point five second dormant period at that moment, so Connor didn't see me blushing furiously.

I pulled out my key and unlocked the door. It swung open. I hesitated, just a moment, before I said, "Come on in. I love the library at night."

He stepped over the threshold and shut the door behind him. Charles was nowhere to be seen. That was unusual; he normally ran for the door as soon as he heard my key in the lock. I liked to think it was because he missed me, but I knew what he was really excited about was a refill of the food bowl.

I felt Connor's hands on my shoulders. His warm breath touched the back of my neck. "Lucy." The word was a whisper. I turned. His blue eyes were focused on my face, his lips were partially open. "Lucy." He pulled me toward him. I went willingly. He touched my face, ran his finger across my mouth. Then he bent his head and kissed my lips. A shock as powerful as if a bolt of electricity had hit me went through my body. I shuddered, and lifted my arms to the back of his head.

I settled into the kiss, but he pulled away. "I've been waiting almost twenty years to do this again." His voice was deep and ragged. His eyes burned.

His phone rang. He mumbled something into my lips.

"Leave it," I whispered.

"I will," he said.

My phone rang. I felt his body shiver as he laughed. "Leave it," he said.

"I will." I couldn't help cursing the spirits of modern technology. When I wanted a cell phone signal in this blasted building I couldn't get one.

The library phone rang.

Connor and I pulled away from each other. "Something's happening." He reached into his pocket and pulled out his phone.

I crossed the room and grabbed the one on the desk. "What!" I might have spoken somewhat sharply.

"Thank heavens I got you, Lucy," Bertie said. "Pat's just called and I'm going around there right now. Stephanie has been arrested. Amos and Ellen aren't at home, and I don't have his cell number. I've left a message, but I need you to contact Amos and then go down to the police station and find out what you can." She hung up.

I stared at the receiver in my hand. I heard Connor say, "On my way."

I turned.

"That was Butch," he said. "Stephanie's been arrested for the murder of Will Williamson."

Chapter 13

Connor and I ran out the door together. By the time we got to our cars, Louise Jane was emerging from the marsh at a fast clip. I'd forgotten all about that dratted Louise Jane, but I was thinking about her now. If she'd come knocking a few minutes ago, I might have killed her.

Killed her.

Just an expression we all use when we're angry at someone. It doesn't mean anything. Until it does.

"I heard the news," Louise Jane said. "Wow. So Stephanie killed Will after all."

"I thought you were hunting for ghosts, Louise Jane," Connor snapped. "Doesn't taking a phone call spoil the atmosphere you need to commune with the spirits?"

"I can do two things at once, Mr. Mayor." She looked between Connor and me. The edges of her mouth turned up. "Looks as though you guys were interrupted in the middle of something *important*."

Connor ignored her. "Better go in separate cars," he said to me. "Who knows how long we'll be tied up."

"Right."

Louise Jane waved good-bye as Connor sped away. Before starting my own car, I found Uncle Amos's cell number on my phone and called him. He and Aunt Ellen, he told me, were having dinner with friends. He'd be there as soon as he could.

I knew from past experience that Sam Watson wasn't going to inform me as to what was going on, much less allow me to be with Stephanie while he questioned her. He probably wouldn't even let me past the inner doors. Still, I felt as though I needed to be doing something. Pat would be frantic with worry. Hopefully it would all be a misunderstanding, and I'd be able to bring Stephanie home.

It was late, but traffic was heavy through town as people returned from or traveled to their Friday-night revelries. I didn't mind because it gave me time to think. I knew Stephanie hadn't killed Will, so what on earth would Watson have on her that would allow him to arrest her? Was the real killer attempting to frame Steph? That had to be it. Watson was no fool; surely he'd be able to see through a ruse such as that.

Up ahead I saw the right-turn indicator of Connor's car start to blink. I slowed down, made my own signal, let a giant SUV go by, and turned into the police station. Butch was standing on the steps in his uniform, waiting.

Butch really was a great guy, I thought. He didn't like Stephanie, but he'd called for help for her anyway. Connor was the mayor, so of course he couldn't get involved in a police investigation, but he could have a word with the chief and find out what was going on. Butch smiled as he saw me jump out of my car. Oh, dear. If Butch wasn't such a great guy, I wouldn't feel so bad knowing I was going to hurt him. "Lucy, what are you doing here?"

"We were having dinner," Connor said, "when I got your call."

Butch's eyebrows rose. He looked from one of us to the other. I tried to smile at him. I felt dreadful. Regardless of what happened between Connor and me, I would have to tell Butch that we could only ever be friends. And I'd have to tell him soon. Now, however, didn't seem to be the quite the right time.

"The phone lines are burning up," Connor continued. "Bertie called Lucy. Even Louise Jane knows about it."

"You were having dinner with Louise Jane?" Butch said.

"That," I said, "is a long story." No matter how dreadful I felt, I had to remind myself that Stephanie was in a heck of a lot more serious predicament.

"What's happening, Butch?" Connor asked.

Butch led the way across the driveway to the bench Watson and I had sat on earlier. I sat in the middle, Connor on one side, Butch on the other. It was, I had to admit, an extremely comfortable place to be.

"This is not for the town grapevine, right?" Butch said. We nodded.

"I was with Watson when he first interviewed Stephanie about her whereabouts the night of Will Williamson's murder. She told him that after you, Lucy, and Bertie left her, when she'd learned that Williamson was her father, she stayed in, put her mother to bed, drank a bottle of wine, watched TV, and fell asleep in front of the TV."

"That's right," I said.

"She lied," Butch said bluntly.

"What?"

"We've been canvassing the neighborhood where Will was living. Marlene told us that Will went out after getting a phone call late that night. We were hoping to find someone who saw him meeting someone."

"Did you?"

"No. But we did get a call later from someone who saw Stephanie Stanton outside Will's house."

"He's lying!" I said.

Car lights swept the driveway. I recognized Uncle Amos's Camry and breathed a sigh of relief. He spotted the three of us sitting under the beech tree, but didn't come over. He raised his hand in a lazy greeting before strolling up the stairs, as if he didn't have a care in the world. I wanted to yell at him to run, to hurry. But Uncle Amos never ran, unless it was after a tennis ball. He never seemed to be in any sort of hurry at all. He moved at his own pace, thought before speaking, and when he did speak it was in an unhurried Louisiana accent. And then he'd simply destroy hostile witnesses and prosecuting attorneys with the speed of his mind.

"I'm sorry, Lucy, but it's true," Butch said. "A neighbor was walking his dog. He noticed Stephanie because she was looking very harried. He said she was crying and looking confused, staring at the houses, as though she was searching for something."

"It must have been someone else," I said.

Butch shook his head. "It was Stephanie. He picked her out of a photo lineup."

"So she went out for a drive. Okay, she shouldn't have been driving if she'd been drinking, but . . ."

"Lucy," Connor said. "Regardless of why she was there, the point isn't as much that she was, but that she told Sam she hadn't left the house all night. She lied to the police."

That would mean she'd lied to me also. "Why did this so-called witness call the police anyway? Not at the time, but a day or two later—have you wondered about that?"

"You can be sure Watson has considered it," Butch said. "The paper mentioned the street Will was renting on. The guy saw it and remembered the agitated woman of the night Will died. So he called."

"The phone call!" I said. "What about the phone call Will got that night after they got home? The one that made him go out. You can trace that call, can't you? I'll bet you anything it wasn't Stephanie who called."

"The phone was a burner. Impossible to trace, particularly if the user has tossed it. Which he, or she, would be an idiot not to."

"This looks bad for Stephanie," Connor said. "But there's a big step from pacing up and down someone's street to killing them. There's nothing we can do tonight. I'll call the chief in the morning for an update."

"She hasn't been charged," Butch said. "Not yet, anyway, just brought in for more questioning."

"At this time of night," Connor said, "it's pretty much the same thing."

"I'd like to stay," I said.

"You won't be allowed to talk to her," Butch said.

"I'll only stay until I know if they're going to hold her. Someone has to tell her mother what's going on."

The two men exchanged glances over my head. "Don't try to talk me out of it," I said. "Stephanie is my friend. I believe in her innocence, and I intend to be here for her."

I was left cooling my heels in the reception area at the front of the police station. I called Bertie to check in, and she told me Pat insisted on waiting up until there was news.

When I'd run out the door after Connor, I hadn't even stopped to throw a book into my purse. To give me something to do while I waited, I loaded an e-book onto my iPhone, but I scarcely read a word of it. Either the little screen wasn't conducive to paying attention or my mind was occupied elsewhere. I'd texted Uncle Amos to let him know I was waiting.

Inside the police station at night, the lights are dimmed, and a sense of calm peace fell over the place in the absence of the daytime bustle of office work. Unlike the beautiful serenity of the empty library, an underlying tension filled the police station, even when no one was visible. Doors kept opening and shutting, voices were heard and cut off, cars turned into the cruiser lot at the back.

No one came out to check on me. I was beginning to doze off in the hard, uncomfortable plastic chair when I heard voices approaching. I leaped to my feet. Uncle Amos and Sam Watson came through the inner doors. To my enormous relief, Stephanie walked between them. She was wearing a pair of scuffed sneakers, and her tiny frame was dwarfed by the two tall men on either side of her. She looked, I thought, like a ten-year-old who'd been called down to the principal's office, though there was no youthful mischief in her face. The shine had gone out of her hair, and deep dark bags lay beneath her eyes. She managed to give me a weak smile. "Amos told me you were here. Thanks for coming, Lucy."

I gave her a hug. Her body shook, but when we broke away her eyes were clear.

"Now see here, Detective Watson," I said. "I insist you listen to me about those lights I saw Monday night."

"You insist, do you? You can insist all you want. Good night, Ms. Stanton. Amos."

Watson turned and walked away, leaving me sputtering in righteous indignation.

"Come on, Lucy," Uncle Amos said.

"I'll take Steph home," I said.

"Good," he said. "We'll talk tomorrow, Stephanie. My office, eight o'clock."

"I'll be there. And thanks."

"You don't have to talk about it, if you don't want to," I said to my friend once we were in my car.

She turned her head away from me and sat looking out into night as I drove through the empty back streets, past houses wrapped in darkness. Then she groaned and threw up her hands. "I was a fool. A total and complete idiot. Yes, I went out after Mom was in bed. Her keys are kept by the back door, so I just grabbed them and jumped into her car." She sighed and leaned against the headrest. "I'm lucky I didn't kill someone, driving in the state I was in. I went to the street where Will told us he was staying. For some stupid reason I got it into my head that I had to meet him. Then and there, that night. I wanted to look into his face, see if I could find myself there, I guess. Maybe I wanted him to break down and tell me that he'd been thinking of me all these years and regretting not having been there for me. I didn't know which one was their house, so I guess I was hoping he'd be standing in a window or coming home or something. Anything. I wasn't there long, fifteen minutes maybe, before I realized that not only was I wasting my time, but in danger of screwing this up. When I did confront him I wanted to be in full possession of my faculties. Not some babbling idiot that would make him glad he'd run out on us."

"Oh, Steph," I said.

"When Watson asked me if I'd gone out after you and Bertie left, I lied without thinking. I lied to you too, Lucy, and I'm sorry about that, but I guess I wanted to believe it myself. In the moment, I was able to convince myself that I might not have been lying. I had such an awful headache that morning, and I barely remembered what had happened the night before. I thought I'd dreamed it all. Unfortunately, I didn't. But I do know that I didn't kill him. I suppose my mom called you?"

"Bertie did. Pat phoned Bertie and she went right over. Butch called Connor."

"He did? He was the one Watson sent to pick me up. Didn't he just love it?"

"Butch isn't like that."

She didn't reply.

When we got to Pat's house, all the downstairs lights were on, and Bertie was standing at the window, peering out.

"Thanks, Lucy," Stephanie said. "You don't need to come in."

"I . . ."

"I'd rather you didn't. My mom and I need to be alone."

"Sure," I said.

It had been an awful day (well, most of it anyway) but it wasn't to be over yet. The driveway to the lighthouse is long and headlights can be seen well before an approaching car reaches the parking area. Louise Jane stood waiting for me in front of the library, feet apart, hands planted firmly on her bony hips. A miner's style flashlight was wrapped around her head.

I was barely out of my car before she said, "How am I supposed to attract the spirits if you keep popping in and out all night? Lighting up the place, slamming doors?"

"Please, Louise Jane, not now. I'm tired."

"You think I'm not? I've been up all night, you know."

"I'm going to take a wild guess that you didn't find anything."

"Patience, Lucy, is a prime component of communing with the supernatural."

"Good thing I have none then. Good night, Louise Jane."

"What happened with Stephanie?" she asked.

"You seemed to know mighty quickly that she'd been taken down to the police station for more questioning—not arrested, I might add. How?"

"That's the thing about having deep roots in a place, Lucy, that you'll never fully understand. I know people. People know me. My grandmother's friend, Myrna Schmitt, lives across the street from Pat Stanton. Myrna knows that I'm interested in uncovering *the truth* about what happened here that night, so naturally she phoned me when she saw police activity."

I had an image of Myrna standing by her lace curtains with curlers in her hair, wearing a flannel nightgown, binoculars trained on Pat's living room window.

"Not," Louise Jane went on, "that I'm not surprised to hear Stephanie wasn't arrested. You and I both know other forces are at work here."

"Good night, Louise Jane." I started up the path.

"Sleep well, Lucy. I'm sure you're perfectly safe inside the lighthouse, but don't venture out at night, please, sweetie. Until I've determined what exactly we're dealing with here."

I didn't dignify that comment with a response. When I crossed the threshold of the library, Charles was standing at the door with a look on his face that resembled nothing so much as my mother when I'd get home five minutes after curfew. "To bed," I said. He ran lightly up the stairs ahead of me.

I did not run lightly. I didn't run at all. I was bone-tired, desperately worried for my friend, yet still exhilarated by the memory of Connor's kisses. Tonight, the hundred steps to my apartment might have been a thousand. I gripped the iron railings and dragged my weary body and confused mind up. It was four o'clock and I had to be at work, bright and cheerful, for opening at nine. If there was one good thing about the lateness of the hour, it was that Louise Jane would probably sleep all day (so she could maintain her self-appointed rounds at night) and therefore, wouldn't be hanging around bothering us.

I finally made it to the fourth-floor landing and

fumbled to put my key into the lock, while Charles waited impatiently at my feet. I froze.

Was it possible?

No. I was so tired my brain wasn't working properly.

I opened the door and Charles charged into the kitchen. A loud meow informed me that his food bowl was empty. I filled it, struggled out of my clothes and into my pajamas, brushed my teeth, and washed my face. I crawled into bed. Charles finished his dinner and joined me.

I wanted to think about Connor. I wanted to remember every moment of our dinner together, relive every second (brief though they had been) I had been in his arms.

But all I could think about was . . . Louise Jane.

Louise Jane was obsessed with the paranormal history (or fantasy) of the Outer Banks, of this lighthouse, and the surrounding marshes in particular. If she even believed some of the rubbish she spouted, I didn't know and it didn't matter. Louise Jane was also obsessed with getting a foot in the door of the library, and that meant (in her mind) getting rid of me.

How far would she go to make people accept that she was an expert in communicating with the paranormal? To scare me away so my job would be available? Louise Jane was the only person who believed the story of the wrecker's lights. She believed it because she wanted to believe it. It would validate everything she worked so hard to make others believe. Had she taken it one step further?

Had Louise Jane McKaughnan killed Will Williamson so as to deposit his body mysteriously in the marsh?

Charles dug his sharp claws into the duvet and kneaded

at the fabric. I pulled my arm out from under the covers and scratched his favorite spot at the front of his head, right above the eyes.

No. Even Louise Jane wouldn't be that obsessed. Or was she? I thought of her out in the marsh at night, creeping around in the dark in her pink-and-purple boots and a miner's lamp on her forehead. My misgivings wouldn't go away.

I, and everyone else, had accepted her story of being in the marsh searching for spirits without question. But suppose that wasn't the truth? Had she dropped something before or after killing Will and was she searching for it under the pretense of being a ghost hunter?

No. I didn't like Louise Jane, and she certainly didn't like me. But she was no killer. I might, however, try to find out what exactly she was up to out there.

Chapter 14

Saturdays are always busy at the library, particularly with families and children. Locals who have the day off work or school drop in, weekend residents pay us a visit, and Ronald puts on several children's programs for the school-age set. I particularly enjoy days when the library's full of excited chattering children beginning (we all hope) a lifetime of reading.

This morning, the rising sun was barely visible behind a bank of dark, threatening clouds, and the forecast was for rain all day, so we'd see more families through our doors than on a regular sunny Saturday.

Before heading downstairs, I opened my window and held my phone out so as to send Stephanie a text:

Call me if you want to talk.

I pushed SEND, and then the phone beeped with an incoming text sent while I'd been out of range.

I'm tied up with a fund-raising function tonight. Picnic on the beach tomorrow?

It was from Connor.

I replied: Great idea!

I went to work with a skip in my step.

Being busy kept my mind on my duties and off my worries. Only one incident threatened to spoil my day. It was late afternoon and children were arriving for Saturday's natural history time. Last week Ronald had asked the kids to bring a single piece of Outer Banks nature with them today. They arrived laden with broken shells, bags of sand, insects in bottles, gull feathers, and even a rock or two. Bertie stood by the door, exclaiming in delight over every treasure, while proud parents and grandparents beamed. The children ran up the stairs and many of the parents settled down to chat for an hour. When the only evidence of children in the building was the sound of excited laughter coming from over our heads, I dragged the returns shelf around the main room to return books to their proper places.

I was tucking the newest Krista Davis book into the mystery shelf when, from the other side of the partition, I heard mention of the name that had been filling my mind (and my heart and my soul) all day. I held my breath and listened.

"You don't really think Dr. McNeil capable of something like that?" a woman said.

"These days, I wouldn't be surprised at anything anyone does," replied a second woman. "Particularly when it comes to politics. You know, Mary-Alice, that I'm not one for gossip. But my niece's husband's brother is friends with Bill Hill and Bill told him that Dr. McNeil was enraged at what he saw as Will Williamson's betrayal. And, well, we all know what happened to Will, don't we?"

Who the heck was Bill Hill?

"Nonsense. You're letting your tongue run away with you, June. What I hear is that it was a mob killing. Poor Will had an unfortunate resemblance to someone the New York mob is after, and they killed him by mistake. The location of the body, in that boat, proves it."

"It's that lawyer girl," a third woman put in. "Pat Stanton's daughter. I always said Pat had airs above her station. Imagine, a girl with a single mother going to law school."

"I happen to know Pat well," the first woman said with a pronounced sniff, "and Stephanie is a lovely young girl."

Behind the stacks, I nodded. I was about to thank June for having a head on her shoulders when she said, "Stephanie had no reason to kill Will. I'm not saying Connor McNeil did, but Bill Hill says . . ."

"Bill Hill is paid to think the worst of Dr. McNeil," Mary-Alice said. "Besides he'll do anything to win an election. Sometimes, I swear that he's more power hungry than that mayoral candidate of his."

Bill Hill, I remembered, was Doug Whiteside's assistant, Billy.

"Far be it from me to make judgment without evidence," said the poisoned-tongued June, "but where there's smoke . . ."

"I suggest you not be spreading that around," Mary-Alice said. "Now, if you'll excuse me, I'm looking for a new book. I'm in the mood for a nice light cozy."

I darted out of my hiding place as the three women came around the corner. I expected June to slither, but she walked on two legs just like the others.

This was definitely not good. Rumors were spreading, and fast. And Bill Hill, doubtless encouraged by Doug Whiteside, was fanning the flames.

The children had left, along with their parents and grandparents, and the last of the patrons were checking out their books when Josie, Grace, and Stephanie came in.

"This is a surprise," I said. "Let me finish up here and I'll be right with you." I helped an elderly lady put her weekly stack of books into her canvas tote bag. "Thank you, Mrs. Brady. See you next week."

"If you're talking to that nice Mayor McNeil, tell him I don't believe a word of what people are saying about him," she said to me.

"I will," I said.

"What are people saying about Connor?" Stephanie asked once Mrs. Brady had left.

"That he killed Will Williamson when he realized Will wasn't going to donate to his campaign," Josie said.

Stephanie laughed. She stopped laughing when she saw the looks on our faces. "You're not kidding."

"No, we are not," I said. "I overheard several people talking about it earlier today. Only one of them seemed to take the idea seriously, but one is enough to start a stampede."

"What did you do?" Grace asked.

"Do? What could I do?"

"Throw them out on the street and tell them never to darken your door again?" Josie suggested.

"I just might do that next time. And there might well

be a next time. That assistant of Doug's is spreading muck all over town, and I've not the slightest doubt Doug put him up to it."

Ronald clattered down the stairs. For natural history day, he'd dressed in Bermuda shorts, a multipocketed khaki jacket, a trilby hat, and white socks inside sandals. "Hi, ladies. Have a nice Sunday." He breezed on by.

"He's a lovely man," Stephanie said.

"That he is. And very happily married," Grace said.

"The story of my life," Steph sighed.

"What brings you three here?" I asked.

"Girls' night!" Josie said. "I insisted that Steph come with us. I deliberately didn't call ahead so you couldn't refuse."

"Your cousin can be very persuasive," Stephanie said. "She brought her mother to our house to sit with Mom."

"We've got microwavable pizza, supermarket salads, and a tub of Ben and Jerry's Chunky Monkey in the car," Grace said. "I'll run out and get it."

"And I'll bring in the wine," Josie said.

Once they'd gone, I smiled at Stephanie. "I'm glad you came."

"I feel like I've been kidnapped. Between those two and my mom I didn't have a heck of a lot of choice."

"Kidnapping's nicer these days than it was in David Balfour's time," I said. "All you have to face is an excess of Ben and Jerry's, not be tied up in the hold of a leaky brig, wrecked at sea. Did you hear from Detective Watson today?"

"No. Amos said that my being in the general vicinity of Will's home the night he died is evidence against me, but not enough for them to take to court on its own. He warned me that the police will be going back to that neighborhood to question everyone, hoping to find someone who saw me doing something . . . incriminating. They didn't find my fingerprints in either Will's car or that boat. But as we lawyers know, absence of evidence . . ."

"Isn't evidence of absence."

"What's this about suspecting Connor, of all people?" she asked.

"Connor. Terrorists. New York mob. You name it; someone has a theory of why they did it. Normally, I'd say it doesn't matter what the gossips say, but with the election coming up, this could hurt Connor."

"It's a mess all around," she said.

"Have you heard from your employers?" I asked. "You can't do better than have Amos O'Malley acting for you, but is your firm prepared to help out?"

Stephanie's laugh was bitter. "Help? Hardly. Yes, my boss called. They are not happy about this cloud hanging over my head, and would like to ensure that I clear myself of all suspicion before continuing with my work. The briefs I am currently working on will be assigned to other lawyers in the meantime."

"You can't mean they're firing you! Is that even allowed? You haven't been charged with anything."

"Not fired, no. Just advised to continue with my leave of absence." She shrugged. "No one goes into the law expecting it to be a warm and fuzzy work environment, but I have to say I'm disappointed in them. I called one of my so-called friends, another new lawyer who started the same time as me, to find out what people are saying, and she was, shall I say, frosty. Couldn't get off the phone fast enough."

"Her loss," I said. "You know you have friends, real friends, right here, don't you?"

She touched my arm with a sad smile. "I know. I'm starting to think Raleigh isn't the place for me anymore."

"What do you mean?"

"Law's a tough career, like I said, but it hasn't made Amos O'Malley hard in the way it's making me feel jaded. Let me think about it. When we get all this cleared up, I can make some decisions."

Josie and Grace fell through the door laughing and laden down with bags and coolers.

I took my friends up to my apartment. There weren't enough chairs, so we settled in a circle on the floor with a delighted Charles in the center. Fortunately, I own four wineglasses. As Josie poured she said, "I drove us here, but Jake's coming to pick me up when the restaurant closes. So I can indulge, indulge. I'll be back sometime tomorrow to get my car." To Josie, indulge meant about a half glass of wine. She worked unbelievable hours at her bakery, seven days a week in season, from four a.m. until closing at three. Jake worked equally unbelievable hours, but his were the opposite of Josie's. He started in the early afternoon and would be at the restaurant until after the kitchen closed at midnight.

I couldn't imagine how they managed, but they were clearly happy and very much in love. Sacrifices now, Josie sometimes said, to prepare for their future.

We drank wine, ate tasteless pizza and delicious ice

cream. We laughed and chatted. Grace kept going to the window, hoping to see Louise Jane's light as she crept through the grasses of the marsh, but outside nothing moved. As delightful as the evening was, we couldn't avoid the topic on all our minds forever. When Grace said, "We need to make this a regular thing," Stephanie sighed and replied, "if I'm not in jail."

We leaned in for a group hug. When we separated, I said, "The way I see it there's no shortage of suspects."

Grace crawled across the room on her hands and knees to get her bag and pulled out a notebook and pen. "Let's get our thoughts in order and maybe we can come up with something no one's thought of. Go ahead, Lucy, you seem to be closest to all this. Other than Steph."

"Blue sky?" I said.

"Total blue sky. We'll get it down, no matter how crazy the theory."

"Okay," I said. "First of all, if some people believe Connor was capable of killing Will over a campaign donation, then why not say Doug Whiteside did it to frame Connor?"

"Good one," Josie said.

"Marlene's happily spending Will's money. Maybe she figured she'd prefer to have the money and not put up with him anymore." Grace made notes as I spoke. "Teddy Kowalski had a business deal with Will that fell through."

"Teddy?" Josie said. "Out of the question. We all know, Teddy. He's a pussycat."

"I can't see Teddy doing it either, but we said blue sky, remember. As long as he had a motive, he's on the list," Grace said.

"I wouldn't have figured Mr. Out-on-the-rigs-in-the-middle-of-winter to be a book collector," Josie said.

"Rare books can be an excellent investment." Grace jotted Teddy's name down.

"And then there's Louise Jane." I explained my reasoning. I have to admit, my friends looked pretty doubtful. "And, last of all, someone we don't know about. Will wasn't a nice man. I've been hearing that he liked nothing more than to pick an argument with people and threaten to sue them."

"Like Ralph Harper," Stephanie said.

"Old Ralph?" Grace said. "What's he got to do with this?"

I explained about the confrontation in the library parking lot only hours before Will died. Grace added his name to the list.

"It's possible someone from Will's past never forgot a grudge," I said. "I asked your mom to look into that, Josie. Do you know if anything came up? She said she'd call if she found anything, and I haven't heard."

Josie shook her head. "When I asked her to sit with Pat tonight, Mom said she wanted to talk to Pat anyway. Throw around some ideas, see if Pat can remember any other girls Will might have been having affairs with, or if he ever told her about someone he was fighting with."

"Then," Stephanie said, "there's me."

"You are not a suspect," I said.

"I am to Detective Watson. He had to admit that considering I am a respected member of the legal profession, and have no police record of any sort, it's unlikely I would have killed Will because I was angry at him."

"Exactly," I said. "Now who . . ."

"But," she continued, "Watson wanted to know what I thought when I realized that Will was a wealthy man. Did I decide it was time he paid up for all the years my mom and I went without? I told him the thought had crossed my mind, but if he was dead that door would be closed, wouldn't it? Watson disagreed. He said there have been cases in which unknown illegitimate children were found to have a claim on an estate. Maybe, he said, I decided to get what I was owed without waiting another twenty or thirty more years."

"That's ridiculous," Grace said.

"Yes, it is, for me. But it makes me wonder if there are other so-called-illegitimate children out there wanting a piece of the action."

"Impossible for us to know, unless Aunt Ellen and her friends remember something."

"You said Will has a son?" Grace said. "What about him? He might have killed his dad, not wanting Will to joyfully discover that he had a long-lost daughter and cut her in on the inheritance."

I shook my head. "Timing doesn't work. Will didn't know Steph was his daughter. You were sitting right next to each other at book club, and he didn't even blink."

"*Bored disengagement* is the phrase that comes to mind," Steph said.

"The only person who knew, until Wednesday night, was Pat," Josie said. "Besides, if the son did know, and was the type to think that way, he'd be more likely to kill Stephanie, an intrusive stranger, than his father, wouldn't you think?"

We nodded.

"I have a brother," Stephanie said. "Imagine that."

"What I'd like to know," Grace said, "is how Will got into that boat. Someone must have lured him down to the marina at night. He wouldn't go with just anyone."

"As Detective Watson won't tell me what clues he's coming up with," I said, "we simply don't know. He might have been killed anywhere, and the body dumped into the boat. I'd like to know how the killer got away after tying up the boat. He wouldn't have walked back to town, so did he have an accomplice? Either someone in on the killing, or who he called after the fact? Hey, I've just remembered something."

They looked at me, eyes wide with interest. Even Charles's ears stood to attention.

"What?" Stephanie said. It almost broke my heart to hear the hope in her voice.

"Boats. Who knows boats better than the coast guard? Marlene told me Will threatened to sue the coast guard guys who rescued them the night of the storm. Not just Ralph Harper but all of them."

"He really was a piece of work," Grace said. "I'd say no loss to anyone, if we didn't have friends involved."

"Is it possible that Ralph and the coast guard made a mistake?" I asked. "The sort of mistake a man like Will would delight in jumping on? And did one of the guys, or all of them, decide to take Will out of the picture before he could lay a complaint?"

"That's ridiculous," Josie said.

"No more ridiculous than some of the other things we've heard," Grace said. "Blue sky, remember. Anything's on the table."

"Josie," I said. "Aaron volunteers with the coast guard, right?"

She nodded. Aaron was her younger brother.

"Could you ask him to find out who, in addition to Ralph, rescued Will that night? Maybe one of us can go around and ask a few discreet questions."

"Questions like, 'Did you murder Will Williamson so you wouldn't be arrested for negligence?'" Josie said.

"Put like that, it does sound rather silly," I said. "But if we have the names maybe all I need to do is place another word in Watson's ear. I told him what happened between Will and Ralph, but I don't know what happened about that."

"Can't hurt," Josie said. "Sure, Aaron'll be glad to help. He's making noises about becoming a police officer."

Stephanie groaned.

"Yeah," Josie said, "you and my dad both."

"I've nothing against the police," Grace said. "I wouldn't mind getting to know Butch Greenblatt better. But I think his mind is elsewhere these days." She gave me a look. I busied myself gathering up the empty ice cream bowls (Charles had already washed them).

"Butch?" Stephanie said. "Surely you don't mean Lucy's interested in that big lug? Lucy has enough common sense to stay well away from the likes of him. Cops are relationship poison. Particularly the big handsome macho ones. They're on far too much of a power trip."

"Butch isn't like that," Josie said.

"I don't intend to find out," Stephanie said.

"Butch is so much like his older brother," Josie said. "Neither he nor Jake have anything to prove to anyone.

And, speaking of Jake"—Josie checked her watch—"he said to be ready at quarter after. It's almost that late now."

Reluctantly, my friends got to their feet. They helped me carry the last of the dishes and glasses into the kitchen, and Charles and I went down with them to lock up.

Grace stuck her head out the door. "I don't see Louise Jane's car. Drat, I was hoping to make rustling noises in the grass and moan." She did a terrible imitation of a tormented ghost and we laughed.

Headlights swept down the driveway.

"Looks like Jake's got someone with him," I said. The car pulled up and two men got out.

Beside me I heard Stephanie let out a soft grunt I took for disapproval.

Jake and Butch. Jake was shorter and slighter than his younger brother but the resemblance between them was unmistakable. They might have been twins.

Extremely good-looking twins.

Josie ran up to Jake and they greeted with a kiss. "Did y'all have fun?" he said when they separated.

"Sure did," Grace said. "Hi, Butch."

"Hi." Butch gave me a smile. He ignored Stephanie, which seemed to suit her, as she ignored him. They stood in the center of the parking lot like two blocks of ice. These people were two of my best friends and they hated each other. I wished I could do something to convince each of them that the other was a nice person.

But I suspected that the differences between them ran too deep.

Josie leaped into the front passenger seat of the car, leaving Butch, Grace, and Stephanie to get in the back.

Jake drove a Honda Accord. If not for the look on Butch and Stephanie's faces, I might have laughed. Grace got into the back first and didn't move from beside the window. Stephanie crawled into the middle seat, and Butch was forced to squeeze his six-foot-five, two hundred pound frame·between the door and a steaming Stephanie.

I could already tell that for my friends, it was going to be a long ride home.

Chapter 15

I woke to the feel of something rough and wet on my face. I opened my eyes and found myself staring into Charles's expressive blue orbs. "Geeze," I said. "Go back to sleep, will you?" He lifted one paw and swatted my cheek.

"No," I said. "I refuse to get up. It's Sunday and I have the right to sleep in. I have an exciting day ahead of me and I need my beauty rest." Unimpressed, he swatted me again. That was unlike Charles. He was usually content to wait for me to make getting-up noises. I rolled over, thinking of my date with Connor. A picnic on the beach. Could anything be more romantic?

The phone rang. I rolled back over. Charles smirked, and leaped off the bed. I answered the dratted phone.

"Morning, Lucy. I apologize for calling so early." It was Connor. My heart moved and I snuggled deeper into the bed, feeling a nice warm glow in my chest.

"Not a problem," I said. "I was up."

"I'm really sorry, but I'm going to have to cancel our picnic."

A bucket of cold water drenched my nice warm glow. "Oh," I said.

"I have to meet with Dorothy, my campaign manager. I don't know when we'll be finished. There have been some not-promising developments in the campaign this week."

"You mean Doug Whiteside?"

"Yes, I do. Are you hearing anything more?"

I told him what I'd overheard in the library stacks yesterday.

"That's what Dorothy says people are talking about. I want to confront these rumors head-on. Maybe even have the chief make a statement. Dorothy fears that doing so will only be adding fuel to the fire. Regardless, I have to be out there most of today, pressing the flesh, convincing voters that I'm not a cold-blooded killer."

"I understand, Connor." And I did understand. Totally. But I couldn't help being disappointed.

"Thanks, Lucy. Can I call you tonight and let you know how it goes? Hopefully we can do something next week."

"Of course," I said.

"Enjoy your day." He hung up.

I refrained from hurling the phone across the room. Blast that Bill Hill and his sneaky insinuations. If anyone had something to hide in this campaign, it would be Doug Whiteside.

Now that the prospect of more sleep had been ruined, I rolled out of bed and pulled back the curtains. Oh, great, a perfect sunny day. I would have been a lot happier if a snowstorm was bearing down on me.

There is only one thing a woman can do in the face of such profound disappointment.

Pay a visit to Josie's Cozy Bakery.

"That was fun last night," my cousin said to me.

"It was. I noticed your car was gone this morning. How was the ride home last night?"

"You mean other than when Stephanie told Butch he was deliberately taking up too much of her space, and he said, 'Excuse me for living, but could you get your elbow out of my ribs'? It reminded me of when you and your brothers would visit and Dad would try to stuff all of us into the back of the van."

"It's too bad those two don't like each other. Makes things awkward."

"What time are you meeting Connor?" Josie asked. I'd told my friends last night about our plans for today.

I explained what had happened, and she pulled a face. "Can't be helped I suppose. What are you up to today then?"

"Lucy, one extra-large latte," Alison called, placing my drink on the counter. I shifted the paper bag containing a breakfast sandwich to the other hand and grabbed the cup. "I plan to do some politicking of my own. See you later."

Before leaving home, I'd gone online and searched for the information I needed: the location of Doug Whiteside's campaign office. I'd then spent an hour catching up on e-mail and Facebook posts with friends back in Boston, until I figured it would be time to find the office open.

I munched on my sandwich as I drove across town. I expected Doug's campaign headquarters to be a hive of activity, but only one rusty car was parked outside when I pulled up. The office was located in an unattractive strip mall, next to a nail parlor. I had no trouble identifying it, because giant posters of a grinning Doug graced the windows. The smile was so fake, the teeth so white, I wondered if they'd been Photoshopped.

By contrast, Connor's official pictures played down his extraordinary good looks and made him look older than he was. Maybe his team feared that older voters wouldn't take such a young, handsome man seriously.

I pushed open the door and marched in. An elderly lady, dressed in a lilac twin-set and pearls, her blue-rinse hair crimped and tightly curled, was seated behind a desk. The office wasn't big, one room with a door, now open, leading off into a small meeting room. Tables were covered in election signs and promotional handouts. Numerous boxes of those ubiquitous fridge magnets were piled high. The room was painted industrial beige, the carpet brown and worn thin in places. The only decoration was a banner pinned to the back wall that read in big letters, DOUG FOR NAGS HEAD.

"Help ya, honey?" the woman asked.

"Is Doug in?"

"Not yet. If you want to talk to him, why don't you leave your number and I'll tell him to call you. He always returns every phone call."

"Okay. I'm here because I'm uh . . . interested in renting a space for my boat at a marina on Roanoke Island and I'm wondering if there are any taxes on that."

"What?" She looked confused. As well she might. Even I didn't know what I was talking about. On the drive over I'd decided that if fortune favors the brave,

I'd have to be brave. In the cold light of day I didn't believe Doug had killed Will to make Connor look bad. But Doug was perfectly happy to take advantage of the situation. I wanted to let him know that two could play at that game.

"I'm sure he doesn't know," the woman sniffed, "what folks get up to on Roanoke."

"Oh, sorry. I thought Doug would know. He has a berth there, doesn't he? At the marina near Wanchese, I was told."

She started to shake her head (not a single strand of her hair moved) and then, like a bulb coming on, light flooded into her eyes. "That's where that man was killed."

"Someone was killed there?" I gasped. The police weren't saying where exactly the murder took place—if they even knew. I wondered if this woman had inside information or was speculating based on the theft of the boat. But, I reminded myself, that wasn't why I was here. "You don't say. How awful. Was it near Doug's slip?"

"Doug doesn't have a boat slip."

"Maybe it was Bill Hill I'd heard about then?"

"Don't think so."

"Really? I could have sworn. Oh, well, never mind."

"What'd you say your name was again?"

"I didn't. Thanks. I'll pop in later."

I attempted a hasty exit. So hasty, I almost bumped into Doug and Billy coming in. "Sorry," I said.

"Not a problem. I run into voters all the time," Doug chuckled. "But they're rarely as pretty as you. Ha-ha."

Ha-ha. Even Billy had the grace to look embarrassed.

"Oh," Doug said. "It's you again. Lucy from the library,

right? Thanks for dropping in. Sorry I wasn't around to greet you. Here to volunteer, are you? Billy, why don't you get this young lady a coffee and show her to a table and a phone?"

"Another time," I said, squeezing past them. In an almost empty parking lot, Doug had managed to park his Cadillac Escalade at such an angle that I could barely get my door open, and I had to suck my stomach in and wiggle myself into my own car.

Before I could get the engine started my phone rang. To my considerable surprise, it was Marlene. She didn't bother with greetings. "Lucy, something absolutely dreadful has happened."

"What? Are you okay? Do you need me to call the police?"

"The police have just been here. Can you come over? Right away?"

"Sure. But, why are you calling me, Marlene?"

"I . . ." Her voice broke. "I don't have anyone else to ask, Lucy."

"I'm in town now, so I can be there in a couple of minutes. Is it Mike? Have they arrested Mike?"

"Mike? Who cares about Mike? It's much worse." She hung up.

I switched the engine on and put my car into gear. Before driving away, I glanced up at Doug's office. He was standing in the window, his real face next to the campaign picture giving him a strange double-headed appearance. Bill Hill was standing slightly behind him and looking over Doug's shoulder. They were watching me, and neither of them was smiling.

* * *

There was little point in speculating as to what had happened at Marlene's, but I couldn't help myself from doing so anyway. The police had called on her, bringing upsetting news. She said they hadn't arrested Mike, and obviously they hadn't arrested Marlene if she was still at home, so what could it have been? Had they warned Marlene she was under suspicion? Were they calling off the investigation? Had they concluded that Will's death had been suicide? It hadn't looked like suicide to me, but what did I know? I'd had only a quick glance at the body—and one glance had been more than enough—so I might have missed important clues.

At Marlene's house, no cars were in the parking area, but that meant nothing as the double garage doors were closed. I ran up the steps and pressed the bell. Marlene threw open the door almost immediately. She was again dressed in a bathing suit and the turquoise robe. Today her hair was undone and blond tresses curled around her shoulders. It made her look older and somewhat harder than the casual, cheerful ponytail she usually sported. Then again, her eyes were red and her face streaked with the tracks of tears. It wasn't a look that would make anyone, other than a toddler, look young.

"What's happened?" I said.

She threw her arms around me and sobbed. I hugged her back and tried to mumble words of comfort. Finally she pushed herself away. She dug a tattered tissue out of her pocket, blew her nose, and wiped at her eyes. "Come on in, and I'll tell you. Oh, Lucy, it's simply dreadful."

We went upstairs. Mike was in the great room, pacing up and down in front of the glass wall. He wore jeans and a tight-fitting T-shirt and held a glass half full of a smoky liquid. When I came in, he swallowed the drink in one gulp.

Marlene threw herself into a chair with a moan.

"Don't be such a drama queen," Mike said, heading to the bar for a refill.

"Is someone going to tell me what's going on?" I said.

"It's gone. All gone," Marlene moaned.

"What's gone?"

"Will's money. He hasn't got any."

"What?"

"I went out to dinner last night and my credit card was refused. It was embarrassing enough to be sitting in Owens having dinner all by myself, never mind the smirk on the stuck-up waitress's fat face when she brought my card back. Fortunately I had enough cash on me to pay the bill, although the look she gave me when I didn't leave a tip was simply hideous. I called the bank this morning, and they said the card has been suspended until"—she gulped—"the outstanding interest charges are paid."

Some crisis. I'd been dragged halfway across town in a panic so Marlene could tell me her credit card bill was overdue. "Pay the charges then."

"I have nothing to pay it with! I don't keep track of those things! Will pays my card off every month. That was our arrangement."

I glanced at Mike. "What Marlene means," he said, "is that Dad told her he was paying it off. It would seem he was lying to her. As well as to everyone else."

Marlene grabbed a fresh tissue out of a box on the side table and blew her nose enthusiastically. Mike's face twisted in disapproval.

"I still don't understand," I said.

"I don't know why Marlene called you," Mike said. "I don't believe in washing a family's dirty laundry in public. Then again, Marlene's hardly family, are you?" His sneer was probably equal to the waitress's when she realized she wasn't going to get a tip from what had, no doubt, been a high-spending and high-demanding customer. Mike turned back to me with an attempt at a smile. "Regardless of Marlene's histrionics, it was nice of you to come over, Lucy. As long as you're here, you might as well know what's happened. Your pal Detective Watson paid us a visit. He'd obtained a warrant to look into my dad's bank accounts and did so yesterday. He found nothing."

"Nothing wrong, you mean. That's good isn't it?" I figured it was standard procedure for the police to investigate a murdered person's financial affairs. They'd be checking for unusual amounts of money going out that might mean blackmail or coming in that might mean up to no good.

"Nothing!" Marlene wailed. "No money. Nothing."

"You mean . . ."

"Yup," Mike said. "Dad was dead broke. Worse than dead broke, he was drowning in debt. That silly little car he said he'd bought Marlene—only a lease. The boat he wrecked, rented. This house that was supposedly paid up until the end of the year? Nope. I expect we'll be evicted as soon as the rent check bounces."

"Wow," I said. "He had nothing?"

"Nothing but bad investments, loans coming due,

and a couple of small GICs that are locked in. He was probably on the verge of cashing them in, and taking a big penalty for doing so."

Marlene sat on the couch and wept. "He won ten thousand dollars in one night of poker in Vegas. Right after we met. He said I was his lucky charm."

"He lost, the cops say, more than two hundred thousand in the week he was there," Mike said.

"Wow," I repeated.

"All this time," Marlene moaned, "I thought he was playing computer games. I asked if I could play with him once—just to keep him company, like? He said he played to get rid of stress and wanted to be alone."

"And you were too busy to push it?" Mike sneered. He nodded to the stacks of fashion and gossip magazines covering all the tables. "Too stupid and self-absorbed, more like."

"You can't talk to me like that," she said. "I don't interfere where I'm not wanted."

"That," he said, "I'm glad to hear."

"Hold on," I said. "I don't understand. What's his computer got to do with anything?"

"The cops searched the computer," Mike said. "It seems that Dad was a regular visitor to almost every online gambling site in existence. His accounts show a couple of small wins here and there. And major losses everywhere else."

"Isn't gambling illegal in North Carolina?" I asked.

"Not online gambling, no. But even if it was, that's hardly going to stop anyone," Mike said. "They don't call it the World Wide Web for nothing. As for retiring? Turns out that was a lie too, as the cops found out by placing a single phone call to the boss at his old company. Dad was fired. Told if he left quietly the company wouldn't take him to court for embezzlement. Fired for cause, which means he got no pension and no benefits. Turns out dear old Dad's gambling habit didn't start when he hit Vegas."

"What are you going to do?" I asked Marlene.

She peered at me through red eyes and wet lashes. "Look for a job, I guess."

"You won't find it easy around here. Tourist season's ending. Jobs dry up for the winter."

"Mike?" she said with a sniffle.

"Don't ask me," he said. "I'm not helping you out. I figure you're not entirely blameless here, Marlene. You were happy enough spending Dad's money without asking where he was getting it."

"I don't ask a man about his finances!"

"No. You only spend it."

She opened her mouth to reply, and judging by the look on her face it wasn't going to be a polite one. I was not getting into the middle of this. Time for me to take my leave and let these two have at it without me as witness. "Guess I'll be going," I said. Tough on Marlene, but she wouldn't be any worse off than she'd been before she met Will. Mike probably had expectations of his dad, but he wouldn't be the first heir to find the vaults empty when the will was read.

"Don't go, Lucy," Marlene said. "I don't want to be alone. Please."

Mike finished his drink and slammed the glass onto the table. "Don't leave on my account. I'm outta here."

"Are you going home?" I asked.

"No. The cops haven't released Dad's body yet, but

when they do I'll have to make the arrangements." He gave Marlene a poisonous look. "No one else to do it, is there? Might as well enjoy this house while we can. I can't order you to leave, Marlene, but stay the heck out of my way. I'll have to call my mom. Might as well make her mad at Dad one last time." He headed up the stairs.

When he was gone, Marlene dabbed at her eyes and said, "Drink?"

"I don't think so."

"Oh, come on. There's some Prosecco in the fridge, the last bottle of the case Will bought. I might as well drink it while I have it."

"No, thanks, but you go ahead."

"You'll stay for a while, though, right?"

I wanted to go home. I didn't want to be involved in this woman's life. But she looked so sad and so lonely that I gave in and said I'd keep her company for a while.

I couldn't help but reflect on the irony. Instead of enjoying the day with Connor—a delicious picnic spread out on a blanket on a deserted beach, walking on the wet sand (holding hands?), splashing in the surf, spreading sunscreen on each other's backs—I was spending my Sunday sitting on Marlene's lounge chair watching her drink and listening to her bemoan her lot in life.

It was hot, and the sun beat relentlessly down on the deck. I struggled to put up an umbrella to sit under, although Marlene seemed happy to stretch out in the sun. I refused yet another entreaty to have a glass of wine, but eventually I was persuaded to try on a bathing suit. I went to the guest bathroom (huge open rain shower, stone countertops, and ceramic tiles in desert colors of tan and ochre with matching towels) and Marlene brought me a stack of bathing suits. "How many of these do you have?" I asked. Even my mom, who has plenty of money and the drive to spend it, vacations with only two suits. Three if she's feeling indulgent. Maybe four if it's a long vacation.

"A bunch," Marlene replied.

Some of the bathing suits still had price tags attached. I dug through skimpy bikinis and one-pieces that were more lace than solid fabric, and found a tankini in dark blue with a sedate red stripe. The top was far too large for me and I had to wiggle unhappily into the bottom. But it would do, as long as we weren't going out in public.

Back outside, Marlene was in the pool. I leaned on the railing and watched as she did laps with a powerful crawl before flipping onto her back to float with her face to the sun and her eyes closed.

"As much as I don't like her, I can't help feeling sorry for her, just a little bit," said a voice behind me. Mike put his hands on the railing. "Dad did lie to her."

"Did he make any promises to her, about the future, I mean?"

"Marriage? I don't know. If he did, and she believed him, she's even stupider than I thought shc was."

I didn't think Marlene was stupid. Naive perhaps, too quick to trust. Then again, maybe not. She was no worse off than she was before Will Williamson walked into that restaurant in Vegas. If she sold some of her jewelry, returned the unworn bathing suits, she could hop on a bus to Nevada. Maybe she could even get her job back, and return to her old life with a couple of months of high living to brag to her coworkers about.

"What are you going to do?" I asked Mike.

"I've taken time off from my job to take care of Dad's affairs. Soon as things are sorted, I'll go back to Raleigh and continue as I always have."

"What do you do?"

"I'm a manager at a branch of Great Eastern Bank."

"That's nice," I said.

He laughed. "It's not. Not nice, I mean, dull as dirt actually, but it pays the bills. Which is more than my father could say. Speaking of nice, it was kind of you to come when Marlene called. I'm sure you had plans for the day."

"My plans were canceled."

"I'm glad to hear that."

I turned and looked at him. "Why?"

"Because you're here." He gave me a sheepish smile. "Look, Lucy, I'm sorry you had to witness that scene earlier. It wasn't my idea to drag you into my dad's mess, but I'm glad you came. Maybe we can get to know each other better. Without certain *other people* interfering. Are you free for dinner tonight?"

"What?"

"I'm asking you out to dinner. Unlike Marlene, my dad didn't pay my credit card bills. Don't worry. I won't be inviting her to join us."

The hot sun beat down on my head. I tugged at the edge of my too-tight tankini bottoms. "No," I said. "I mean, no, thank you. I'm . . . busy."

"Tomorrow then?"

"Uh . . ." This was awkward. I didn't want to be rude,

and Mike seemed like a nice enough guy. Nothing had been said between Connor and me, but even if Connor didn't declare his intentions, I had decided he was the man for me. "I'm seeing someone."

Mike studied my face. Those gray eyes. Stephanie's half brother. So far she hadn't indicated that she wanted to meet him. I wondered if I should arrange to introduce them. "It's just a dinner," he said.

I hoped Stephanie'd be pleased. I hoped Mike would want to get to know her. Stephanie wouldn't have to worry about being all alone in the world when her mom died. "Do you have children?"

He blinked. "I'm not married, if you're asking."

"I was just wondering. About kids, I mean."

"I don't have any children. Not yet. I'm divorced, have been for some time. Does that mean you'll say yes and have dinner with me?"

"Sorry, but no."

"Lucy, come on in. The water's heavenly," Marlene called.

"Be right down! Are you coming?" I asked Mike.

"No, thanks. I'll stay up here and watch."

I swam with Marlene for a while, and it was heavenly. Not as nice as a day at the beach, though.

We were toweling off on the deck when Marlene said, "I'm starving. I think we have some chips and salsa in the cupboard. Want some?"

"Not for me. Thanks. I need to get home," I said.

"Why?"

Because I want to. "I'm sure you have things to do."

She pouted and dropped into a lounge chair. "I've nothing to do but sit here until I get thrown out like last week's garbage. We're almost out of wine. Mike, be a sweetie and go to the store, will you?"

"No," he said. "The bank of Williamson, all branches, is closed, Marlene. Permanently. I'm getting a beer. Want one, Lucy?"

"No, thanks."

Once he'd gone into the house I said to Marlene, "Did Detective Watson tell you anything more about the night Will died?"

She shook her head. "Watson doesn't *tell* anyone anything. He just asks questions. I don't think he's at all competent. He's running around in circles if you ask me. It's the same questions every time."

"He's hoping you'll remember something important," I said, wondering why I was defending Sam Watson.

"Whatever. I like it here, on the Outer Banks, I mean. I'd like to stay for a while. If you hear of any jobs, let me know, will you?"

"Sure. Do you have any guesses as to who might have phoned Will that night? Who he might have been going out to meet?"

She lowered her sunglasses. "Lucy, these questions are getting tedious. I don't know and I said I don't know. I told Watson to trace the call. They can do that, can't they? He said the phone was a throwaway, meaning no record of the owner. I think that's suspicious—don't you?"

"It might be." Then again, not everyone who bought a burner phone was planning to use it for criminal purposes. Some people didn't like their phone conversations to be traceable. Or so I've been told.

I went in search of my clothes and dressed quickly. When I came out, Marlene was lying back in her lounge chair, stretched out in the sun with her head back and her sunglasses in place. She'd refreshed her glass. The empty bottle of Prosecco had fallen over and was rolling back and forth across the table. Mike was nowhere to be seen.

"I'm off," I said. Then I added, against my better judgment, "Give me a call if you need anything." Why was I getting involved in these people's lives?

"I'll do that," she said. "I still have the car. It hardly uses any gas at all, but it's almost empty. I shoulda filled up when I had the chance. Don't know what I'm going to do then."

I let myself out.

Chapter 16

If Will Williamson was, as his son had said, dead broke, that changed everything. Financial doom might have been a hurricane on his horizon but, like people who throw hurricane parties instead of heading inland to safer ground, Will seemed to have continued to live the high life, spending money like water. Money he didn't have. He must have been in a total panic underneath, realizing that sooner rather than later his day of reckoning would arrive. One bounced check or refused credit card and the whole edifice would come tumbling down. What might he have done to delay that day?

He'd dropped two hundred thousand dollars (an almost unbelievable sum) in a week in Las Vegas. Had he borrowed to maintain his gambling habit as well as his lifestyle?

Had he borrowed from the wrong people?

He'd been gambling online, we knew that. Marlene had said he regularly went out at night without her. She thought he was drinking, but might he have been gambling? There are no casinos or hotel lobby slot machines on the Outer Banks. All forms of gambling are illegal in North Carolina, but I figured that minor detail wouldn't stop serious gamblers. Was he out at night in a modern equivalent of a speakeasy, gambling with money he didn't have?

Watson must have reached the same conclusion, and he would now be looking for loan sharks or mob enforcers, leaving my friend alone. I headed for Pat's house to give her and Stephanie the good news.

Unfortunately, Watson was also there and, even more unfortunately, he wasn't inclined to see things my way. He was walking down the path, heading toward his car, when I drove up. *Curses,* I thought as he spotted me the minute I turned the corner, lowered his sunglasses, and waited. As long as he was here I might as well give him the benefit of my deductions, in case he hadn't reached the same conclusions as I had.

"Every penny of Williamson's money, or lack thereof, is accounted for, Lucy," he said to me when I'd finished blathering about illegal gambling parlors, the Vegas mob, and hit men. I might have even speculated that they'd stolen the boat with the intention of taking Will out in the Sound and fitting him with a pair of "cement overshoes" when they'd been interrupted for some unknown reason. "Men with solid reputations, blue-chip investments, and adequate means don't have to frequent loan sharks. You've been watching too much TV."

"I never watch police shows on TV," I said. "Too unrealistic. I prefer novels."

He raised one eyebrow.

"Besides," I went on, "Will didn't have a good reputation or blue-chip investments; that's my point. He'd been fired from his job and thus didn't even have an income."

"Not that it's any of your business, Lucy," he said, "but for some reason I find myself telling you things my wiser nature tells me not to. Will Williamson had been a moderately wealthy man, a high-level executive in a solid oil company, with property and investments. Then, about five years ago, he developed a gambling habit that very quickly spiraled out of control. He's not the first to fall prey to online gambling and he won't be the last. It's a curse. His was the same old story I've heard a thousand times. He began losing, a little here, a little there. Then more and more. Initially he could afford the losses, but not for long. He had to sell stock he'd been given as part of his compensation package at a bad time in the market. He lost the lot. So he sold more and lost even more and entered the downward spiral. He began taking bribes and kickbacks. He wasn't a particularly clever crook, the desperate ones never are, and when his bosses found out they fired him. They didn't do him any favors, far as I'm concerned, by not laying charges or making the firing public. Williamson told everyone he'd had enough of Alaska and had taken a generous retirement package. He owned a vacation home as well as a nice house in Anchorage. He sold those, taking the first offers he got and thus another financial hit, and headed for Vegas. He lost almost all of it there. Everything he lived on for the last couple of months was debt. He had a fistful of credit cards, and ran them all up to the max. Same with a line of credit. His debts were enormous, but all aboveboard and easily traceable. If he went to the mob, they turned him down." Watson laughed. "They have more sense than many banks I could name."

The front door of the house opened, and Stephanie came out. "Everything okay here, Lucy? Is this man harassing you?"

Watson rolled his eyes. "Just exchanging pleasantries, Ms. Stanton. Now, Lucy, if you have no more wild theories to share with me, I have real police work to do."

"Officious jerk" was Stephanie's comment. But she wisely waited until Watson was in his car and disappearing down the street.

"He told you Will Williamson had no money?"

"Yeah. He implied that I was angry when I realized I wouldn't be getting a big bequest. First I supposedly killed him for my inheritance, and then I supposedly killed him because I wasn't going to get anything. All this about a man I didn't even know. Watson's fishing." Stephanie laughed, but there was no humor in it. "What brings you here anyway?"

"I thought the revelation of the state of his finances would break the whole case open, but Watson doesn't seem to think it makes a bit of difference. Everything okay here?"

Stephanie touched my arm. "Other than still being under suspicion of murder, you mean? We're as okay as can be. I was on the phone earlier with Amos. I find his small one-man practice fascinating. Do you know, his secretary called me "honey," put me through right away, and I didn't hear the sound of billable minutes being counted as we talked? Amazing."

"Not all lawyers fit the sharklike stereotype," I said.

"So I'm beginning to realize. Why don't you come in and say hi to Mom. Do you have time for a glass of tea?"

"Sure."

Pat Stanton was seated in her lounger, her feet up and her legs covered by a blanket, a pile of books from the library stacked on the side table beside her. More books and magazines were scattered on the floor. I leaned over and gave her a peck on the cheek. She had that musty smell of an invalid confined to the indoors, her face was pasty, and her skin was lined with deep marks of worry. On top of the pain she must be in all the time, and the frustration of not being mobile, she had Stephanie's troubles to worry about.

I took a seat while Steph went for the drinks. "What'cha reading?" I asked.

"Reading?" She waved her hand at the side table. "Some silly thing that isn't keeping my attention. Oh, Lucy, I'm so tired of being stuck in this house." She burst into tears. "More than anything, I just want to go for a lovely long walk on the beach."

I was so shocked I didn't know what to do. Strong, capable Pat Stanton, a mighty force of strength and reliability, was crying. I jumped up and went to her. I crouched in front of her chair and took her hands. "It's all going to be okay. We know Steph didn't kill anyone, and Watson will figure out who did soon. And then everything will get back to normal." I tried to smile. It wasn't easy.

"Normal? I wonder what that even means. Will's dead. Things will not be normal for him, not ever again."

"Did Watson tell you what he learned about Will's finances?"

"Oh, yes. The stupid fool. I was surprised to hear about the gambling, but I suppose a man changes over thirty years. Will was never one to lose control. He knew what he wanted and was determined to get it. I wasn't surprised, though, to hear that he kept spending money he didn't have. Appearances were important to Will." She wiped away a tear. "My poor dear Will. For all his faults, he didn't deserve to die. I loved him once, Lucy. No matter what happened over the years, I haven't forgotten that." Her face was etched with pain. More pain, I realized, of lost love and forgotten youth, than from her injuries. She pulled a tissue out of her sleeve and blew her nose. "Where is that tea?" She raised her voice. "Stephanie?"

"Hold your horses, Mom," came a shout from the kitchen. "I'll be right there."

I got up off the floor and took my seat on the couch as Stephanie came through with a tray balancing three glasses, an ice-filled pitcher, and a plate of store-bought cookies.

"I was telling Lucy," Pat said, "that if I wasn't stuck in this house or that hated wheelchair, I'd be out pounding the pavement myself trying to clear your good name." She gave me a smile, but the smile was forced and her eyes glistened with tears.

With a shock, I realized that this was the first time I'd seen anyone showing any emotion at all over the death of Will Williamson.

Poor Will, indeed. What a sad legacy: the only one who shed a tear for him was a woman he'd wronged so badly so long ago.

* * *

I was dead beat when I got home. It's more tiring, I think, dealing with other people's emotions than it must be to walk headfirst into a hurricane.

I hadn't eaten since the breakfast sandwich in my car, so I fixed myself a bowl of mushroom soup and sat at my small table with *The List*—the list of suspects my friends and I had drawn up last night. Charles curled up in the window alcove to bask in the sun.

I studied the list as I sipped my soup. Things had changed since last night. Watson might not think the revelations about Will's finances were important (or he might and he wasn't telling me what was on his mind) but I was convinced they had to be.

Doug Whiteside. I'd wanted to believe Doug capable of killing Will, but had dismissed him as a suspect because it was a stretch to think he'd killed Will in order to frame Connor. But now? Had Will promised Doug a big campaign contribution? Had Doug already spent money he hadn't received? If he had he'd look like a fool and a mighty bad money manager to boot, when Will turned around and said, "You're outta luck. Sorry." Even if Doug hadn't spent the money, he might have been furious at being tricked. Doug had a ready-made accomplice, someone to pick him up from the marsh after tying up the boat: Billy. That was a thought. I added Bill Hill to the bottom of the list. Maybe I had things backward, and it was Billy who'd killed Will, either to frame Connor or because he was worried about the threat to Doug's chances of winning the election.

As the campaign manager, Billy would know everything about the candidate's finances, particularly who was donating what. And who was not.

I made a second column on the page and headed it LIGHTS. I was convinced, although no one else was, that the mysterious lights the night of the storm were an attempt to kill Will. I put a determined tick beside Doug's name. Doug had lived on the Outer Banks his entire life. My mom and Aunt Ellen had known his sister in high school. He'd know these waters as well as his way around a boat. I knew absolutely nothing about Bill Hill. Tomorrow, I'd see whether he'd have been capable of manning a boat, but for now, I put a tentative tick by his name.

Ralph Harper. I put a big X beside his name in the new column. Ralph may have been mad enough to kill Will *after* the storm, but he would have had no reason to set the lights that caused Will to wreck his boat.

Marlene. Marlene certainly hadn't set the lights so she also got an X in that column. As for motive, she was on the list because I'd wondered if she got rid of Will, hoping to keep his money for herself. That might still be the case, as she appeared to be totally blindsided by the news that he didn't have any. Was it possible that had all been an act? Had she known he'd lost all his money? She had nothing to gain by killing Will if he was broke, but she would have been furious. Angry enough to kill? I'd seen her when Watson broke the news of Will's death, and I'd swear she was surprised. But what did I know about Marlene? Nothing, other than what she chose to tell me. Of all people, Marlene was best positioned to talk Will into a late visit to a marina. We had only her word that he went out alone that fateful night.

I ran my eyes down the list. I finished my soup, washed up my bowl, then headed for the phone. On the other end, the phone was picked up and a posh English accent rattled off the last four digits of a phone number.

"Theodore? Hi, it's Lucy."

"Lucy? To what do I owe the pleasure of this call?"

"Have you heard the news? About Will Williamson's financial situation, I mean?"

Theodore's sniff was enough to tell me that he had. "I was due to go around to the house a short while ago for one last desperate attempt to resume negotiations. I was preparing to leave when I got a call from Will's son telling me not to bother. Marlene has no money to purchase my books, or anything else. Will Williamson, it turns out, didn't have so much as two shillings to rub together. His estate is, shall we say, as dead as he is."

"How do you feel about that?"

"Miffed, if you must know, Lucy. Highly miffed. I have to once again begin the entire tedious process of finding a buyer for the Christies. Oh well, can't be helped. Why are you ringing?"

"No reason. Bye." I hung up. I put a tick, a small one, but still a tick, beside Theodore's name. It was possible that he found out Will was going to renege on their deal. Will probably hadn't intended to buy the books in the first place. What had Pat said about him? Appearances were important to Will. He couldn't just tell Teddy he wasn't interested in buying a bunch of old books after Marlene had gushed over them; he had to put on a show of being a big spender. Teddy, like Doug, was a lifetime Banker. He'd know the shoreline and the old stories of the wreckers. It was difficult to imagine the nautically challenged Theodore out in a boat at night by himself, particularly with a dead body in the bottom. Difficult, but not impossible. Who knows what people can do when they believe they have to.

My next call was to Ellen and Amos's house.

"Lucy, honey," my aunt said. "I'm glad you called. I'm sorry I haven't gotten back to you, but I don't have anything to report about Will's past. I've been asking around, and either folks have forgotten him or don't have much to say. He didn't have many friends in school, and what friends he did have lost touch as soon as he left Nags Head. He married a local girl and they had a baby, but once they moved away, no one seemed to have spared him another thought. No one said that they'd ever heard he'd so much as come back for a visit. The only interesting thing I learned isn't news to us: there'd been talk that he was cheating on his wife. Some folks said they knew it was Pat, and that they'd guessed Pat's baby was Will's although she never said—but the way they talked about it, it was more like folks remembering something they'd forgotten all about than gossip they'd cherished all these years."

"No other women?"

"If there was, he kept it secret. And, considering that his affair with Pat wasn't much of one, except maybe to his wife, I have to think there weren't any others."

Looked as if that line of inquiry was a dead end. No one seemed to even remember Will until prompted, much less carry a grudge that would end in murder all these years later. Reaching into his past had been only a faint hope, but I couldn't help feeling a pang of disappointment.

"I agree." I sighed. "Thanks, Aunt Ellen. Is Aaron in?"

"Let me get him," she said.

"Hey, Lucy," my cousin said. "I bet you're calling about the coast guard, right?"

"Josie told you what I'm interested in?"

"Yeah. I went down to the station this morning and found the guys who'd been out that night. They said Williamson had been acting like a real jerk. He threatened to sue them for causing him to wreck his boat." Aaron laughed.

"What did your friends think about that?"

"They thought it was darn funny. There he was, soaked to the skin, surrounded by wreckage, and trying to pretend it wasn't his fault. Apparently he had some woman with him he was trying to impress."

"And that was all?"

"Pretty much, although they said Ralph Harper got awful mad. As mad as Ralph ever gets anyway." Aaron said good-bye, but before I could hang up my aunt was back on the line.

"Ralph Harper. What's he got to do with this?"

"He was with the coast guard when they rescued Will. Will got blustery and threatened to sue. Ralph came to the library the night Will died and confronted him. Why?"

"I totally forgot until this very minute. But now it's all coming back. Ralph and Will were not what you'd call friends as young men. Ralph was in school with us, but he quit to help his father fish as soon as he was old enough. He didn't spend much time on his homework and was restless and irritable in class, because all he wanted was to be out on the water. Even back then, the sea was all he cared about. Because his grades were bad, and he failed a couple of times, he had the reputation for being slow, as in not very smart. Which he wasn't. He simply wasn't interested in learning about the wider world. He wasn't a big boy, but he spent a lot of time working on his dad's boat, so most of the boys left him alone. But Will made fun of him, his fishing family roots, his love of the sea. I seem to remember talk about them coming to blows behind the school one day. Will got the worst of it, but that didn't stop him from mocking Ralph. Although he did start being more discreet about it. In Ralph's hearing, anyway."

"That's interesting," I said. "Do you think Ralph's the sort to carry a grudge?"

"For all these years? Absolutely not."

"Still, I'd like to talk to him. Do you have a number for him?"

"No, honey. I don't even know where he lives. I haven't spoken to Ralph in a long time. Hold on, Aaron's waving."

My cousin came back on the line. "If you're looking for Ralph, Lucy, you could drop by the coast guard station sometime, but he's not usually there unless there's a storm coming in. I've heard that he eats his breakfast most every morning at the Shrimp Shack, at least the mornings when he has a fishing trip lined up. It's open early and is near his boat slip."

"Thanks, Aaron. That's great. Say bye to your mom." I hung up, feeling as though I might be making progress.

Ralph Harper hadn't been high on my suspect list because he'd argued with Will after the wreck. But in light of what I'd just learned, I was wondering if Ralph might have been responsible for lighting those lamps. It was highly unlikely that Ralph would want to kill Will over some high school bullying, but they might have had a confrontation recently that I hadn't heard about. Maybe Ralph hadn't intended that Will die in the storm but only wanted to frighten him into acknowledging that Ralph had used his knowledge of the sea to save him. Of all the people I'd considered, Ralph was the most likely to know about the intricacies of this shoreline, and the behavior of a small boat in a storm.

And then when, far from being grateful for his intervention, Will had threatened to sue Ralph and to mock his reputation in public, had Ralph decided to put an end to Will's bullying? Permanently?

The phone was still in my hand when it rang. Connor. I took a deep breath and answered. "Hello!"

"I am finally finished with meetings and handshaking and baby-kissing. Are you free for dinner?"

"Yes."

"How about something casual and comfortable so I can forget I'm mayor for a night?"

"I'd like that."

"Is six too soon?"

"I'll be ready." It was ten after five now. I could forget about Ralph Harper and the case tonight. I ran for my closet. Charles leaped off the window seat to join me. We peered at the racks of clothes. I was aiming for casual and comfortable, yet drop-dead gorgeous. A difficult feat. I pulled clothes off hangers, held them up in front of me, and tossed them behind me onto the bed.

Everything I owned was suitable for wearing to work in a library, hanging out with girlfriends, or going to a party or to the beach. What did casual and comfortable even mean? I tried to think of what my mom would do in this situation. My mother would never allow herself to be caught dead without the perfect outfit. When she had been here during the summer she even had the right accessories to wear when being interrogated by the police.

I found a flowing calf-length skirt in colorful swirls of blue and red. I'd bought it because it was on sale, but had never worn it. When I got it home, I decided it was too hippie, as though I was about to head down the road to Woodstock in a gaily painted Volkswagen Kombi. Of course, having gotten it at seventy percent off, I couldn't return it.

I was about to toss the skirt onto the rapidly growing pile, when Charles meowed and jumped onto the bed to land beside a plain black short-sleeved T-shirt with a deeply scooped neck. I picked the T-shirt up and held it against the skirt. Charles gave an approving meow.

I jumped into the shower, washed my hair, and gave it a quick blow-dry. There isn't a lot I can do with the mass of black curls I consider my curse, so I bunched them up into a loose knot at the back of my head and pulled a few tendrils free. I applied a touch of pale pink lipstick and some blush, dressed in the skirt and T-shirt, and chose a small gold chain and gold hoops for jewelry. Because I was going for casual and comfortable I could avoid the high-heeled sandals I hate (but force myself to wear anyway) and slipped on black ballet flats.

I twirled in front of the mirror. I thought I looked

pretty good. I needed a second opinion. "How do I look?" I asked Charles, who was watching from the bed.

In answer, he jumped down and went to inspect the empty depths of his food bowl.

I had just finished feeding him when the doorbell sounded. "Don't wait up," I called to the cat.

Chapter 17

"Tell me again why I want to be mayor," Connor said to me.

I laughed. "Because you're good at it?"

"I'm okay with the mayoring part, but sometimes I hate the politicking part."

We had gone to the town of Duck where, as Connor said, he was less likely to be approached by voters, and were comfortably settled in a restaurant near the boardwalk overlooking the calm waters of Currituck Sound.

"Did you run into any problems today?" I asked, sipping my glass of wine.

"Plenty of people had heard Doug Whiteside's insinuations, but no one, so they told me, believed them. What they didn't tell me, I can guess."

"You don't seriously think anyone believes him, do you?"

"People who don't like me will believe it, and people who want me to keep on as mayor won't. The big problem with that sort of insinuation is that it turns people off politics. Good people who don't believe in the integrity of their elected officials and wash their hands of the whole thing, saying we're all crooks."

"I'd love to go door-knocking for you sometime," I said. "I can help hand out literature and stuff like that."

He smiled at me. "I'd like that very much, Lucy."

"Do you know anything about Bill Hill? He's Doug's assistant or campaign manager or something. Seems to follow Doug around everywhere."

Connor shook his head. "Never heard of the guy until recently. Why do you ask?"

"The women I overheard in the library spreading that muck said Billy had been the one who mentioned it. Not Doug."

"Is that right? I'll ask Dorothy to look into it. Sometimes the paid staffers can be even more ruthless than the politicians themselves. They can have as much, or more, invested in winning than their candidate does. And often they have nothing to fall back on if he or she loses."

"Did you hear that the police have learned Will didn't have any money?" I asked.

"Yes, I did. For some reason I find myself not at all surprised you know about it, Lucy. At least once that news is made public, no one can say I killed him because he threw his support behind Doug. More likely Doug was mad because Will threatened to make him look like a fool and a sucker. That, of course, is between you and me. The last thing I want to be accused of is spreading dirt about my opponent." The waiter asked if we were ready to order, and we spent the remainder of the evening chatting about our lives. No more was said about Doug Whiteside or politics or the subject of who might have wanted Will Williamson dead.

On the way to Duck, Connor had played Aerosmith on his iPhone through the car's Bluetooth system, but heading back he switched the music off and we drove in comfortable silence, watching the night pass by.

"Sometimes I see deer along the highway at dusk," I said as we left the bright lights of Nags Head behind us and turned onto Highway 12. Thick clouds filled the sky and the darkness on this stretch of road closed in on us. "So drive carefully."

"I will," he said.

He pulled up in front of the lighthouse. My heart pounded in my chest and my hands were clammy. I took a breath. I'd decided before we left the restaurant what I was going to do at this moment. "Would you like to come in for a drink?" I asked.

He turned in his seat and faced me. His hand reached out and he ran a finger lightly across my cheek. "I'd like that."

A tap sounded on my window. I yelped and Connor's hand jerked away. I whirled around to see a white face peering into the car. Louise Jane. She wiggled her fingers at me. I might have made a very unladylike noise.

"Hope I didn't interrupt anything," she said, once Connor and I were out of the car. "There'll be no moon tonight, so it's a perfect night for me to be on watch."

"On watch for what?" Connor growled.

"For whatever's out there." She hefted her pack onto her back, lowered her miner's light, and switched it on. The light hit me full in the face, stinging my eyes. I turned away. "I'll be around most of the night, but you two mustn't spare me a thought." She made no move to leave. I hoped something very nasty was in the marsh, lying in wait for Louise Jane and her blasted light.

"Have fun," Connor said, through gritted teeth. "I need to be going anyway. I have a busy day tomorrow. Could I please take a rain check on that drink, Lucy?"

"Sure," I said. "Thanks for the dinner."

He got in his car. Louise Jane and I watched while he drove away.

"Gee," she said, "I hope I didn't chase him away."

I went into the lighthouse without a word. Drat that Louise Jane. I'd decided it was important to go slowly with Connor. I'd been dating Ricky for many years, and I knew the breakup with him made me vulnerable to rushing too fast into something with the next attractive man who presented himself. This burgeoning relationship with Connor had, to me at least, the potential to be the real thing, and I was determined to make it work. Slow and careful. When I invited him in for a drink, a drink was exactly what I meant. Not that I would have been adverse to a few kisses.

Even if my intention had been for Connor and me to fold campaign leaflets all night, there was nothing quite like knowing Louise Jane was prowling around outside (no doubt watching to see if the interior lights went out) to ruin a girl's mood.

Connor, obviously, felt the same.

I refrained from yelling at Charles when I got to my apartment and found that he'd made himself a comfortable nest of the black wool pants and black cashmere sweater that had been a Christmas gift from a friend in Boston. My fault for not putting the clothes away. Not

Charles's fault that Louise Jane had ruined the end of my evening.

I went to the window and peered out. All was pitch dark; no glimmer shone from Louise Jane's light, but I was facing the wrong direction. When the thousand-watt bulb came on above me, it illuminated a bank of thick clouds, moving fast across the night sky. I kicked off my ballet flats, stepped out of the colorful skirt, and pulled on the cat-hair covered black pants, thick socks, and hiking boots. I topped it all with a heavy dark sweater, grabbed a flashlight, and let myself outside.

It was time to find out what Louise Jane was really up to out there in the night. I will admit I found it hard to believe she'd killed Will, a man she'd met only a few hours before, in order to give her ghost stories some veracity. But, who the heck knew what Louise Jane was capable of? It was possible she might accidentally come across something the police would want to know and spoil the crime scene. I hadn't thought to mention to Watson or Butch that she was prowling around out there.

By now I knew the staircase and the main room of the library so well that I didn't need to switch on any lights. I stopped on the third floor to peek out the west-facing window. A small yellow light was bobbing along the path to the Sound. I ran lightly down the rest of the stairs and through the library. Once I was outside, I switched my flashlight on. I kept it at the weakest setting, aimed it toward the ground at my feet, and headed for the boardwalk.

I walked slowly, trying to make as little noise as possible. I wasn't exactly scared, but I did keep my free hand clenched on the phone in my sweater pocket. I turned at a bend in the path, and the light of Louise Jane's headlamp came into view. I crept forward. I felt a drop of rain hit my head, and then several more in rapid succession. In less than a minute the clouds had opened, rain came pouring down, and I was drenched right through. Feeling even more of a fool, I crept forward. Louise Jane had stopped moving. I was debating jumping out and yelling boo, when I heard her voice. "Now what? It's starting to rain, is that going to be a problem?" She was on the phone, which surprised me. I didn't know ghost hunters used smartphones. Nothing wrong with keeping up with the times, I guess. I switched off my light.

"Yes, I have them here. I'm at the dock, Grandma."

After a long pause Louise Jane said in a voice that was almost plaintive, "But I don't want to sit out. It's raining. It wasn't supposed to rain so I didn't bring an umbrella. No, I don't want to knock on the lighthouse door and ask Lucy for one. She'll laugh at me. No, Grandma, they moved the hidden key over the summer and forgot to tell me where they put it."

Rainwater was forming into an icy river at the back of my neck. I shivered and took an involuntary step backward. My foot slipped on a wet rock and I grunted softly. I dropped to a crouch. There are no trees in the marsh, and I was out in the open.

"Something's moving," Louise Jane said. "Hold on, Grandma." She raised her voice. "Spirit!" The command was strong and powerful. Despite myself, I shivered. "Show yourself."

I held my breath. The lighthouse light came on. The beam's powerful enough to be seen some thirty miles distant, but it's constructed to direct the light out to sea and remarkably little of it shines on the ground. Then it switched off, and we were plunged back into darkness. Wet, cold, miserable darkness, I might add. My sweater was not waterproof, I had nothing on my head, and the sudden deluge was creating muddy puddles beneath my feet.

"Nothing, Grandma," Louise Jane said at last, "Must be an animal. You're sure Great-grandmama said this was what I had to do? Did you tell her it's raining? Wake her up then!"

I'd seen, or more to the point heard, enough. Louise Jane was following her great-grandmother's instructions, as interpreted by her grandmother. By the sounds of it, she'd be happier if I popped my head up over the grasses and invited her in for a hot chocolate and a turn with Charles on her lap.

If I hadn't known she'd be absolutely furious at me for spying on her, I would have done precisely that. Instead, I waited until the light went into its twenty-two point five second dormancy and crept away. I'd been out for about half an hour. I was cold and I was wet, but my time had been well spent. Louise Jane had been nothing but a footnote on my list of potential killers, but I could now confidently cross that footnote off.

A cup of steaming hot chocolate with two marshmallows bobbing on the top and a purring cat curled up on my lap was exactly what I needed right now.

Chapter 18

Even Charles was asleep when my alarm went off. I briefly considered giving up my mission and going back to sleep, but my better nature (or maybe just stubborn curiosity) got the upper hand and I struggled out of my lovely warm comfy bed. Charles opened one eye and promptly closed it again.

Aaron had told me that Ralph Harper liked to have his breakfast at the Shrimp Shack on the days he was taking out his boat. Most fishing charter boats, I knew, left harbor at five. Shudder. I guessed that Ralph would get his boat ready for the day, and then leave his crew to wait for the clients, while he went for his breakfast. Meaning, he'd be at the Shrimp Shack around four thirty.

Therefore, so would I. If he wasn't there today, I'd just have to try another approach.

Shower, makeup, and proper clothes could wait until later. I splashed water on my face, gathered my hair into a ponytail, pulled on jeans, T-shirt, and sneakers and headed out.

The sun wasn't even up yet when I drove toward town, and there was no traffic on the highway. I turned left at Whalebone Junction and crossed the low bridge onto Roanoke Island. A few cars joined me—fishing people, I suspected. Who else would be foolish enough to be up this early?

I'd looked up the Shrimp Shack last night before going to bed and jotted down some directions. They were located near Pirate's Cove Marina, where Ralph kept his boat. I found the restaurant with no trouble, parked close to the doors, and got out of my car. I took a deep breath and went in. I was immediately overwhelmed by the scent of frying bacon, warm toast, and sizzling grease. Yummy.

A wall of glass specked with salt spray overlooked the edges of the marina. This was obviously a place that catered to the serious fishing crowd. The photos of men (and a very few women) that lined the walls were packed so closely together I could scarcely see the cracked and peeling paint beneath. The tabletops were scarred and the red vinyl seating at the booths was so badly worn and torn in some places that the stuffing poked out.

All the booths were taken by a mixture of genuine old salts and tourists trying to pretend they were serious fishermen in their brand-new clothes and clean hats.

No one so much as glanced up from their food when I came in.

"Be with you in a sec, hon," the waitress called as she came out of the kitchen, bearing a tray loaded with plates piled high with eggs and bacon or stacks of pancakes.

The booths were full, but there were still some empty

stools facing the long counter. My luck was in. I spotted my quarry by himself, next to an empty seat.

I waved cheerfully to the waitress and crossed the room quickly. "Is this seat taken?" I asked Ralph.

He grunted without looking up from the magazine propped beside his plate. A quick glance showed me pictures of big fish leaping out of the water. I hopped onto the seat and grabbed the menu standing between the ketchup bottle and the napkin dispenser. I opened the menu and pretended to study it. Then I, ever so casually, turned to the man beside me. "Oh, hi. I didn't notice you there for a moment. Ralph, right?" I smiled.

He turned his head. "Yeah." He studied my face. "How ya doin', Lucy?"

I was momentarily taken aback that he knew my name. "Good. I'm good. Thanks. I didn't get a chance to say hi the other night in the lighthouse parking lot." I continued to smile. I decided it would be best not to mention the circumstances of our meeting. Ralph Harper looked, I thought, a lot like Gandalf the Grey in the *Lord of the Rings* movies. Long shaggy gray beard touched with the memory of youthful black, equally long and shaggy hair, and eyebrows that might well have a life of their own. His face was a deep nutty brown, as craggy as a walnut shell, evidence of a life spent on the sea. Aunt Ellen had said he'd been in school with Will Williamson. If I hadn't known that, I'd have said the fisherman was a decade older. His eyes were a soft blue-gray, the color of the ocean as the fog began to lift.

He gave me a smile that made me think of Gandalf when he looked at the hobbits, not as he faced the fire-breathing Balrog. "Sorry for not being more polite that evening. Had things on my mind. I'd heard you'd come back. I was glad of it."

"Come back?"

"To the Outer Banks. You're a sea woman, Lucy. You need to be here." His voice was deep and rolling, like waves crashing into the rocky shore in a storm.

"I've lived in Boston all my life," I said.

He studied my face. "And in all your life in Boston, how many times did you go to the beach?"

"Uh . . ."

"Do they even have a beach in Boston? No matter, you couldn't hear the sound of the waves from where you lived or worked, you couldn't pop down to the beach any time you had the inkling to get the sand between your toes and let the surf wash away your troubles. Might as well have lived in Kansas for all the attention you paid to the sea." Ralph shuddered at the very idea of landlocked Kansas. "No, you belong here, Lucy. I'm glad you realized that."

I was stunned. He seemed to know a lot about me. And it was true. To me, the Outer Banks was the beach; it was the sea. Boston was where I went to school and later where I worked. I enjoyed going down to the Charles River for a walk at my lunch break, and I'd often meet friends for dinner in a restaurant or bar overlooking the water. But it wasn't the beach, and the ocean was never more than a pleasant background view.

"Can't say I've seen you in here before. What brings you in today, Lucy?"

"I couldn't sleep, so wanted to go out for a drive. Someone told me this is a good coffee place."

Ralph lifted his cup. "If you like it strong and not fancy."

"Ready, hon?" The waitress stood in front of me, pencil poised.

Ralph was having fried eggs, sausages, hash browns, and wheat toast. My stomach turned over. I didn't think I could face that much food this early. "Just coffee please."

She reached for the pot and poured me a cup. Ralph's concentration returned to his breakfast and his magazine.

Okay, the "fancy running into you here" routine wasn't working. I'd have to try the direct approach. "Actually, Ralph," I said. "I was wanting to talk to you."

"Figured it was somethin' like that," he said. "Shoot, young lady."

"Will Williamson."

"Figured it was that too," he said, slicing off a hunk of sausage and popping it into his mouth. "Knew him when we were kids. He was a miserable boy. Didn't change much when he grew up."

"You helped rescue him the night of the big storm."

"Shoulda let him drown. Probably woulda if I'd known it was him." He turned to look at me. The eyes were still warm and blue. "Nah. Man takes an oath to the sea, gotta fulfill it."

"Oath?"

"The sea is a beautiful mistress, but her rages are terrible to behold. She can turn from one face to another fast as a man can blink. I was just a boy when my father told me we never were to let her claim a man, not if we could save him. We fear her and respect her always, but never let her think she can defeat us. That's the only thing she respects in return."

"Oh," I said. "Is the Sound part of the sea? I braced myself to run as he focused those intense blue-gray eyes on me. But instead of seeing a storm raging in their depths, I saw waters so calm a toddler could play in them. "The cops spoke to me, Lucy. Asking my whereabouts after I spoke to Will that night. I told them: I went home to my bed."

"Can your wife verify that?" I said, feeling bold.

"Never married. I have my mistress. She's a harsh one, but a loving one all the same." He waved his hand toward the window. Outside, boats bobbed gently in the protected waters of the marina. It was still dark, but lights lined the wharf and were on in many of the big charter boats as they prepared for a day's fishing. "Don't matter. That Sam Watson, he knows how things work around here. A waterman isn't out prowling around in the middle of the night. Morning comes early." He wiped up egg yolk with his last piece of toast. "Now, if you'll excuse me, young lady, I got to get going. We leave five o'clock on the dot, whether all the customers have arrived or not." He threw money on the counter and swung off his stool, the lightness of his movements a sharp contrast to his wizened appearance.

"Will got nothin' but what he deserved." Ralph looked down at me. I sucked in a breath, wondering if he was about to confess. "I wasn't surprised to hear Will had been found on the water. He disrespected the sea awful bad that night. But she takes care of herself. She don't need no help from me nor any man. You have a nice day, Lucy. Coffee's on me. You want to go out on a boat one day, let me know. I'd be happy to take you, 'cause I know you for a water woman."

He left, rolling from side to side as though he was already feeling the swell of the ocean beneath the boat decks.

It wasn't even five thirty when I got home. I climbed out of my clothes and climbed back into my bed. But sleep didn't come. Ralph had moved up on my suspect list. I decided that it wasn't impossible to think that he, on discovering that the sea didn't have any particularly malicious feelings toward Will Williamson, would have to be the one to give her a helping hand. Everyone I'd met seemed to like Ralph, and someone had said he was a gentle soul. That might have been true, in the past, but was his grip on reality slipping a bit? Not to mention that Wanchese Marina, from where Will had departed on his last journey, is not far from Pirate's Cove, where Ralph keeps his own boat.

After an hour of staring at the ceiling and thinking about murder, I got up for good. I fixed myself a breakfast of yogurt, granola, and berries. The conversation with Ralph had been interesting, and perhaps illuminating, but I did have other suspects to consider.

As I ate, I poked around on the Internet, trying to find out what I could about Doug Whiteside's assistant, Bill Hill. The Internet may sometimes seem to be the source of all knowledge, but that can also mean way too much knowledge. With a name as common as Bill Hill, I got millions of hits, including a Bill Hill Road in Connecticut. I tried narrowing my search down to North Carolina, and then to Nags Head, and came up blank. I tried Doug Whiteside of North Carolina and my computer screen filled with pages of data. I clicked on images and was overwhelmed with pictures of Doug's beaming face. As

I'd hoped, Bill was in several of them, sticking faithfully to the background. One newspaper photo had been taken at a fund-raiser at a local golf course, and this one featured Bill with his arm around the shoulders of a woman with a strained smile that failed to reach her eyes. The caption read, "Whiteside's friend and campaign manager William Hill and his wife, Jill, greet guests."

Armed with that small amount of knowledge, I finished breakfast, rinsed my dishes, and Charles and I went downstairs to work.

I took advantage of a brief lull, before the crowds started to arrive, to check the library's circulation files. As I'd dared hope, we had a patron by the name of Jill Hill, although she'd last taken out a book about three months ago. Judging by the books she borrowed, her interests leaned heavily toward gardening and Native American history. I glanced around the room. No one was requiring my attention. I grabbed the phone before I could think better of it, and placed a call. It rang several times, and then a woman's voice said, "Hello?"

"Is this Jill Hill?" I asked.

"Yes."

"This is the Bodie Island Lighthouse Library calling. I wanted to let you know that your book on . . . the currents around the Outer Banks has arrived."

"Book? You must have the wrong number. I haven't visited the library for some time."

"Perhaps it was delayed," I said, "or your husband requested it? Do you have a . . . uh . . . boat?"

"My husband and I own a small boat, yes, although he doesn't have much time to get out fishing these days.

He doesn't use the public library. Obviously there's been a mistake. Good-bye."

I heard the click of the receiver being replaced. I let out a long breath. So, Bill Hill did have a boat. His wife hung up before I'd been able to find out where the boat was kept. Wanchese Marina maybe? I could hardly call her back and ask. I drummed my fingers on the desktop.

Had Billy murdered Will with or without Doug's knowledge? Had his wife, Jill, been an accomplice? Had she followed in their boat to take Bill back to town once the deed was done?

Had Bill and Jill Hill killed Will?

I was debating phoning Detective Watson to ask him if he'd checked up on Billy when a smiling man, dressed in Bermuda shorts and a lurid Hawaiian shirt, asked me if I could recommend a nice place to take his wife to dinner. By the time I'd given him directions to Jake's Seafood Bar a line was forming at the desk, so I went back to work. When I had time to think about it again, I decided not to call Watson about Billy. What could I say but that I suspected a man who lived in Nags Head of being a ruthless killer because he owned a boat? I'd have to think up a more subtle way to let the detective know Bill Hill would be worth investigating.

Stephanie phoned a short while later to invite me around for dinner that night.

"I'd love to come," I said. "Time?"

"How about six?"

"We close at five on Mondays so six would be perfect. I'll see you then." I hung up with a smile. I was looking forward to seeing Stephanie.

After closing, I went upstairs (love that commute!)

to feed Charles and to change. At quarter to six when I came back down, everyone had left and the library was settling quietly into the night. Apart from my Yaris, two other cars were in the parking lot: a beat-up old van over by the boardwalk and a nondescript beige sedan tucked into the trees in the loop where the driveway curves back on itself.

I got into my car and headed into town. The sedan pulled out behind me and followed, staying behind in the turns, and keeping well back in the light traffic heading into Nags Head. I paid it no mind.

When I got to her house, Stephanie explained that she wasn't much of a cook. Luckily, her mom shouted instructions from the living room, so she'd managed to throw together the ingredients for a curried chicken casserole with rice, which she served with a tossed salad of kale and arugula. The meal was delicious and I told her so. By unspoken agreement, we kept away from the topic of Will Williamson and his untimely demise. Dessert was a selection of tarts from Josie's Cozy Bakery, served with a tub of vanilla ice cream. I said the time-honored words of "not for me—thanks" before allowing myself to be persuaded to have "just one."

"I don't know if it's my place to say anything," I said, scraping the last drops of ice cream off my plate, "but I think it's something Steph should consider." I looked at Pat.

"Go ahead," she said.

"Will's son by his first wife is named Michael. He lives in Raleigh, but he's in town now, making the arrangements. I've met him and I think he and Steph might like to meet."

Stephanie leaned forward, her face lit by excitement. "My brother."

"Half brother," Pat said.

"What's he like?" Stephanie said.

"Ordinary guy," I said. "Seems nice enough. He's a bank manager. Divorced, no kids. He's staying with Marlene at the house Will rented, although they'll probably be evicted soon. If you'd like to meet him, I can arrange it."

I glanced at Pat. Her face was still. She said nothing.

"Mom?" Stephanie said. "Would you mind?"

Pat shook her head. "You do what you want to do, dear."

"I would like to meet him. Imagine, my brother. Does he look like me?"

The resemblance was strong. I decided to play that down. I studied my friend's face as if I had to give it some thought. "The eyes are similar. You probably want to meet in a neutral place the first time. Why don't I call him tomorrow, suggest he come to the library in the afternoon? You can go for a walk on the boardwalk or find a quiet alcove. Then, if you want to, you can go for coffee or something. Can you get away?"

"Mom, would you mind? Just an hour or so. If we want to talk more, we can arrange another time."

"That would be fine, dear. Now, if you'll excuse me, I'm very tired."

I pushed my chair back. "I'll let you know what he says. I need to be going too. Thanks, Steph. Dinner was great."

"I'll make a cook out of her yet," Pat said with a soft smile. I didn't blame Pat for being wary of her daughter meeting Will's son. It was bound to disrupt the close relationship between the two women. But Stephanie deserved to know her family, and Pat was smart enough to recognize that.

I said my good-byes and walked out into the soft night air. I drove toward home deep in thought about Stephanie and Pat and Michael and Marlene. Even if the police never charged Stephanie with the killing of Will, if they didn't arrest someone else, the cloud of suspicion would hang over her for the rest of her life. She was already getting grief from her employers about it. I wanted to help, but I didn't know what else I could do. I'd tried, but all of my poking around had come to naught. Maybe it was a random thing after all. Maybe an old enemy from Alaska had followed Will here, and had slunk off back to wherever he'd come from. Maybe we never would know what had happened that night and William Williamson would join the cold case files deep in the police station archives.

I turned at Whalebone Junction and all but one car dropped away. No traffic was coming toward me. I drove carefully, keeping an eye out for deer. A burst of light flooded into my car, bouncing off my rearview mirror directly into my eyes. The vehicle behind was coming up fast and had turned its high beams on. I slowed slightly, intending to let him pass. To my surprise, he slowed also, but he didn't turn his lights down. He was way too close, almost sitting on my bumper. I glanced in my mirror but could see nothing but white light. *What an idiot,* I thought, *and probably drunk at that.* I was planning to report it to the police as soon as I got home when a shock ran through the car and up my spine. He'd hit me! The car dropped back, and I took a deep breath, trying to keep myself calm. *Almost home, Lucy. Almost home.* The car accelerated again, and hit me again, harder this time. I swallowed panic and fought to keep my little Yaris on the road. I was approaching the turn-off to the lighthouse and all I wanted to do was run home, but I didn't dare make the turn. I could not lead my pursuer down that dark and lonely dead-end road, although nothing much better lay ahead of me. I was heading into the wilderness with a maniac close behind me. My phone was in my purse, and I'd tossed the purse into the passenger side footwell. I was gripping the steering wheel so tightly my knuckles were turning white. Another jolt traveled through me as my car was rammed from behind again.

What was he, if it was a he, playing at? He had to be trying to force me off the road. I didn't dare contemplate why. The ground on either side of the highway was completely flat, so flat that in high winds waves washed over the road. There are no cliffs. If I went off the road, all that would happen would be that I'd sink a few inches into sand or muddy marsh grasses and get stuck. The car pulled back slightly as we came into a straight stretch. Instead of bracing myself for another blow, I steadied the Yaris as best I could and dove for my purse. I grabbed the bag and then the steering wheel. My car was fairly new and the alignment was perfect. I was still safely on the road. I opened my purse and fumbled around, trying to find the phone. Papers, notebook, pens, wallet, lipstick, sunglasses, compact, hairbrush, the book I'd grabbed after being stuck in the police station without anything to read. I could have wept. All the detritus of my life lay at my fingertips but not my phone. Up ahead, the dark night broke as a set of lights came into view. It was impossible to tell how far away the approaching car was. A mile maybe? This, I decided, was my chance. I'd make a U-turn, try to follow the other car, and alert them to my distress. Then to my overwhelming relief I found it. My fingers closed on the hard case of the iPhone. I pulled it out and swiped the lock screen. My hand shook so badly, I missed the EMERGENCY call button.

The car behind me pulled back. For a moment, I dared hope he was giving up, leaving me alone, but then it accelerated, and I knew he was aiming to hit me for real this time. I put my foot on the gas. I was going too fast to make a safe U-turn, but what choice did I have?

My headlights caught a dark shape at the side of the road to my right, emerging from a scruffy patch of stunted trees. It turned, and bright eyes reflected light back at me. It leaped into the air, directly in front of me. I screamed, and instinctively wrenched the steering wheel to the right. I felt my tires sink into soft sand. The car following me shot past. It squealed to a stop and began to turn.

The brakes of the truck coming toward me groaned as the driver slammed them hard, trying to avoid the leaping deer. The animal disappeared into the night, and the truck tumbled off the highway, coming to rest almost exactly opposite where I was. All the doors flew open and to my infinite relief four men jumped out. The vehicle that had been after me flew down the center of the road and its rear lights faded away.

I clambered out of my car on shaking legs.

"Are you okay? Is anyone hurt?" The men surrounded me. Four men. Young, strong, men. They were dressed in overalls, orange vests, and heavy boots. A work crew heading home at the end of the day.

"I'm fine," I said. "Just a bit shook up. Are you all okay?"

"I didn't hit it," one of the men said. "Gave me a heck of a shock though. Blasted deer."

"Oh, please, Ray. You'll use any excuse to come to the aid of a pretty young lady."

The men laughed. I laughed too. I laughed so hard, I couldn't stop. The men watched me through eyes full of concern. I gulped and fought to swallow tears.

"You don't look like you're stuck too hard," Ray said. "We should be able to push you out. Are you able to drive?"

"I . . . Yes, I'm fine, but I am a little unsteady. That was a close call." *In more ways than one.* "Would you mind following me home? It's not far. I live at the lighthouse."

"You live at the lighthouse? You must be Lucy. My mom visits your library all the time. Ruby O'Reilly?"

"Sure, I know her."

Another vehicle approached, coming from the north. I held my breath, but when it entered into our circle of lights I could see that it was an SUV, not a sedan.

"You need any help there?" a woman called.

"We're fine. Thanks," Ray said. I waved in agreement. She carried on her way with a cheerful toot of her horn.

I climbed back into my car. The engine was still running. I threw it into gear and touched the gas lightly. The right front wheel spun in the sand, trying and failing to get a grip. The men gathered around, bent their backs to my little Yaris, and with one mighty shove, I was free.

I could have wept with relief. I waited while they piled back into the truck and then I led my small honor guard to the lighthouse. The men remained in the truck, and Ray focused his headlights on the path, lighting my way to the front door. I thanked them again, invited them to pay the library a visit sometime, and let myself in. Once I had the door shut and the locks turned, the truck drove away.

Only then did my legs collapse, and I sank to the floor. Charles crawled into my lap and buried his head into my chest while I cried.

Chapter 19

I don't know how much time passed before I staggered to my feet and almost crawled up the stairs. I let myself into my apartment and immediately phoned Butch. I related what had happened, although I didn't really know *what* had happened. A car had chased me down the highway, hitting my Yaris several times, apparently trying to force me off the highway. I skidded off the road, another vehicle arrived, and my pursuer drove away. That was all. Butch was working and said he'd file a report for me. He also said he was coming to the lighthouse right now to have a look at my car. There would be damage to my bumper that they might be able to match to the car that had hit me.

"Thanks, Butch," I said.

"You don't need to come downstairs," he said. "I can tell by your voice you're shook up. Make yourself a hot sweet drink and go to bed."

And that is exactly what I did.

*   *   *

I went to bed, but I didn't sleep. I kept seeing the lights of that sedan getting closer and closer, feeling the jolt as it hit me, again and again, and saw that animal leaping into the road. The men's truck had suffered no damage so they hadn't hit the deer, and for that I was very thankful.

After an hour of tossing and turning I switched on my light, got up, and went to the kitchen. *The List* was on the counter where I'd left it.

At first, I'd assumed some lunatic saw a woman alone in a small car and decided to have some fun. But the more I thought about it, I began to realize he might have been after me specifically. When I'd left the lighthouse for dinner with Stephanie and Pat, a beige sedan had followed me into town. I'd paid it no attention, so hadn't noticed if it stayed behind me all the way to Pat's house.

Was it possible he'd waited outside for me to leave, and then followed me to the highway?

The only reason I could think of why someone would target me personally had to be to stop me from asking questions about the death of Will Williamson.

I'd decided earlier that I was wasting my time and achieving nothing. Perhaps I was getting a lot closer to the truth about what happened than I realized.

I studied *The List*, running over the events of the past few days. This morning, I'd openly asked Ralph Harper about his whereabouts the night of Will's death. I'd moved him up on the list, but now I struck a solid black line through his name. Maybe I'm naive, but I didn't believe anyone with eyes that soft and gentle would try to harm me. It was still possible that Ralph might have killed Will because of some notion of an insult to the power of the sea, but if tonight's incident was related to the death of Will, and I was convinced it had to be, then Ralph was off the list.

Who else then?

I'd gone to Doug Whiteside's campaign office, and Doug and Billy had seen me there. The receptionist would have told them I was inquiring about the marina. Bill's wife, Jill, might have told him about the strange phone call from the library. I hadn't given her my name, but it would have taken no genius to figure out that it was me calling.

I'd asked Marlene about the phone call Will supposedly got the night he died.

I'd phoned Theodore, asking if he knew Will had turned out to be broke. But no—as with Ralph, I would not believe Teddy would do anything to harm me.

I'd followed Louise Jane through the marsh. Could she have known I was there all along, and was she only pretending to be on the phone talking about spells and paranormal events? No, not Louise Jane. I scratched her name out with a firm, solid line. If she'd known I was spying on her she would have dragged me out of the undergrowth and put me in my place with a withering remark. I studied the list again. *What was I missing?*

I was woken by the ringing of the phone. I blinked and tried to stretch. My neck was as stiff as Louise Jane's smile when she pretended to be friendly to me, and I found myself twisted into a very awkward position. I was sitting at the kitchen table. I'd fallen asleep with my head resting on *The List*. I fumbled for the phone and groaned out a "Hello?"

"Lucy. Butch told me what happened to you last night. Are you okay?"

"Detective Watson, is that you?" I recognized his voice, but I certainly didn't recognize the concern in it. "I'm fine, although a bit stiff and my neck hurts. Gosh, what time is it?"

"Ten after eight. We found the car that hit you."

"Great! Are you sure? Who was it?"

"It was located in a dark corner of a shopping center lot. The damage to the front bumper matches yours, thus we have no doubt it's the right car. The vehicle had been stolen sometime yesterday. The owner is an elderly lady who didn't even know it was missing until an officer knocked on her door."

Clearly it had been too much to hope for that my pursuer had calmly gone home and parked his car in his own driveway, front bumper facing the street. "I was hoping the car would lead you to him."

"Lucy, I have to tell you that this is the first I've heard of anyone chasing lone women down the highway at night, or otherwise causing that sort of trouble. I have to conclude that it might have something to do with the Williamson case."

"I've been thinking that too. It seems to me that . . ."

"Lucy, stay away. I know you've been poking around and asking questions, and I know you're trying to help your friend. In other circumstances, I might find that admirable. But in a matter of a murder investigation, I do not. You've made someone mad at you, and you're not equipped to handle it. Stop acting on your own, Lucy."

"Okay," I said in a very low voice.

"What was that? I didn't hear you."

"I'm done being the Lone Ranger," I said.

"Glad to hear it. I promise when I have something to reveal I'll tell you about it. How's that?"

"That's good. Bye."

He hung up.

I ached. My upper back, shoulders, and neck were nothing but a ball of tight muscles and pain. I would have been sore this morning anyway, after the way I'd clenched the steering wheel and the jolts my spine had taken, but falling asleep with my head on the table hadn't helped much. I got to my feet, moving very slowly. I stood under a hot, steaming shower for a long time.

I couldn't face food this morning (although Charles had no such qualms) and huddled over a cup of coffee, looking out the window and watching the sun rise in the sky.

"Lucy, what on earth happened to your car?" Ronald said the moment he came through the front door. I was walking down the stairs, moving carefully so as not to send any shock waves into my neck.

"I was rear-ended," I said. "I haven't even looked at it yet. Is it bad?"

"Pretty bad, yeah," he said. "Are you okay?"

"I'm fine."

"You obviously are not." Bertie had arrived with Ronald. "You're walking like an eighty-year-old woman."

"A touch of whiplash, I think."

"My office, now," Bertie ordered. "Ronald, you can open up. But first make Lucy a cup of my special tea, will you please?"

Bertie ordered me to sit in the visitor's chair in her office and take off the sweater I'd put on over my blouse. She came up behind me and laid her warm palms on my shoulders. "Tell me if it hurts."

It didn't hurt. It so much didn't hurt that I felt myself falling asleep as her strong, capable fingers kneaded my neck and shoulders.

I heard the door open and Ronald slip in. He handed Bertie a cup and she gave it to me. I cradled it in my hands, enjoying the warmth, if not the scent. "Drink it all," she ordered.

It was a lukewarm watery green liquid that tasted as dreadful as it smelled. I did as ordered.

"Did the police charge the person who hit your car?" she asked.

"Ummmm. No, it was a hit-and-run. Stolen car. Ummmm."

"I don't think you've damaged anything," she said. "You just need to keep that area warm and relaxed and you'll be as good as new in no time."

"Ummmmm."

"Oh, to be young," she said, "and so resilient." She slipped my sweater over my shoulders and tucked the throw she kept behind her desk around me. "You rest for a while, honey. Come out when you're ready."

When I woke, the clock over Bertie's desk said it was almost noon. I'd slept the morning away, while Bertie stayed out of her own office and my coworkers did my work for me.

I tossed off the throw and moved my shoulders. I felt almost normal. What on earth was in that tea?

Bertie was sitting behind the circulation desk when I came out. She smiled. "Feeling better?"

"Much. Thank you. I'm sorry I slept for so long."

"You needed it." She got to her feet. "Stephanie called for you about half an hour ago. I said you were indisposed."

Shoot. I was supposed to call Mike Williamson and arrange a meeting with Steph. I'd totally forgotten about it. Bertie went to her office and I took her place at the desk. A couple of patrons were chatting by the magazine rack, and I heard the murmur of voices from the cookbook shelves. No one needed my attention at the moment, so I made the call.

"Hi, Marlene. Lucy here."

"Lucy! How nice to hear from you. Are you coming over for a swim? I found another case of wine in the garage."

"I'm working today." Must be nice, I thought, to simply assume a person could drop everything and rush over for a swim and a glass of wine in the middle of the day.

"Come after work then," she said.

I didn't bother to reply. I wasn't calling to set up a social engagement. "I need to speak to Mike, but I don't have his number. Is he there?"

"No. He went to the bank. Some details of Will's estate. Not that there is any estate. The owner of this house called this morning and left a message. There's some problem with the rent, she said. I didn't call her back, but it won't be long before I'm out on the street. Hey! I've just had the best idea ever! Do you have a roommate?"

I ignored the question. "What's Mike's number?"

"I don't know. I haven't needed to call him since he's been here. When I phoned to tell him that Will had died, I called his house in Raleigh."

"Will you ask him to contact me soon as he gets in?"

"Why?"

"Please, Marlene."

"Oh, all right. As long as you promise to think about the roommate thing."

"I promise." I wasn't lying. I had thought about it. I thought that even if I had the room, which I don't, about the last person I'd want to live with was Marlene. When the final bottle of Prosecco ran out, I could guess who'd be expected to buy more.

I phoned Stephanie and told her I hadn't been able to talk to Mike, but I'd let her know when I did, and then lowered my head and concentrated on doing my job.

Shortly before four, a steady stream of cars and vans began pulling into the parking lot, disgorging preteens for their book club. Almost everyone who'd come into the library this afternoon had stopped at the desk to ask me what had happened to my car and inquire if I'd been hurt. I hadn't gone outside to check out the Yaris. I was afraid of what I'd find. I hadn't noticed anything loose or any strange noises when I'd driven home last night after the near-crash, but I hadn't exactly been paying attention to the condition of my vehicle.

The preteens had run upstairs and their parents were either standing around gossiping or looking for books for themselves, when Mike Williamson strolled in. He spotted me behind the desk and gave me a wink and a big grin. "Marlene told me you wanted to talk to me, so I figured this would be a good chance to see where you work. Busy place."

I thought Charles had gone upstairs with the kids, since he loves nothing more than story time, but he leaped onto the desk. The hair along his back stood on end. He arched his spine and hissed at Mike.

Mike drew back and lifted his hands. The grin had disappeared. "Geeze, a cat. I can't stand cats." He made a shooing gesture toward Charles. Charles showed him his sharp teeth.

"Sorry," I said. "I don't know what's gotten into him. He's usually very friendly."

"Let me take him, Lucy," one of the parents said. "My daughter's allergic to cats, so I can't have one. I have to get my fix with this guy every chance I get." She scooped Charles up and carried him off, cooing soothingly. The look on his face indicated that he did not want to be soothed.

"I do want to talk to you," I said to Mike, "but it isn't something we can discuss in public."

The grin returned, and he leaned across the desk. He lowered his voice. "Let's go someplace private then. You can skip off early. No place more private than the beach. Unless you want to show me where you live?"

I sucked in a breath. My skin crawled and the hair at the back of my neck was standing as high as Charles's had. And not just from Mike's slightly slimy insinuations, or from the cat's reaction to him. The minute Mike walked through the door, I realized that I *had* seen Will Williamson's son before. Every time Mike and I had met, he'd been wearing long pants. Today, perhaps with the idea of luring me to the beach, he was in a short-sleeved T-shirt and board shorts that came to his midthighs. His thin legs, accented by knobby knees, looked like two saplings with burls in the middle. They were also excessively hairy.

Mike Williamson had been on Coquina Beach the afternoon before the big storm hit. He'd been alone, studying the shoreline with binoculars. He'd stared at me as I walked past, making me so uncomfortable I left the beach early. A few hours later, Will and Marlene's boat had been led onto the shore by false lights.

He'd been here all along, before his father was killed.

I'd briefly considered that Mike might have been responsible for his father's death, not wanting to share his inheritance with Stephanie. But I'd dismissed that because Mike wouldn't have known he had a long-lost sister. Besides, I thought Mike had been in Raleigh at the time of Will's death. Marlene had phoned him at home the next morning to break the news. But Raleigh was only a three-hour drive from Nags Head—easy to make it back under the cover of night after having killed a man.

"Something the matter?" he said now.

I blinked and shook my head. I leaned forward and lowered my voice. "I can't exactly sneak out, Mike. My boss would notice and she's a real dragon. We close at seven tonight. Why don't you come around at eight, once everyone has left, and we can . . . talk." I tried to sound seductive. I failed.

But he didn't seem to think so. He grinned even wider. "Eight o'clock it is. Nothing like a walk on the beach in the dark." He gave me an exaggerated wink and an unattractive leer and left.

I dropped back into my chair. Good heavens. What had I done?

"My son said you ran into a bit of trouble last night, Lucy."

"What? I mean oh, hi, Mrs. O'Reilly. Yeah, a deer ran into the road in front of me. I didn't hit it, thank goodness. It was great of Ray and his friends to help me out."

"He phoned me this morning and told me to look in on you. He wants to be sure you're okay."

"You can see that I am."

She put a stack of hardcovers on the desk. "In that case can you recommend something for my husband? He's started to get interested in the origins of the First World War."

"Has he read *The War that Ended Peace* by Margaret MacMillan? It's excellent."

"I don't think so."

"Let me get it for you. It was returned earlier and I didn't see it go out again." I went to the history shelf, found the thick book, and brought it back. Mrs. O'Reilly thanked me and left.

At five, the kids came clattering downstairs, and a lineup formed as they and their parents checked out their books. When they'd left, laughing and chattering, I called Ronald. "Would you mind taking the desk for a while? I've something important I need to do."

"Sure."

I went outside with my iPhone. On the spur of the moment, I'd come up with a plan to deal with Mike Williamson. I knew I should go to Watson with this information, but what could I tell him? That Mike gave me a creepy feeling? That I'd seen those skinny, hairy legs where they shouldn't have been?

I didn't think the police had leg lineups.

I'd promised Watson I wouldn't play the Lone Ranger anymore. And I wouldn't. No, for this plan I needed allies.

I called Butch first. "Can you come to the library at seven tonight?"

"Sure. What's up?"

"I can't explain on the phone. I need you to trust me. It's very important. You mustn't be late."

"I'll be there."

My next call was to Connor. I made the same request. He didn't hesitate for a moment before agreeing to come. I went back inside, but had a hard time concentrating on my job for what remained of the day. I said nothing to my coworkers about my plans. They'd only worry.

I was worrying.

At five minutes to seven I announced closing time. The last of the stragglers checked out their books. Bertie came out of the back carrying her keys and bag. "Do you have any plans for tonight?"

"No," I said.

She studied my face. "You still look strained. Take it easy for a few days. You should come to the studio. I have a gentle yoga class at six thirty tomorrow morning."

The door opened and Butch and Connor came in. They eyed each other suspiciously, and me even more suspiciously. "Is something going on here?" Bertie said.

"Nope."

"I don't believe you," she said, "but I trust you're in good hands, Lucy. Good night."

I walked to the door with her and glanced out. Dusk was lengthening and the first and brightest stars were appearing in the blue-black sky.

I turned and faced the two men. I took a deep breath. "Mike Williamson killed his father." No point in beating about the bush.

"Are you sure?" Connor said.

"How do you know?" Butch said.

I explained about seeing him at the beach, and how I hadn't recognized him until today, when I saw him wearing shorts. "He was there, deciding where to place the lights. I'm sure of it. He needed daylight to check out that stretch of the coast, and with the storm coming he would know that everyone would be heading home soon. He must have stayed until it was dark and he figured his dad's boat would be passing."

"This is the first I've heard of any lights," Connor said.

"You remember at book club Will told us that lights on the beach had made him turn toward what he thought was a small boat harbor?"

"That's a story. A story Louise Jane told to make herself sound important."

"But it wasn't just a story. I saw them too."

"Why didn't you tell me or Sam Watson?" Butch asked.

"At first I didn't think it was important. Then, when I realized it might have been a deliberate attempt to wreck Will's boat, it was after Louise Jane had grabbed the old tale and run with it, so no one believed me."

"Fair enough," Connor said. "We'll go with you to Detective Watson."

"Actually," I said, "I've got an idea. Look, Watson's not going to arrest a guy because I said he has hairy legs."

"You've got that one right," Butch muttered.

"So, we're going to trap him." I checked my watch. Seven fifteen. "He'll be here at eight. You'd better move your cars."

"What?!"

"Are you nuts?"

"Hide your cars in the loop. He won't notice them in the dark. I'll wait for Mike outside. You two can conceal yourselves nearby."

"Why would we want to do that?" Connor said.

"Remember in *Kidnapped* when Alan made Ebenezer Balfour confess to cheating David out of his inheritance while David and the lawyer hid and listened? We'll do the same."

Butch and Connor looked at each other.

"That," Butch said, "is the craziest thing I've ever heard."

"Hear me out. Mike is a vain and boastful man. He thinks I'm interested in him. I don't expect him to break down and confess, but I'm counting on him telling me enough, thinking he's impressing me with how clever he is. Then, once he's said something we can take to Watson, you two leap out of the bushes and Butch arrests him." I smiled at them.

"First," Connor said, "allow me to point out that there are no conveniently located bushes."

"No, but you can hide around the corner. I'll turn off the light above the door."

"Even better," Connor said, "I'll talk to him. I'll say I'm looking for you, but you seem to have gone out.

And then I'll say, 'By the way, Mike, did you kill your dad?'"

"He is not going to say anything in an attempt to impress you," I said. "It has to be me."

"This," Butch said, "is the stupidest idea I have ever heard."

"But?" I said.

"But, it's worth a try. Connor and I'll be here in case he tries anything. At best he'll say something about setting the lights and at worst he'll say nothing incriminating at all."

"I can't say I approve," Connor said, "but I'm not going to drive off and leave you two to carry out that plan by yourselves."

"Good," I said. "Now, move those cars."

I checked my watch again. Seven thirty. Charles was sitting on the returns shelf by the door, his eyes fixed on my face, his tail moving slowly back and forth. "What?" I asked. "You want to object too?"

The big cat wisely said nothing.

Chapter 20

By quarter of eight we were in position. I wasn't going to take the chance of getting trapped inside the lighthouse while my rescuers waited outside, so I positioned myself on the front step. Connor and Butch had concealed their cars in the loop and themselves in the deep shadows of the lighthouse.

When I'd left the building, Charles had tried to dash outside. That was unusual. People came and went all day, and he knew better than to try to escape. I lunged for him and snatched him up. He spat and hissed and scratched at my arms.

"Wow! Calm down there," I said. "What's gotten into you?" I deposited him on the desk and dashed for the door. He tried to make a leap for it, but I was faster and slammed the door in his furious little face.

"Everything okay?" came a deep voice from the darkness.

"Fine. Charles decided that tonight of all nights, he wants to hunt for mice."

I'd switched off the lamp above the door. It was a cloudless night, for which I was grateful, and the moon cast a pale white light. I took a deep breath, bounced on my toes, and swung my arms. My neck and shoulders were stiffening under the tension, but I tried to ignore that.

It would all be over soon.

At five to eight, lights came down the drive. I held my breath. It might be someone looking to enjoy the marsh on a quiet night. Heck, it might be Louise Jane. If it was I'd kill her.

The car swung toward us and my heart sped up. It pulled to a stop directly in front of the path to the library.

"Showtime," Butch said.

The car door opened and someone got out.

"Hey, Lucy." Stephanie.

I ran toward her. "What are you doing here?"

"You didn't call me about Mike. Mom has a friend over to watch a movie tonight, so I figured I'd drop by and ask if you talked to him. To my brother, imagine that. Did you?"

"Yes. No. Never mind. You have to leave. Now. Quickly." I grabbed her arm.

She pulled it away. "What's going on, Lucy?"

"Nothing."

"Too late," Butch called. "Someone's coming. Get her over here."

"Who's that?" Steph peered into the dark. "What are you people doing? Oh, it's you. I should have known."

"Hide. Now," I shouted. Headlights were coming down the drive.

I shoved Stephanie toward the men. An arm reached out and she was dragged into the shadows. "Will you let go of me!" she said. "You can't touch me like that. Oh, hi, Connor. You're here too? What's going on?"

"Will you be quiet for once," Butch shouted. "And do what you're told."

"Do what I'm told? I have no intention of doing any such thing, and certainly not when I'm being told by the likes of you."

"Please, Stephanie," Connor said. "It's important, and everything will be explained soon enough."

"See, Butch? Now I'll listen," she said. "All you had to do is ask nicely."

Butch groaned. No one said anything more.

The car came to a stop beside my Yaris. The door opened. Mike Williamson got out. He walked slowly up the path, swaggering in his confidence.

"Hi, Lucy," he said. "Why are you standing out here in the dark?"

"It's a beautiful night. I thought I'd wait for you here."

"Nice to know you're that eager," he said. "Let's go inside."

"I've been inside all day. I need some fresh air."

"We'll go to the beach then. We can have a nice quiet walk. I bet you know some private spots."

"That would be lovely, but let's wait a couple of minutes and enjoy the moment."

"Okay. I'm enjoying every moment I spend in your company, Lucy. I hope we can have lots more moments together."

I giggled. At least I tried to giggle, but I fear it may have come out more like a strangled choke. The lighthouse beam flashed and I could see Mike smiling at me. His smile was broad, but there was something behind those eyes. I shivered and wrapped my arms around myself.

"Cold? Maybe we should go inside after all."

"I'm fine. I guess you'll be going home to Raleigh soon. Once you get your father's affairs sorted out."

"I might stay for a while. If you give me reason to, Lucy. My father's affairs are something I would rather not spend much time thinking about."

I shifted my feet. We could stand here all night, Mike pretending to flirt, me pretending to respond.

Obviously he was thinking the same thing. "Why don't you get a sweater and then we can go for that beach walk. It's a nice night for it. You said you had something you wanted to talk to me about?"

"Uh," I said.

He climbed the step and stood beside me. I could see his face in the moonlight. The edges of his mouth turned up in what he probably thought was a smile. I was amazed that I'd once thought him attractive. He glanced around us, taking in the dark, the quiet. The total, or so it appeared, absence of anyone else. "Whose car's that?"

"What car?"

"The one beside yours."

"It belongs to a library patron. It wouldn't start so she got a lift home and will send a tow truck out tomorrow. How do you know which one's mine?"

"I figured a cute little car like that would belong to you, Lucy. Looks like you've got some damage to the back bumper. How do you find a car that small handles? Ever have any trouble staying on the road?" The playful spark had gone out of his eyes. The gray was as cold as chips of ice. He almost snapped the words out, as his composure slipped. Mike might have wanted me to think he was trying to seduce me, but he couldn't hide the menace that practically radiated from him. His plan was to go to the beach, all right. But only one of us would be coming back.

"No." I cleared my throat. "I mean, no. Do you come to the Outer Banks often?"

"Now and again."

"I was wondering because I thought I saw you recently."

Something rustled in the grass. A grunt followed by a squeak.

"What was that?" Mike twisted his neck and peered behind him. Fortunately at that moment the thousand-watt light high above us went into its dormancy.

"Mice. We get lots of mice around here. That's why we have a cat in the library. I was out for a walk a few days ago, I don't remember quite what day, and I saw this guy. Well, let's say it might have been you. I noticed him. I thought he noticed me too."

"I might have seen you there, yeah."

I tried to give him a flirtatious little laugh. I wiped clammy hands on my hips. "It wasn't far from where your dad wrecked that boat. Do you sail too, Mike?"

"I used to have a fishing boat. Lost it in my divorce settlement. But I wouldn't exactly say my dad sailed. More like splashed in the water on a boat he couldn't handle and couldn't afford."

"Why do you think he would have gone out in such bad weather, if he was a poor boater?"

"The thing about my dad, Lucy, was that he wouldn't

let anyone tell him what to do. As far as he was concerned, he knew it all. I knew his absolute self-absorption would get him into trouble one day. And so it did. Why do you want to talk about my father, anyway? Let's go." He reached for my arm. I pulled it away. I had to keep him talking. The minute he touched me or tried to get me into his car, Butch and Connor would be on us, and all chance of a confession would be gone.

"It was a clever trick," I said. "Setting those lights, knowing someone unfamiliar with the area would think it a small boat harbor. A place to seek refuge."

"Dad always did underestimate me. His mistake. I learned a long time ago that I could talk him into doing things he didn't want to do by appealing to his vanity. Gee, Dad, it looks bad if your son can't go to that sports camp with the other kids; what will their parents think? Gee, Dad, what will Marlene think of you, now that you've got a big fancy motorboat, if you don't take her out to sea?" He laughed. My skin crawled.

"He crashed the boat because he followed false lights," I said.

Mike laughed again, a laugh without the slightest trace of humor. "I knew he'd be too vain to try to learn how to properly navigate the thing. He intended to just crawl around the canals or stick to the sound. I called him that morning, said it was going to be a great day, why didn't he take the boat out for a test drive, show Marlene what he could do with it? Didn't work out so well for good old dad, did it? Another thing you can say for my dad. He'd always had luck on his side, although it seems to have run out as far as the gambling tables go. He and Marlene got themselves to land, although the boat wasn't so lucky. Still, I knew his luck had to run out sometime."

I was desperately trying to think of something I could say that would get him to incriminate himself. He'd implied that he'd set the lights, but not come right out and said he had. I changed direction. "Marlene's nice, don't you think?" I said. "What do you suppose she's going to do now? Poor thing."

"Marlene." He almost spat. "The sooner she's out of my life, the better. All she was after was my dad's money. What little was left of it."

The money! That had to be at the center of all this. "You told me you work for a bank. That must be so interesting."

"It can be useful. But sometimes not useful enough. My dad went through his money mighty fast; it was almost all gone before I found out what was going on."

I took a deep breath. It was now or never. "Did you call him that night and say you wanted to talk it over? After the trick with the false lights failed?"

He grabbed my arm and gave it a hard twist. "Enough talking. Let's go, Lucy. You're like a rabid dog with a bone and are far too nosy for your own good. I tried to warn you off last night, but you don't seem to be able to stop asking questions."

"Last night," I said. "That was you on the road last night? You could have killed me!"

He said nothing, only tightened his grip on my arm.

"Are you taking me for a boat ride?" I said. "Like the one you took your dad in? You're the person who called him the night he died, aren't you?"

"Yeah, I called him. Told him I was thinking of

buying a boat and needed his advice. Like I said, all I had to do was appeal to my dad's vanity and he wouldn't question why we had to look at the boat in the middle of the night. A buddy of mine has a slip at Wanchese. I've been down there with him several times, know my way around in the dark." He jerked on my arm so hard I was yanked off my feet. "Enough talking. Let's go!"

A shout of rage pierced the night. Mike staggered backward, dragging me with him. I fell hard.

"You killed him! You killed my father!"

"It's okay, Steph. It's okay. I've got him," said Butch's voice.

Strong hands grabbed me, soft fingers ran over my cheeks and stroked my neck. "Lucy. Lucy. Say something."

"Something," I croaked.

A light came on. Connor was crouched beside me. His hands cupped my face and I looked up into blue eyes full of concern. Mike Williamson lay on the ground, facedown. Butch straddled him and was snapping cuffs onto Mike's wrists. Stephanie had Butch's police-issue flashlight trained on the scene. Her hands were perfectly steady.

"I'm okay, I'm okay," I said, struggling to stand up. Connor jumped to his feet and pulled me after him.

"Mr. Mayor," Butch said. "Call nine-one-one. I know someone who wants to talk to this guy."

"Every word I said was a lie," Mike shouted. "That stupid woman was coming over all coy, wanting me to tell her that I'd been a bad boy. So I did what she wanted. This is a setup, pure and simple."

"We'll let the detectives sort it out," Butch said.

"Looks to me," Stephanie said, "that they'll have a pretty good case."

Mike twisted his head to look at her. "Who are you?"

"Me?" Stephanie said. "I'm your sister."

Connor kept his arm around me while he pulled out his phone. He called 911 first, and told them Butch needed assistance. Then he called Watson and told him to get down to the station immediately. He put his phone away and wrapped his arms around me and pulled me close. "Lucy. My darling, precious, Lucy," he whispered. "Don't you ever do anything that foolish again. I couldn't bear to lose you."

Now that it was over, I began to shake. I couldn't believe I'd been so brave. And so foolish. Connor stroked my back and whispered words of comfort. I felt his strong heart beating against me. I didn't want to move. Not ever again.

I heard sirens coming our way. Reluctantly, I pushed myself back from Connor. I looked into his eyes and gave him a smile. I touched his cheek. His lips formed the word "Lucy" and then he released me.

Butch stood up and pulled Mike to his feet as the sirens got close and blue and red lights washed the tall pines lining the driveway.

"That was quick," I said.

"I gave them a call when I was moving my car," Butch said. "A heads-up that I might need assistance."

Mike stared at me with such vehemence that I took a step backward. "You. I should have finished you off last night. I'll get you for this."

Connor stepped between us, and Butch said, "Where you're going, you won't be getting anyone, buddy. Steph, do you know a good lawyer?"

"Nope," she said.

Chapter 21

Sunday dawned bright and clear. And that was a good thing because it was decorating day at the Bodie Island Lighthouse.

Charlene had bought up all the red, white, and blue bunting available in half the state; the fire department arrived with a truck, a ladder, and numerous volunteers; library patrons brought excited kids and picnic baskets. Doug Whiteside and his wife were there, him in white shirt and dark tie, grinning though gritted teeth, her looking perfectly bored in a pink suit. Bill Hill rushed around, trying to get Doug in the center of every photograph. Bill's wife was with him, a stout, red-faced woman dressed in jeans and a sweatshirt. I noticed Bill pointing me out to her, and she came over.

"Do you work at the library?" she asked.

"Yes, I do."

"I'd like to pick up my book when you have a chance."

"What book?"

"The one on ocean currents around here? Someone

called to tell me it was in. I didn't ask for it, but it reminded me that I've not been out in our boat for a long time. Bill's not keen on the sea, but I used to enjoy it so much."

"Oh, that book. I . . . uh. You weren't interested, so someone else took it out. Sorry."

"That's okay," she said. "I'll reserve it again." She looked around her, at the happy crowds, the laughing children climbing all over the fire truck. I started to edge away. I couldn't remember if we even had a book on ocean currents. "I've missed this, you know," Jill said. "I'm sorry about that. I love this library, but Billy told me Doug wants to close it down so it would be better if I stopped coming." She gave me a smile. "I think I'll tell him that Doug needs to get rid of that idea instead."

"Thanks," I said.

She wandered away. I saw Ralph Harper, rolling across the grass as though he was on the deck of his boat, and gave him a wave. He came over at his usual leisurely pace.

"She's pleased," he said.

"Who is?"

"The sea. The lighthouse is honoring her, and she likes that."

"This isn't . . ." I was about to explain the purpose of the decorations, but I decided to let Ralph believe what he wanted. "I'm glad to hear it."

"It'll be good weather for the next couple of weeks." He touched the brim of his salt-encrusted hat and strolled away.

"Quite a crowd." Connor slipped up behind me. He put his arm around my shoulders and pulled me close. I snuggled against him. It had been very late by the time we finally left the police station the night of Mike's arrest. Connor had driven me home, and he'd come inside with me. We sat downstairs for a long time surrounded by my beloved books, sipping hot tea, playing with Charles, talking about all that had happened, and so much more.

"Now that I've found you again, Lucy," he'd said, as he stood at the door, ready to leave, "I'm not going to let you go."

"No worries," I said, smiling up at him. "I have no plans to leave."

Charles had meowed his approval.

"A photo, Mr. Mayor," a man shouted now, "of you and your fair lady."

Connor and I smiled at the camera. "Am I your lady?" I asked, once the photographer had moved off.

"I certainly hope so," he said with a hearty laugh. He took my hand in his, and it felt so very right being there.

Most people had come out ready to pitch in and help in shorts and T-shirts, but some families looked as though they'd come directly from church. Mrs. Fitzgerald was dressed as though she were presiding over a garden party, in a belted pastel dress, stockings, pearls, and a wide-brimmed hat. She even carried a parasol. A small circle consisting of Diane, Curtis, and Louise Jane was gathered around the folding chair at which she held court, talking intently. I did not want to know what the topic under discussion might be.

Ronald, dressed in purple shorts, an orange shirt, and a pink tie, was attempting to entertain a group of children with card tricks. He was a mighty poor magician, and all but the smallest kids soon found something more interesting to take their attention. Charlene was with the fire chief, both of them gesturing wildly and studying the lighthouse structure with the same intensity as if they were planning a campaign to storm the fortress. Men were gathered around them, offering helpful advice. Charity, the eldest Peterson girl, had joined them, her eyes shining with interest. The eyes of the baggy-panted boy from the YA book club were also shining, but he was watching Charity rather than the preparations.

Sam and CeeCee Watson spotted Connor and me and came over. "If the idea is to get everyone talking about the election," CeeCee said, "I think y'all have succeeded, Lucy."

"Talking about it is one thing," Connor said. "Getting out and voting is yet another."

"Speaking about talking," Watson said, "I've hardly been able to get Mike Williamson to shut up. He's got a lifetime of grievances he thinks I'm interested in hearing."

CeeCee rolled her eyes. "No shop talk."

"This time shop talk is okay," I said. "I was there, remember."

"True. In that case, I see Bertie. I'm going to ask what time we're getting under way." CeeCee walked away, her long colorful skirt swirling around her legs, a big straw hat protecting her face.

"You've charged Mike with murder?" I asked Sam Watson.

"Yes. He tried telling us that you'd tricked him into saying things that weren't true, but once Butch reminded us that Mike obviously knew about the attempt on you the other night, the details of which are not common knowledge, he broke down and confessed all."

"Did he say why he did it?" I asked. "I mean, kill his dad. I can assume he intended to kill me because I was getting close to uncovering the truth."

"If it helps, he says he'd intended only to frighten you on the highway, Lucy. But I suspect after that failed, he decided he had to get serious. You hadn't figured out that he was the killer and had allowed yourself to be alone with him, so he was prepared to kill you too."

I shivered. Connor muttered.

"As for why he killed his father. Mike had always believed his dad was wealthy, and being the only child he, Mike, would inherit it all someday. When he found out through his banking contacts that Will had lost almost everything, Mike was furious. There were a few CDs and some hard-to-redeem investments left, but Mike knew Will would tear through them soon enough. Particularly as he now had Marlene wanting to live the good life."

I shook my head. "That's so sad. I've been wondering all along how Mike got away after leaving his dad and the boat tied up in the marsh. Did he tell you that?"

Watson nodded. "He simply tied a small rowboat behind the fishing boat. Left the bigger boat—with his dead father—at the pier and rowed himself back to the marina under cover of darkness. Will was already dead, by the way, when Mike loaded him into the boat."

Connor felt my shudder and gave my hand a comforting squeeze.

"Why bring it here? Why didn't he just push the fishing boat out to sea?" Connor asked.

Watson shrugged. "I guess he thought it a fitting place, for some reason. He did mention that his dad had been chattering on about some book club Marlene and he had gone to at the lighthouse."

"Do you know how Marlene's doing?" I asked.

"See for yourself." Watson pointed behind me.

I turned to see Marlene dashing up the path toward us. She was dressed casually and comfortably in shorts, a T-shirt, and flat sandals. Her designer sunglasses were over her eyes and her hair was pulled into its usual high, tight ponytail. "Hey," she squealed. "Isn't this fun!" She gave me a big hug. "Did you think any more about that roommate idea, Lucy? We'll have such a great time living together! I hope it's okay if I can borrow your car sometimes. The repo men came for the Smart car last night."

"Roommate?" Connor said.

"I . . . ," I said.

Marlene glanced at Connor, and her eyes slid down to our clasped hands. "Oh, I guess not. You'll let me know if the room becomes free, won't you, Lucy?"

"Connor and I aren't . . ." I began.

"Oh, firemen! I wonder if they need help." Marlene skipped off.

The fire truck was maneuvering into position underneath the lighthouse walls. Excited children ran along beside, while Ronald, helped by Theodore and various parents, tried to ensure they didn't get too close. Charlene opened boxes of flags and bunting; people packed up their picnic baskets; and everyone gathered at the foot of the lighthouse, awaiting instructions. A great cheer went up as the ladder on the fire truck began to rise into the air.

The ever-well-organized Charlene had drawn up a sketch of the lighthouse and a list of orders for everyone who would be helping. Connor and I were to be positioned at my apartment window. He'd earlier hammered several large nails into the window frame, and when the bunting swung past us, we'd grab it, secure it to the building, and send the next section on its way. I would be given a huge rosette to hang in the window. With all the comings and goings, we'd decided that Charles had to be locked in the broom closet for the duration. His cries of protest had been heartrending to hear.

"Showtime," Connor said. "Let's get ourselves into position."

I glanced around the lighthouse grounds, but didn't see the faces I was searching for. "I'm so disappointed they didn't make it."

"Me too," he said, with a glance over his shoulder. "Hey, someone's coming. It might be them." A van drove slowly through the crowded parking lot and stopped at the path. "It's them. I'll tell Bertie and Charlene to hold off a couple of minutes." He ran off, and I went to meet the van. Butch had been driving, and he was now maneuvering a wheelchair out of the back while Stephanie held the passenger door open for a beaming Pat.

"Sorry we're late," Steph said. "The rental place didn't have the van ready."

I gave her a hug. "You're not late."

Butch positioned the wheelchair, and he and Stephanie helped Pat into it. Bertie ran up to join us. "I'm so glad you made it," she said. "You're right on time. Here, let me take Pat. I assume you all have jobs to attend to?"

We nodded.

"All I have to do," Bertie said with a laugh, "is supervise." She pushed her smiling friend down the path to the lighthouse.

I watched them go, and when I turned back to Butch and Stephanie, they were pulling apart with embarrassed grins. I hid a grin of my own as he took her hand and she gazed up—way up—at him with a radiant smile.

Butch had come to the library before opening the morning after the arrest of Mike Williamson and asked me to join him for a walk in the marsh. He'd blushed and stammered and shifted his big feet and didn't look into my face as he said he was hoping we could continue to be friends. But, he'd told me, not able to hide the look of sheer wonder on his face, he was in love with Stephanie Stanton.

I had refrained from saying, "I know."

"I have some big news," Stephanie said as we walked up the path. She linked her free arm through mine. A few very brave souls, Josie and Jake among them, were leaning off the top edge of the tower, preparing to unfurl the first stretch of bunting. Aunt Ellen's head was thrown back and she was facing the top of the lighthouse, but both hands were placed firmly over her eyes. The longest ladder on the fire truck wasn't long enough to reach the top; it would be used to get people in position to maneuver the bunting from one window to another and secure it in places on the outside.

"What news?" I asked.

Butch placed a kiss on top of Stephanie's head. She grinned. "I've quit my job."

"What? Can you afford to do that?"

"I want to be close to Mom. She's doing great. The doctors say her progress is remarkable and she'll be running that marathon in no time. But it's time for me to come home. I've been offered a partnership in a small local law firm."

"Where?"

"O'Malley and Stanton. Like the sound of it?"

"You're going into business with Uncle Amos? That's great. He's been wanting to reduce his workload, and he's been looking for someone to help out. You guys will be so good together."

"God help the cops and prosecutors of Dare County," Butch said with a groan.

"Against my far better judgment," Stephanie said, her eyes glowing with happiness, "I'm going to take a chance on this big lug." She dug her elbow into Butch's ribs.

I smiled at them both. "I'm delighted for you."

Connor was waving at me from the lighthouse door. "Catch you later," I said to my friends and ran to join him.

Before I could get inside, Louise Jane slid up beside me. "You'll be awful thrilled to hear, Lucy sweetie, that I got the final approval from Mrs. Fitzgerald and the rest of the board for my Halloween exhibit. It's obvious that your silly election decorations won't last for more than a few days in the wind and salt spray." Louise Jane looked mightily pleased with herself. I knew I should pretend disinterest, but I couldn't stop myself from saying, "I'm sure that will be fine. We can put out a few books about the paranormal history and Ronald will have his groups dress in costumes that week."

"Oh, Lucy, honey. I always forget how small-minded you can be sometimes. It's so charming. No, Mrs.

Fitzgerald, Diane, and Curtis have approved a full Halloween display with a generous budget to match."

I tried not to imagine Bertie's reaction to news of this budget expenditure. "A full display," I croaked. "Of what?"

She gave me her barracuda smile. "A haunted lighthouse, of course."

ACKNOWLEDGMENTS

Since the publication of the first book in the Lighthouse Library series, *By Book or by Crook*, I have been overwhelmed by the enthusiastic support of the entire cozy community, authors, readers, and reviewers. What marvelous people you all are. Thanks also to my agent, Kim Lionetti, and to Laura Fazio, my marvelous editor at Obsidian, who worked hard to make this a better book.

Margaret Kramer sat at my table at Left Coast Crime in Portland and won a name placement in the book. Thanks for joining us for dinner, Margaret, and I hope you like your character.

Curious to see how
Lucy's sleuthing habits began?
Read on for a sneak peek at
the first delightfully puzzling mystery
in the nationally bestselling
Lighthouse Library series by Eva Gates,

BY BOOK OR BY CROOK

Available now from Obsidian.

Chapter 1

Only in the very back of my mind, in my most secret dreams, did I ever dare hope I'd have such a moment.

Too bad it was being ruined by the cacophony of false compliments and long-held grievances going on behind me.

The party was a private affair, a viewing of the new collection for staff and board members of the Bodie Island Lighthouse Library, as well as local dignitaries and community supporters, before the official opening tomorrow. We were celebrating the arrival of a complete set of Jane Austen first editions, on loan for three months.

Jane Austen. My literary idol. So close.

I tried to block out everyone and everything and concentrate. I rubbed my hands together. Perspiration was building inside the loose white gloves. That, of course, was the purpose of the gloves: to keep human sweat and other impurities off the precious objects.

I took a deep breath, closed my eyes. And I touched the worn leather cover.

I imagined I could feel the very power of the words themselves coming up through my fingers.

"Incredible," a voice beside me said.

My eyes flew open. I snatched my hand back, embarrassed to be caught in a moment so emotional, so *personal*.

"Go ahead, honey," Bertie said, with a laugh. Her eyes danced with amusement. She understood. "Open it."

"Am I allowed to? I wouldn't want to damage anything."

"These books are precious, to be sure. But they'll be put back in their cabinet as soon as the party's over. And they've been cherished, cared for, and thus aren't as fragile as some would be at that age. Enjoy, Lucy. Enjoy. But don't spend too long here. I have people I need you to meet."

The head librarian touched my arm lightly, gave me another smile, and went back to her guests.

I turned the heavy cover, flipped pages with shaking hands, and was soon gazing in awestruck wonder at the frontispiece of the first volume of *Sense and Sensibility*, by "A Lady." A Lady all the world now knew to be Miss Jane Austen. An illustrated first edition, printed in London in 1811. I closed my eyes again and breathed. The scent was of old paper and aging leather, carrying with it memories of the foggy streets of London, the sound of horse's hooves rattling across cobblestones, the gentle rustle of skirts and petticoats, and the crackle of fire.

All I wanted to do was to gather the volume into my hands, spirit it away to a cozy corner with a good reading lamp, and curl up to spend the rest of the night simply enjoying it. Reading it, smelling it, touching it. To be lost in Austen's delightful pastoral England. A world of balls and dances. Of men in handsome uniforms and women in beautiful gowns. Romance and laughter—as well as foolishness and heartbreak. Sense versus sensibility.

With a sigh, I remembered that I had duties. They might be informal ones, but they were still duties.

I closed the book, returned it to its place, slipped off the gloves, and laid them back on the table for the next person to use. I pasted on my fake smile, turned, and stepped forward, ready to plunge into the party.

I was almost knocked off my feet as an excessively thin man shoved me aside. His tiny black eyes blazed with lust as bright as the flashing light on the top of this historic lighthouse. The tip of his tongue was trapped between small browning teeth, and a spot of drool touched the corner of his plump lips. To my horror, he extended an ungloved hand toward the book.

"Excuse me," I said in what I hoped was my best librarian tone. "Those books are extremely valuable. You must put on the gloves. Please don't lean over them like that."

His nose might have been made for peering down at uppity young librarians. "Excuse me," he said with an accent I'd last heard when Prince William visited America. "I am well aware of the proper storage and handling of books. I am, in fact, quite disappointed in Bertie for agreeing to house the collection in this"—he waved his hand as if encompassing not only the crowded room but also the lighthouse we were standing in, the Outer Banks, the moist sea air, and the waves crashing against the sand dunes, maybe even North Carolina itself—"place."

"This is a library," I said. "The proper place for books. Besides, Miss Austen lived near the sea. Her entire country is bound by the sea. I'm sure her books are delighted to be breathing salty air once again."

He sniffed. As well he might. I do have a tendency to get carried away sometimes.

"You," he said, still peering down his long, patrician nose, enunciating each word carefully, "must be the new girl."

His tone wasn't friendly or at all welcoming. But if I was going to get on here, in my new job, my new life, I'd pretend he'd intended it to be. I shoved my hand forward. "Lucy Richardson. I'm the new assistant librarian. Pleased to meet you, Mr. . . ."

He barely touched my outstretched fingers. "Theodore. Everyone knows me as Theodore. At your service, madam. If there is anything you need to know, young woman, about the handling and collection of rare books, you may call on me to enlighten you." He dug in the pocket of his tweed jacket, which emitted a strong aroma of pipe smoke, and pulled out a small square of paper. "My card. Now, if you'll excuse me." He turned away from me. I waited until he was pulling on the gloves and left him to examine the books in peace. I put the card in my pocket without reading it.

"Don't you mind Theodore, honey." My aunt Ellen slipped her arm around me. "We call him Teddy. Drives him nuts. He's just plain old Teddy Kowalski from North Carolina. He was born about ten miles from this very spot, over in Nags Head. Teddy was a smart little tyke; I'll give him that. Always had his head in books when the other boys were tossing balls around. He went to Duke and got a degree in English literature, and came home pretending to be an English lord or some such nonsense."

I laughed. "Did you know him when you were children?"

"Sakes no! He was a couple years ahead of Josie in school."

"How old is he?"

"Thirty-five."

"Really? I would have put him in his fifties." I glanced at the display table. Theodore was bent over *Pride and Prejudice*. He'd propped a pair of reading glasses on his nose.

"He deliberately tries to give that impression. See those glasses? Plain glass. He thinks they make him look more professorial."

"Fool," I said.

Bertie appeared at my side. "Don't take him for that, Lucy." My new boss's tone was serious. Almost warning. "Teddy has airs and pretentions, but he knows everything there is to know about eighteenth- and nineteenth-century English literature. He's a serious collector, or at least he would be if he had the money. A word of warning: always check his bags when he leaves, and if he's wearing a big coat, make him open it. He'll protest, act affronted, but . . ."

"Are you three going to stand here chatting all night

long? You need to introduce Lucy. Everyone's simply dying to meet her." It was Josie, my cousin. If I didn't love Josie so much, I'd hate her. She was everything I am not. Strikingly beautiful, with long, glossy hair bleached by the sun, a pale face full of dancing freckles, cornflower blue eyes that seemed to always be sparkling, perfect white teeth. As proof that life was never fair, Josie was model tall and model thin (except for the generous breasts—more unfairness!). The irony was compounded by the fact that she was the owner and chief baker of the best bakery in the Outer Banks, if not the entire state of North Carolina. Thinking of Josie and her business, I snuck a glance at the dessert buffet she'd catered. I felt a pound settling onto my hips. Hips that definitely did not need further poundage.

"Josie's right, as always," Aunt Ellen said. "You best be meeting folks. Making friendly."

"Come on," Bertie said, "I'll introduce you."

As its name suggests, the library I now worked in was situated in a lighthouse—a fabulous old lighthouse on Bodie Island, part of the Outer Banks of North Carolina. The minute I'd entered the building—long before that; the minute I'd first seen it from the road when I was a child on vacation—I'd loved it. What an imaginative, absolutely perfect place to house a library. All round whitewashed walls, iron spiral staircases going up . . . and up . . . and up, tall windows in thick walls overlooking the marsh on one side and the sand dunes of the shore and the storm-tossed ocean on the other. The shorter back staircase went up only one level, to where the rare and valuable books were housed. The general collection was accessible from the main staircase and filled three floors. Fiction was on the first, as was some nonfiction, with children's books on the second and Charlene's office and her research materials on the third level.

Above that, another turn on the spiral staircase to my own room. Small—pokey really—but absolutely perfect for sipping a cup of tea, reading, gazing out at the ocean, and daydreaming. And worrying that I'd made the worst decision of my life.

From there, the staircase had another hundred or more winding steps to reach the top of the lighthouse. Beyond my room, the stairs were seldom used in this day of electric, computer-programmed lamps.

Since I'd started work here all of four days ago, I figured I'd lost enough weight on those stairs that I could indulge in one of Josie's Cozy Bakery's gooey pecan tarts.

Music, Mozart at the moment, came quietly from the sound system, and the room was full of the low buzz of conversation.

Outside, night was falling, bringing with it a heavy ocean mist carried on a cool wet wind. Inside, we were warm and dry, bathed in soft yellow light. The partygoers were women mostly, with a few husbands dragged along. I smiled to myself at the thought that some of the husbands had probably been persuaded to come only upon hearing that the catering was by Josie's Cozy Bakery. Everyone wore their almost-best, like proper Southern fund-raisers. Colorful summer dresses and heels, primarily, and a few pantsuits, all accented by tasteful and expensive jewelry. Most of the men were in open-necked shirts, but a few wore a jacket and tie.

The majority of the interior lights had been switched off, leaving only a scattering of wall sconces to illuminate the room. Electric, of course. Candlelight would have been perfect, but this was, after all, a public place and a library at that. The alcove against the back wall, where generations of lighthouse keepers had sat to record the weather and the temperament of the ocean, ships passing, and the routine of lighting and extinguishing the great lamps, was now the central display area. Tonight the Austen collection took pride of place. That area was brightly lit and protected by a red velvet rope, warning anyone who wanted a closer look that red wine and gooey pecan tarts did not go well with nineteenth-century paper. When the display opened tomorrow for the public, the rope would mean "Keep back."

"Ronald's been on vacation." Bertie tipped her head toward a short man in his mid-forties pouring himself a glass of wine at the circulation desk that had been converted into a bar for the party. Thick white hair hung in curls around his collar, and he wore shiny black loafers, sharply ironed gray trousers, a crisp white dress shirt, and a giant yellow polka-dot bow tie. "You haven't had a chance to meet. Come on, I'll introduce you. He's the children's librarian and we're very, very lucky to have him." We hadn't taken more than a step before Bertie gripped my arm and jerked me to a halt. "Too late! He's fallen into her clutches." Bertie whirled around. "Who else do you need to meet?"

I craned my neck to see over her and the crowd of partygoers. A stately Southern matron, of the sort I—a born-and-bred New Englander—imagined them to be, was waving her finger in Ronald's face. He smiled and nodded, but I couldn't help but notice that his eyes were jerking around the room, looking desperately for an escape. And not finding it.

"Who's that with him?" I asked Bertie.

She dropped her voice. "Mrs. Peterson, one of our most active patrons. She's a newcomer, meaning she might have been born on the Outer Banks, but her grandparents were not. Her husband, however, is a member of one of our oldest families. She thinks Ronald should be her children's personal librarian and reading instructor. She'd just love to have him on her staff. If not for the minor fact that they have no staff, because her husband lost all of his family's money when he sank every penny into a Canadian gold-mining exploration company that turned out not to have a speck of gold in the ground. Poor Ronald. Mrs. Peterson took his vacation as a personal insult. You don't have to worry much about her, honey. She hasn't the slightest interest in adult books. I doubt she's read a single book since high school. When I announced that I'd been able to secure a visit of the Austen collection, Mrs. Peterson actually said, out loud"—here Bertie put on a very good imitation of a snooty, high-pitched voice—"'But why would anyone be interested in such *old* books?'"

We left Ronald, looking increasingly desperate under the barrage of Mrs. Peterson's verbal assault, to his own devices.

"Where's Charles?" I asked, referring to one of my favorite library employees.

"Banished to the closet by the staff break room for the duration of the party."

"How's he taking that?"

"If you listen closely you can hear the howls of indignation from here." Charles (named in honor of Mr. Dickens) was the library cat. A gorgeous Himalayan with a black face and expressive blue eyes in a ball of long, tan fur that must weigh a good thirty pounds (I wondered if he frequented Josie's Cozy Bakery), Charles was particularly loved by the library's younger patrons. "Mrs. Peterson is allergic to cats. Or so she says. She's starting to make noises about her dear little Dallas coming home from the library with watering eyes."

Aunt Ellen chimed in, "If she dares to suggest you get rid of Charles, I'll . . . I'll do something."

"I'm sure you will," I said. I smiled at my aunt.

"Let me finish introducing Lucy," Ellen said to Bertie. "You have your guests to see to."

"True. Although I'd prefer to spend my time with you two." Bertie straightened her shoulders and waded into the crowd.

"So, you're the new one, are you? Let's have a look at you."

"Excuse me?" I blinked. A woman was standing much too close, intruding into my private space, staring boldly into my face, her eyes dark with hostility. I'd never seen her before. The amount of product in her hair, teased and sprayed into a stiff helmet in a shade of red not known to nature, competed with her perfume. Her fingernails were the color of the wine in the glass she gripped in her right hand. Her dress was lower cut than suited her turkey-neck throat and chest and she tottered on stiletto sandals with straps the thickness of dental floss. She had to be well into her sixties, and not going into old age gracefully. She exhaled alcoholic fumes into my face. The party was just getting under way. She must have had a couple of drinks before arriving.

"Diane, I don't think . . ." Aunt Ellen said.

"I don't care what you think. A *librarian*. A *young* librarian. Just what we need in this town. Another one of *them*." She spoke as if "librarian" were another word for "ax murderer." I had absolutely no idea what she was going on about. I was quite proud to be a librarian.

"At least," Diane said, with a snort, "she's not very *pretty*."

That hit a sore spot. I might not be a beauty like my cousin Josie, but I didn't consider myself to be a total dog, either.

"I can't imagine where she got that dress. Her mother's closet, perhaps?"

Another direct hit. I'd bought this dress especially for this party. It cost considerably more than I could afford, but I wanted to make an impression. Apparently I had. But not the impression I was hoping for. The dress was new, but the clerk in the store told me the vintage look was back in style. It was pale yellow, with a square-cut neckline, close-fitting bodice, tightly cinched patent leather black belt above a flaring skirt, and a stiff petticoat that ended sharply at the knees. The shoes were also new, of the same color and material as the belt, and turning out to have been a mistake. My aching feet were reminding me that I should stick to ballet flats and sports sandals.

"Diane, you're creating a scene." Mr. Uppiton, the chair of the library board, took the woman's arm.

She shook him off. She took a hefty swig of her wine. "No, Jonathan, you're the one who made a scene. You think the whole town isn't talking about you? About how this place, this library, is more important to you than our marriage of thirty years?"

All around us the buzz of polite conversation died as people turned to look. Diane Uppiton's face was turning as red as her hair and nails. Her eyes filled with water that threatened to spill over and ruin her heavily applied makeup.

In the sudden silence, I could hear a ghost screaming from the depths of a castle dungeon. Or it might have been Charles the cat, expressing his opinion at being locked in the closet.

"Our marriage," Mr. Uppiton said, with a sniff, "was a mistake from the beginning. I finally came to realize that. I decided to take the blame for its demise myself, to allow you to leave with some medium of dignity. Dignity that you, my dear, clearly have forsaken."

Stuck-up jerk. He was speaking louder than he needed to, and although he was trying to look concerned, the corners of his mouth were in danger of curling upward. He, I realized, was playing to the audience, and thoroughly enjoying every minute of it. My sympathy shifted and I felt very sorry for Mrs. Uppiton.

"Our marriage"—the tears began to flow—"was my world. I gave you my youth, my beauty. My life. But you, nothing mattered to you more than this cursed library. Nothing."

"In a library, at least, one can have silence," Mr. Uppiton said, with the exaggerated sigh of a martyr. A few people tittered, more in embarrassment than in enjoyment of the joke. But Mr. Uppiton looked pleased with himself indeed.

"Come along, honey." Bertie plucked the wineglass from Mrs. Uppiton's fingers and passed it to the closest person. Me.

Unfortunately that had the result of turning Mrs. Uppiton's attention back to me. "You." She stabbed one of those potentially lethal nails in my direction. "Stay away from my husband."

"That's soon-to-be-ex-husband, I'll remind you," he sniffed.

She ignored him. "Do you hear me? I know your kind."

I refrained from mentioning that about the last person I'd ever want to get close to (shudder) was Mr. Uppiton. The crotchety old jerk, he'd made it plain to everyone who'd listen—and many who didn't want to—that he didn't like me and didn't want me in the job. I was, according to him, a flighty debutante. I figured he meant "dilettante," but wasn't about to point out the difference.

"And you," she said, spraying spittle all over her husband's face, "you'll get what's coming to you. See if you don't. I'll dance on your grave yet."

"Come along now," Bertie cooed. "Let's dry those tears."

"Really, my dear," Mr. Uppiton sniffed as his sobbing wife was escorted to the ladies' room. "Credit me with a medium of taste." I suspect he meant "modicum." Again, I declined to correct him.

Since starting work here, I'd come to realize that Bertie had eyes in the back of her head. As she led

Diane away, without even glancing over her shoulder she shouted, "Charlene, don't you dare touch that CD player!"

The reference librarian leapt away from the machine, a look of total innocence on her face.

Charles reminded us he was still trapped in the closet.